AMERICAN NEOLITHIC

Revised Edition

2019 The Calliope Group, LLC

The
Calliope
Group LLC

Copyright © 2019, 2014 Terence Hawkins

All Rights Reserved
Published in the United States by The Calliope Group, LLC
Tulsa, Oklahoma

Trade Paperback
ISBN: 978-1-7336474-2-7
ISBN: 978-1-7336474-3-4 (eBook)

Library of Congress Control Number: 2019946255

Praise for *American Neolithic*

"The political and social commentary throughout this unique novel is razor-sharp, as are uses of imagery and symbolism. The disturbing contrast of nonviolent, contemplative and deeply compassionate Blingbling to the brutality, apathy and ignorance of modern-day America is profoundly moving...A towering work of speculative fiction that will have readers rethinking what it means to be human."

— **Kirkus Reviews**

"This book will break your heart—I cannot lie—but read it anyway. You will be amazed at TH's prodigious imagination, his Bowie-sharp wit, and the skill with which he tells a story that's as morally urgent as it is satirically diverting."

— **Julia Glass**, author of *Three Junes* and *And the Dark Sacred Night*

"Terence Hawkins's *American Neolithic* is a special novel; thematically rich, it also provides all the pleasures of a hard-boiled thriller. The unique premise and lovingly crafted characters will stay with you long after you've closed the book."

— **Rain Taxi**

"This is a one-of-a-kind novel, a bizarre but gripping amalgam of anthropology, political diatribe, and speculative science fiction, a hard-boiled thriller about a Neanderthal who gets arrested by Homeland Security in a nightmare version of the not-too-distant future. Terry Hawkins is a bold and fearless writer."

— **Tom Perrotta**, author of *The Leftovers* and *Little Children*

"About as perfect as a novel gets...If you're going to read only one contemporary speculative fiction novel this year, make it this one."

— **Jason Pettus**, Chicago Center for Literature and Photography

"Part dystopian nightmare, part gritty Bildungsroman, part satire of our current police state, *American Neolithic* is an ambitious Frankenstein's monster of a novel that is as funny as it is terrifying."

— **Nathaniel Rich**, author of *King Zeno* and *Odds Against Tomorrow*

For Bertha Hawkins, Estelle Witt, Yuss Merlin, and Eric Merlin.
May their names always be for blessings.

Foreword
On *American Neolithic*

Books set in the near future are among the great challenges in fiction writing. Whether they are solemn warnings of rolling disaster, mild stories of new possibilities of justice and peace, or merely noir thrillers with added not-yet-developed tech, it is almost certain they will self-immolate in a very short time after publication–at least these days, when the future doesn't lie very far ahead at all, but lurks around the corner waiting impatiently to mug you. Your clever book is (accidental hits aside) not going to survive the season, and the more your near-future is elaborated the quicker it will fade.

On the other hand, a good writer can turn the trope to good use. Terence Hawkins combines the near future of a quite recent past with a past so far that it not only contrasts but complements. The far past is contained in the memory of a Neanderthal, wise, humane (!) and generous, and the near-future/bent-present is in the moment-to-moment experience of the lawyer who slowly comes to understand that he must not only defend but preserve the man of a past aeon. The blend is effervescent and continuously engaging.

Hawkins is one of those writers who are at the mercy of their wit and the surprising turns of language that constitute style. The contrast in *American Neolithic* between the thoughtful and patient Neanderthal's life-writing and the narration of the lawyer who sets out to protect him, whose language is like Marx Brothers' routines rolled into one, is the engine of the book. The Neanderthal's recounting and the lawyer's, the one placid and wondrous, the other shamelessly gag-laden and swift, operate like a comedy tag team, or a Shakespearean king and his fool.

In addition to these elements of style—which I understand are not the reason most people read books—there is a tricksome and cleverly contrived plot, which will not here be explicated, because that isn't done, at least not until you, reader, have reached the last page. It can be revealed that it comprises, along with the comic *noir*, an actually touching family history—of a family that actually can't have had a history, or an existence at all. Hawkins's gentle treatment of these displaced persons, their care for one another, the immigrant troubles so universal we recognize them immediately and then catch ourselves—this family is unrepresented in family scrapbooks and photos. It's unsettling, as it is intended to be, this American tale that isn't like anybody else's even while it's the same tale as always. For what is mostly a comic—or at least humorous—novel, *American Neolithic* is oddly touching in many places. Is it reasonable that a young Neanderthal could, all on his own, come to reason and speak and write like a Cro-Magnon (our modern selves, with added civilization for better or for worse—complex language, remembered history, social analysis, etc.)? No, really, it isn't: an answer that's useless in the context, for in addition to being a *noir* legal thriller in a comic vein, *American Neolithic* can be understood as science fiction (the science being anthropology) and as a fantasy: the return of the lost and buried Old Ones, to save or to take revenge, or maybe both. Does it matter how it's classified? Not a bit. All that matters is the wit and wisdom, the surprise and the satisfaction of curiosity. Few novels deliver more.

John Crowley

Retainer. Manhattan, early March.

The Homeland cops were holding another terror drill in the Holland Tunnel. Rerouted traffic on Canal and West Broadway was sclerotic, with produce truckers and commuters unpatriotically leaning on their horns. A black drone glided overhead, low enough so that I could see Homeland's eye-and-thunderbolts insignia on the fuselage. Twice it playfully dinked pedestrians with its green and red target lasers. Just so everyone knew who was boss.

It was a March morning, wet and raw. The *Times* was a little damp from drizzle by the time I got to my office. Before I spread it out to dry I scanned the front page. Half the counties in Arizona were now officially polygamous, subject to the stringency that sister wives under fifteen needed their fathers' consent to marry. Oh, and the Mississippi National Guard had turned water cannon on a crowd protesting the demolition of an MLK statue. The White House mumbled something about states' rights and changed the subject.

I was ready to start the crossword when Frobisher called. "Hey," he said. "Seen the paper?"

"Got it in my hands."

"*Post*?"

"Not since the lobotomy scabbed over. *Times*."

Frobisher snorted. "Right. Too good for the tabloids. Listen, do yourself a favor. Go downstairs and buy yourself a *Post*. There's a guy on page three needs a lawyer. Informed sources say it could be you."

"Okay," I said. "Thanks." I thought about finishing my coffee and the crossword first, but Frobisher was a good source and I didn't want him to feel taken for granted. I also thought about just going online, but ever since the Paper of Record had shrunk to the size of a suburban shopper I'd developed an obsession with print. So I compromised and took my coffee with me and tried to think of a five-letter word for a fatal Cossack whip.

I got back to my desk. The President was on the cover, grinning around a Marlboro and giving the photographer a thumbs-up.

SMOKIN' HEART!

Prez shows press his new heart is working just fine. Less than six weeks after the transplant ticker was harvested from a Guantanamo detainee, it's ready for the hard-work, hard-play life of Numero Uno.

Knout, I thought. The word is knout. As in knouted to death. As in the Cossacks strapped the serf to a bench and broke his back with their knouts. I bought a paper and went back upstairs.

Right. Page three. Well, it looked like somebody needed a lawyer, that was certain. The article occupied the whole page. Its right half was a nice sharp color photo of state police and plainclothes cops hustling a squat figure into an unmarked car.

HIP-HOP HELL: GUNFIRE RATTLES RAPMASTER'S BEDFORD CRIB
ONE DEAD, TWO ARRESTED
ICON BLINGBLING SUSPECT

Bedford (Special to the Post) The rural peace of rustic Westchester was shattered in the wee hours by something even worse than the filthy "lyrics" of rapper Newton Galileo's hip-hop chart-toppers, Think We Dum Niggazz.

Bedford was used to a lot from the "pimp kulcha" biggie. Late night parties that had to be broken up by the fire department with high-pressure hoses. Pampers and Popeyes boxes hurled from the windows of white stretch limos

I stopped reading for a minute. With its particular style and sensibilities the *Post* sometimes couldn't be appreciated all at once.

I took a deep breath and started again. It didn't take long to finish, what with its wee tiny words that I didn't even have to sound out. I called Frobisher. He picked up right away.

"Guess your caller ID isn't working," I said.

"I got broad standards. Whaddayuh think?"

"Let me ask you a few questions first."

"Shoot," he said. "Keep it simple. I'm busy and not that bright."

"That I knew. At least the last part. Okay, first, just so I know, why is a guy named Newton Galileo fronting a group called Think We Dum Niggazz? In fact how does a guy come to be named Newton Galileo at all? I leave unsaid the most obvious question."

"It's a joke," said Frobisher. "Irony."

"Oh," I said. "I guess that's okay then. And the same goes for the

2

victim? The late Mr. Einstein Spinoza? Wow. Did they make them all up themselves?'

"Beats me."

"All right. But the alleged shooter apparently didn't get the memo. Blingbling?"

"He wasn't part of the group. He was just kind of a mascot. They found him sweeping up hair in a barbershop in the Village a couple of months ago. He's retarded but he can dance great so they kept him around for shits and giggles. They let him on stage every so often. And he showed up on some kind of media feed and wound up with a YouTube channel for about twenty seconds."

"That made him an icon?"

"What can I tell you, it's the *Post*."

"Right. Well, judging from the picture—and sadly according to the YouTube clip I'm looking at right now it's accurate—he is not the best looking guy in the world."

"Not the smartest either. Which I guess is how he got that great job sweeping up hair. But anyway, when the cops showed he was sitting in a corner mumbling and holding the gun by its barrel."

"Well, that'd be probable cause. But this excellent newspaper says they pulled in Copernicus--"

"Galileo," said Frobisher.

"Right. Just wanted to see if you were paying attention. Anyway, they pull in Galileo too. But the paper neglects to tell me why."

"Ran out of space I guess. What I hear is that two days before the same cops broke up a fight between Galileo and Spinoza. Seems a chair got used for something other than sitting and the neighbors didn't like the way it sounded. So the cops thought they'd like Galileo's perspective on the matter too."

"Oh. What was the beef?"

"Apparently money, for a long time. Short term it was that Spinoza had been putting his dick in the wrong place. Galileo's babymama."

"Ah. And how do you know things that even the *Post* doesn't know?"

"The people who want to hire you know them and they told me."

"Oh. Right. Now who do they want me to represent? Wait! I know! The estate of the late Einstein Spinoza in a very nice wrongful death action against the whole world that will allow me to retire in comfort."

"That would be a no."

"Oh. Hmm. Then I guess you want me to enter an appearance for Newton Galileo, his fellow artistes, their record company, and their various insurers with a retainer that will allow me to retire in comfort."

"Let me call. Ring ring ring. Sorry. Another negative."

"Hmm. Witnesses that might be the subject of the Grand Jury's attention?"

"Nope."

"Oh. That leaves a guy holding a gun, with no papers, and I'm guessing one chromosome more or less than the rest of us."

"My God, you really are a great cross-examiner. You just beat it out of me."

I thought about the cigars in my left-hand desk drawer but decided later was soon enough. "Who's got Galileo?"

"Braunstein." It figured. Braunstein got every NFL rapist and Presidential Family drunk driver. I heard he was thinking about buying Spielberg's old place in East Hampton and tearing it down so he could build something really nice.

"How about the estate?"

"Johnson." Equally unsurprising. Before he was in the Senate, before he was shamed out of office for impregnating his dying teenaged daughter's best friend, Johnson had been the first billionaire ambulance chaser.

"Okay. So how am I getting paid?"

"Friends. Don't ask."

I popped open the desk drawer. There were the cigars. There was the cutter. There were the matches. "So Frobisher," I said. "I see a reference in the popular press to the Homeland Police."

"You do," he said.

"So if they file a Person of Interest they can force me to divulge the source of my fee and confiscate it if he's convicted."

"Right."

"And if they get a judge to issue a terror warrant they can charge me as a co-conspirator if we try it and lose."

"You're the lawyer, not me." Frobisher seemed to be enjoying himself.

I punched the speakerphone button. I needed both hands to fire up a Macanudo. I figured it was Saturday and if I left the windows open all weekend my assistant wouldn't be too mad on Monday. "So," I said, "you want me to represent some cognitively chall enged wannabee rapper with a smoking gun in his hands, several witnesses already staking out positions in the papers, TV lawyers representing everybody else, and the Homeland cops sniffing around my fee."

"That would be it."

"And speaking of my fee?"

"Two-fifty. A hundred now and the rest later."

"Half what any sane man would insist on up front."

"Like you say," said Frobisher, "any sane man. That's why I called you."

I blew a couple of smoke rings. I was trying to do the Ballantine Ale logo. When I was in college they said that if you took a picture of the interlocking smoke rings and sent it to Ballantine it was free beer for life.

I decided to ask the big question. "Umm...Think he's guilty?"

"Fuck no."

"But he's, umm, a special needs kind of guy?"

"Fuck yes. Complete retard."

After I winced I blew a couple more rings. Just for an instant it looked as though they linked up in just the right way. If it had been my junior year and I had been in a New Haven bar instead of my office, I would have been a happy man.

I made a business decision. I made it the same way that I make every business decision. The way that got me a walkup office off Centre Street and a assistant with woman problems that kept her down to a twenty-hour workweek.

"Sounds like a good case," I said.

Undisclosed location, two years later

Naturally they will give me nothing to write with. I think they are amused by my pretense to an art quintessentially human. They think that as I trace these words on the wall with my fingertip whispering meanings to myself I merely parrot the master race's skills without comprehension.

Perhaps I am giving them the benefit of the doubt. Perhaps they are aware that I know exactly what I am doing. Perhaps they withhold pen and paper to deprive me of the gift that has set me apart from my people and brought me here. To render meaningless my literacy and the price I have paid for it.

It was, of course, different before the trial. Mr. Raleigh saw to it that I was well-supplied with paper and pens. But that, as they say, was then. I have not seen Mr. Raleigh for two years.

Even in my imaginary tracings, I must write for you. With your high foreheads and smooth skin and ease with symbols. And, oh yes, mastery of the world.

You, for whom we have always been the Other. Our existence buried deep in your racial memories since the time when glaciers girdled the world and the contest between man and animal was yet to be decided. We haunt your legends as we haunt your dreams, misshapen versions of yourselves, bad copies, formerly kobolds or gremlins, now morlocks and Orcs. Why did Phidias choose as his theme for the Parthenon frieze a battle between men and not-men? Unquestionably, because there stirred in his Attic memory a time, less distant then than now, when your people were not the only human species.

And something had to be done about that.

Never having been more than a dozen miles from where I was born—at least until I came under the jurisdiction of the Department of Homeland Security, which plainly has taken me much farther afield—I have not seen the Elgin marbles. In fact, all I know of them is what I learned from a coffee-stained New York *Times* article that I pulled from a garbage can in front of Madison Square Garden. But that told enough to inspire me to wonder whether the heroic battle between man and centaur was how it really ended for most of my people as well; whether we, however slow and timid, suddenly found it within ourselves to defy mankind's bronze spear-points and disciplined phalanxes. Or whether—and I know this is more likely—we fled chittering and weeping before a few bands of half-starved, nearly-naked toolmakers to have our heads unheroically bashed in with stones?

Perhaps that would explain your ambivalence in representations of us. As I said, we have been demons in ancient times as well as modern. But that is not the whole story. The Other has also assumed a kinder, gentler form—fairy, sprite, leprechaun, munchkin. And now Hobbit. A squat hairy people living in burrows, simple and full of virtue. Not the epitaph I would have wished for our people, but not bad. I wonder, do your people continue to sweat and mumble in your dreams with the guilty memory of some Neolithic holocaust in which you chased the last of us down? Or thought you did.

I wonder, too, whether your suppressed memories of our brief coexistence drive your ability to abuse your own kind. How many times my lips twitched as I read of Tutsis massacring Hutus! Or perhaps it was the other way around? Serbs and Croats. And not too long ago, I understand, Flemings and Walloons. Was it prehistoric habit that enabled you to treat another tribe as not fully human? And once you are assured of our final disappearance, the extinction of the true Other, will you at long last relax and be at peace with yourselves?

They give me nothing to read. They say it is because to do so would be inconsistent with the status I have been assigned. Accordingly, I amuse myself as best I can.

Sometimes I console myself with fantasies of an evolution entirely different from that which brought me here. I imagine the center of the country quaking under the lumbering gait of herding landwhales, huge as zeppelins, the descendants of cetaceans that hadn't abandoned the land to wallow back into the sea's supportive embrace. Panting like diesels through the blowholes in the backs of their locomotive heads. Huge square teeth grinding up tons of wild maize, their diet enriched with stunned rodents dug from tunnels shattered by their passing bulk, the plains' flatness broken by their mountainous droppings. The evolutionary niche from which your ancestors evicted mine now occupied by the distant descendants of dogs, whole countries of them blinking contentedly in the sun, canine nations resolving their squabbles with a warning nip to the flank. Yes, I think the world would have been far better had men descended from dogs rather than apes.

Your people think mine stupid and brutal. Not so. True, we could never compete with you. Not for want of intelligence—though I confess that tools and numbers come much more easily to yours than mine—but because we lack your ability to treat our own as abstractions. Perhaps this has to do with the power of abstraction itself. It is as though you can reduce flesh and blood and rich odor to a number. Witness how in the last century your most civilized country nearly abstracted out of existence an entire people, whose few survivors bear on their arms tattooed numerals by which their extinction would be tabulated.

I asked my keepers what it is about my status that prohibits my being able to read. The young ones who bring my daily bucket of food and remove my daily bucket of filth will not answer. Once though, the older one who asks me questions, Captain Graner, was more forthcoming.

"Answer me a question first," he said.

"Yes," I replied.

"Were there thirty-five of you?"

I thought for a long time. No one had hurt me, at least not too badly. Not yet. No doubt because I had told them anything they wanted to know and made it very clear that pain only confused me. As I hesitated, Graner raised his booted foot. I squealed and cowered. He laughed and stroked his little moustache.

"Give me something to count with," I said.

He had been well briefed so that he knew my limitations in this regard. He thought I could not count for the same reason he believed I could not read: That is, he thought that I am stupid. Not so. We evolved in Ice Age Europe, where climate blocked sunlight and the seasons extended night. Accordingly, we developed larger eyes and, with them, larger sections of brain devoted to processing images. Unfortunately, something had to give. The cranial volume taken up by the visual centers was stolen from those given to abstraction. Thus, while we can speak and compose poetry and sing and in a few storied cases read and write, all but the most elementary math eludes us.

Captain Graner reached into his camouflage jacket and handed me several packs of matches. I squatted at his feet and flipped open the first. As I tore off matches I recited with each a name. A younger woman, behind him, clicked busily into a laptop what I presumed were phonetic transliterations of our clicks and murmurs. She did not transcribe, nor could

8

she, the history of smells and touch that each paper stick represented.

At last I was done. "Is that thirty-five?" said Graner.

"I don't know," I said. "Is it?"

"Oh, Christ." Graner rolled his eyes. "You can talk, monkey, but can't you count?"

I cringed at his feet, curled into a ball. "No," I said between the arms folded across my face.

Graner waited a moment to assure himself that my humiliation was complete. "Is that everyone, monkey?"

"Yes."

"Okay, Bonzo. Let me count for you."

He bent over and laboriously counted out my offering. *One. Two. Three. Eighteen. Thirty-five.*

"See, monkey?" he said at last. "Not so hard. For *humans*."

I heard his boots clatter towards the door of my pen, behind them the lighter footfall of his assistant.

"Wait!" I said. "Please."

"Wait? Wait? What for, chimp?"

"You said you'd answer a question of mine."

"That's right," he said. "Monkey, you are so right."

"Why can't I read?"

He was at the door. His assistant already hovered outside. Her lips were curved in a half-smile, ready to laugh; this was going to be a good one.

Graner pursed his lips in mock gravity. He folded his arms over his chest. "Why, monkey," he said. "That's easy. You're an animal. *And everyone knows that animals can't read.*"

My howls were drowned out in the click of bolts and the assistant's laughter.

Client interview. White Plains, later that day.

This time Frobisher surprised me. More often than not his little crushes on fourth tier celebrity clients crumpled on contact with the brute reality of money. I figured that my loose talk about a retainer would give me time to finish the crossword, drink another coffee, and grow a beard down to my knees. But no. Half an hour after I hung up I tapped into my account and there were the twenty thousand balloons I said I needed even to talk to Blingbling.

So I emailed the legal interview notice to the joint and had an early lunch and got to Grand Central in time for the 1:05 to White Plains. Driving was out of the question. The Homeland cops on the bridge were probably having a body-cavity day, and with gas at eleven-fifty after the last Mahdist raids on the Saudi oilfields, I'd've burned up the retainer at a toll booth.

I was glad I took the train. With a Platinum Trusted Traveler endorsement on my Homeland Passport I didn't even have to wait ten minutes to board. The klickety-klack somehow lulled my brainstem enough to retrieve a five-letter word for a czarist dictate. *Ukase*. As in *Ukase of Unkiar-Skelessi*. A phrase I first saw chalked across a blackboard my sophomore year. Diplomatic history, in a time so distant that the professor brought to his lectern an ashtray for the droppings of the three Camels he would consume in less than an hour.

Happy days. Or at least days happier than these. Odd how quickly the Republic crumpled into a police state, or at least a Police State Lite. One fine afternoon in May the FBI says it thinks there's a dirty bomb in a container ship in Long Beach. The next day they don't find a bomb, but rather a radioactive hotspot on a vessel whose last port of call was Karachi. Which is even worse, they say, because we know there was a bomb but now we don't know where it is. A mere forty-eight hours of blubbering hysteria later a special session of Congress declares a state of national emergency and the President federalizes the National Guard to kind of help look for it. And while the pesky thing refuses to show up, the general feeling is that we should find room on Rushmore for Mussolini. Because these constitutional amendments they're talking about on Fox sure would take the handcuffs off the good guys, wouldn't they? And streamline government, too!

So before you know it there was a forty-state landslide ratifying the

Patriot Amendments. Not surprising, really. We'd been heading in that direction in fits and starts for a generation, regardless of which team was in office, each waterboarded and renditioned. The next used flying robots to kill Americans and whoever they happened to be standing around with so long as they were in Elsewhereistan. And from there it wasn't a big step to ignoring the Supreme Court and invalidating elections. So no shock then that the flying robots were now circling Cleveland and Office of Media Accuracy popups critiqued every article in my news feed.

Sometimes I blamed myself. Maybe if I hadn't switched stations during NPR pledge drives.

Frobisher's discretion had been as hard to crack as a Rite Aid suitcase lock. The "friends" who were coughing up a quarter mil in Bling's defense were neither the NAACP nor what little was left of the ACLU. Nor were they benevolent spinsters who'd liquidated a few shares of Berkshire A in their cats' trust fund.

" Old Skool Killazz?" I said. "Now just what the fuck is Old Skool Killazz?"

"Dude," said Frobisher. With pity in his voice. "Or should I say, *old* dude. Old *white* dude. I know streaming is just too confusing. But do you not have a radio?"

"I do. Oddly enough they haven't shown up on Morning Edition."

"'Shown up on Morning Edition,'" he said. "I keep forgetting that Ivy League thing. Just in case you'd like to join the rest of us in the twenty-first century, Old Skool Killazz has been locked in mortal combat with TWDN at the top of the hip-hop charts for at least three years."

"Mortal combat?"

"Mortal combat. Mortal. We're not just talking trash talk at the BET awards and little girlie shoving matches outside clubs. When LaShette LaFray got gunned down in front of the Killazz studio? That was a TWDN assassination."

"Assassination?"

"You're surprised?"

"Just that you'd call it an assassination. Do they close schools on the anniversary? And I'm surprised that anyone called LaShette hadn't changed his name."

"Very perceptive, Pops. His adoring public knew him as Wun Dolla

Murda."

"Ah. Of course. Do go on."

"Yeah. Anyway. So there's been a lot of bad blood flying around and when the Killazz heard about what went down in Bed-Fly--"

"Bed-Fly?"

"That's what they've been calling Bedford since Galileo moved up there. You know. Like Bed-Stuy."

"Oh. Silly of me."

"Anyway, when the Killazz heard about what went down, well, they seen their chance and they took it."

"Meaning?"

"Meaning they figured if Bling got a good defense and it looked like he got framed maybe Galileo would slip in the shit. They made a call, somebody else called me, I called you."

"Not that I don't appreciate it, but why me?"

"A. We're buds. B. They wanted a serious lawyer, not some A-lister. I figured you're the top of the B-list."

"That's a lot of alphabet. Like I said, thanks." I hung up.

The bull at the desk and I went back to those dewy-eyed days when I was a stumbling junior prosecutor. Nevertheless he asked for three forms of ID— including Homeland Passport—before he buzzed me through. "Sorry, chief," he said. "Word from on high. Already had some assholes from BET try to get through as your guy's lawyers."

"Since when have I looked black? Or entertaining?"

"Entertaining never. Not even interesting. But tell you what, boss, you look blacker than Wild Bill Blingbling."

"No shit?"

"No shit." He hit a button and a bell rang. "He don't look white either. Or Latino. Maybe he's Maltese or something." The barred outer door rolled aside. "Enjoy your stay," he said. "I promise I'll try to remember to let you out."

I've been buzzed through more than a thousand times but it's always the same. Once the last door slams shut behind me I feel like screaming *No! No! It's a mistake! I don't belong here!*.

But I didn't and in a second I was a suit shouldering past the thirty-eight-year-old grandmothers lined up for ten minutes over phones through scratched Plexiglas with men in dreads and orange jumpsuits. Why don't he have to wait like us, they muttered as I settled in the little cinderblock conference room marked LEGAL VISIT. Because I'm a lawyer, I thought. Because I've pissed away an Ivy League education keeping your shitbag boyfriends out of jail.

Bitter? Just a little. When I started out, a very old lawyer told me that you don't get to make many really big choices but one was whether you represent the haves or the have-nots. I figured I'd keep the faith with umpteen generations of coal-mining Raleighs back in West Virginia and vindicate the downtrodden and unjustly accused. So I learned the business in the DA's office and after I'd done my time hung out a shingle. But, sadly, Sacco and Vanzetti are long gone. So instead I represent the guilty—if not as charged, then generally of something much worse. Mom would be so proud.

The legal visit room had concrete walls painted a shade of orange just different enough from prison jumpsuits to make you queasy when your client walks in. It had a metal table bolted to the floor. On the client's side was a metal stool also bolted to the floor. On the lawyer's side was a metal chair not bolted to the floor, demonstrating that as an officer of the court I was trusted not to steal the furniture. Or use it as a weapon.

Or maybe it meant I was entitled to. Food for thought.

I opened the iPad and set out a fresh legal tablet with my pen next to it. An hour passed. Without the iPad I would have stuck the pen through my eye.

Just when I was about to switch from online caselaw to online porn, I heard buzzers and slamming steel followed by the squeak of rubber-soled boots and the swish of paper prison slippers. A bull was at the door. "Got your client," he said. "I'm at the gate when you're ready." Looking at someone I couldn't see, he nodded towards the empty stool. "In there, guy."

A little figure in an orange jumpsuit peeked around the door. "It's okay," said the bull. "He's your lawyer. He's on *your side*." The bull pushed the little figure forward—gently for someone who's used to separating serial killers in shower buttrapes—and closed the door behind him.

The *Post* hadn't prepared me. The desk sergeant was right about my guy. He didn't look African American. Or anything else. He looked *weird*.

I said he was little, but when I got a good look at him I realized that this impression was inspired not by his size but by his obvious timidity.

True, he wasn't tall—a little shorter than me, maybe five-six max—but he was *thick*. Big chest and shoulders, heavily muscled and hirsute forearms sticking out of the jumpsuit's short sleeves, square-nailed hands the size and shape of catchers' mitts. No neck to speak of, so his round head nestled flush between his sloping trapezius muscles.

So far, not so weird. The overall effect was that of an East European Olympian before they got all picky about steroids and gender reassignment.

His face, however, was a different story. When I looked up I almost dropped my pen. I had done as much homework as I could in the hour between the transfer of funds and lunch, but music videos didn't do the boy credit. If credit was the right word.

It was the kind of face you see in a pen-and-ink artist's conception in the Science *Times* on Tuesday or in claymation reconstructions on the Discovery Channel. Nose both long and bulbous, like an heirloom potato. Huge jet black eyes that would have looked right in a manga cartoon, beneath a shelf of brow. Forehead and chin receding. My God, I thought, he looks like a caveman. I jotted a note—*Birth defects? Fetal alc/drug? Shrink/ geneticist?*

Recovering from my momentary shock, I took advantage of my chair's mobility by knocking it over as I scrambled to my feet. "Hey," I said, grinning as I reached across the table. "Glad to meet you. Sorry it's here." The thousandth time for that, too.

My noisy flurry of awkward activity clearly had not proven reassuring. He was just settling cautiously onto his stool when I lunged across the table to shake hands. Rather than giving my extended paw a manly shake, he made a funny chittering noise and rolled off his stool and onto the floor. I froze for a moment, hand still outstretched, until I heard the same sound coming from under the table.

Okay, I thought, maybe there's some guy still in here from the last interview. Or maybe there's a giant raccoon down there. But I bet that's my new client.

I dropped to my hands and knees. Yep. There he was. Curled up in a fetal ball and shaking with explosive sobs.

I didn't need my legal pad. Even the Homeland Czar would agree that this guy was incompetent to stand trial. On the one hand, I'd never see the quarter million I said I'd need to try the case. On the other, I wouldn't have to work very hard for the hundred I knew was coming just to get this misunderstood fellow hooked up to a permanent antipsychotic drip.

Well, I thought, what the hell. I was under the table anyway. Poor bastard got plucked out of a bottom-rung job at a barbershop to serve as a hip-hop court jester. And look what it got him. So I started to pat the poor bastard's heaving shoulder.

He curled up even tighter.

"Take it easy," I said. "It'll be okay. I'm on your side."

He cried harder still. Obviously I am not the most nurturing guy. Trying to remember that he probably had the mental capacity of a puppy I started to rub his back in circles and made the little shh, shh, shh noises I'd heard women use to comfort heartbroken children. Not easy when the heartbroken infant in question appears to have weightlifter's muscles under his prison polyester.

After a minute or two the sobbing had deteriorated into an occasional wet snuffle. Afraid that if I kept massaging the next noise I'd hear would be a snore, I backed up a little. Still on my hands and knees, mind. Under the table. "It's okay," I said again. "I'm on your side."

My client took his forearms from his head and rolled over to face me. His nose was six inches from mine. At this range I was again struck by just how weird he looked. His skin was no color I had ever seen, a reddish brown that verged on orange. His pores were big and his creases, though few, were very deep. It made him look like a basketball.

He opened his mouth. I don't know what made me look in. The fact that I was under the table in an interview room with an accused murderer whose head belonged on NBA hardwood? I mean, why not? Anyway, his canines were, well, canine and his molars were the size of golf balls. And, forgive me, but he hadn't flossed for quite a while. My eyebrows were singed.

Having opened his mouth he decided to use it. "My side?" he said.

As the *Post* article had said and my hurried Googlings confirmed, he was hard to understand. It was as though his words were whistled and slurred.

But I understood what he said, and anyway, I was his lawyer not a speech therapist. "Your side," I said. "*Your* side." I extended my hand again. This time he took it. Nice strong grip. Nice warm hand. It felt like one big callus.

I crawled backwards from under the table. He did the same, though a little more slowly, so I had time to arrange myself in the lawyer chair and get comfortable with pretending that the previous five minutes hadn't happened. By the time my client had re-emerged and gotten himself situated my tie was straight, my hair smooth, my eye steely.

"Now," I said, "let's get started. My name's Raleigh. Some friends of yours asked me to talk to you to see if I could help you out. I want to help you. I *will* help you if I can. But I can only help you if you help me. Is that okay so far?"

He nodded his basketball head.

"Good. This is a great start. Now there are a couple of things you have to understand. First is that if I decide I can help you and take your case then I take my orders from you and only you. Even though your friends are paying me. I'm telling you this because I want you to understand that I'm on your side and only your side.

"I'm also telling you this because once I get into your case anything you say to me or I say to you is strictly private unless this becomes a terrorism case, which I don't think will happen. But it's only strictly private if you don't tell anyone else what I say to you. No judge in the world can make me tell what you said to me, unless you want me to tell. But if you tell some guy in your cell 'hey, my lawyer told me I'm walking because the DA's stupid and the judge is stupider,' all of a sudden our private conversations aren't so private. It's called a waiver. It could mean that the judge might make me talk about what we've talked about.. So don't talk to anybody else about the case. Anybody. Ever. Understand?"

He nodded again. His dark eyes were utterly blank, his leathery features surprisingly calm since his little outburst under the table. Because I knew he spoke English I assumed that I was looking at a grown up crack baby having a psychotic break.

"Good," I said. "Just so you understand. I told you a minute ago that what we say here is just between us unless this is a terrorism case. Now I have to tell you a couple of things that may scare you, but you shouldn't let them scare you because this isn't a terrorism case. But since the Patriot Amendments were passed every lawyer in a criminal matter has to warn his client of certain things. So I'm warning you about things that probably won't happen, but just might, okay?"

He tilted his head. No doubt listening to those other voices inside it.

"Okay. Again, just so you understand. If the Homeland Police decide

you might be a terrorist they can make me file a certificate to say that
we haven't talked about terrorism, which if we haven't I would do. But
if we have I would have to withdraw from your case, because if you were
a terrorist and I falsely said you weren't I could face the death penalty
myself."

He was starting to quiver. Funny. Wonder why.

"And if the Homeland Police thought you were a terrorist planning
something bad to happen in the next thirty days they could go to the
Patriot Tribunal to issue a special warrant. If they issued that warrant
I would have to tell them about any conversation we had about terror
attacks. And you would be transferred to the Homeland Police Special
Interrogation Unit where you could be questioned with any level of force
not recognized as fatal to a reasonably healthy person."

The shaking wasn't getting any better. What a surprise.

"Finally, under very rare circumstances, if you meet a certain secret
terrorist profile and haven't told me to turn you in and the national security
alert level is orange or above, any judge of the Patriot Tribunal can order
you detained in a Freedom Friendly Ally, which is another country that
hasn't joined the International Criminal Court and has repudiated certain
provisions of the Geneva Conventions and the United Nations Charter."

If he started shaking any harder I would have had to put a spoon
between his teeth. I could see from the way he was curling into himself
that he was considering another fetal retreat under the table. I half rose
out of my chair and grabbed a cantaloupe-sized bicep.

"Look. It sounds bad. But don't worry. It probably won't happen. I have
to tell you the very, very worst. They make us tell everyone that so that bad
guys will get scared and confess right away. But they tell me that you're
not a bad guy. Are you?"

The shaking hadn't stopped. But at least it had gone from the DT's to a
shiver. He shook his head. Twice. Hard.

"Okay," I said, releasing his arm and settling back in my chair. "So just
pretend I didn't tell you what I just told you. But I do have to tell you
one more thing. As I said, I'm on your side. I will do everything possible
to make sure you're walking next to me when I leave the courthouse at the
end of your case. But the one thing I can't do is let you take the witness
stand if you told me you did it. If you did it, tell me, and I'll try the case
without you on the stand. But if you did it and you don't tell me and I let

you take the stand I guarantee you things will go very badly."

The shaking had stopped. He nodded solemnly.

"Okay," I said. "Do we understand each other then?"

He hadn't given me anything to understand, and I very much doubted that he understood what I had given him, but he nodded again. Obliging guy. I could just see the cross now. *"You killed him, didn't you? Nod. You wanted to, didn't you? Nod. It felt good, didn't it?"* His head bobbling like a ceramic Great Dane in the bric-a-brac garden on a grandmother's TV. Oh well. My job was to make sure it didn't come to that.

"Okay," I said again, smiling the compassionate smile I reserve for the utterly guilty and entirely stupid. "I read the papers. Tell me what really happened."

He cleared his throat and started to speak in his whistling slur. "Sorry," I said. "Slow down."

He started again. If I strained I could pick out individual words. It was like talking to one of the ghetto boyz with sideways trucker hats and NBA shorts who sat with their legs splayed and eyes anywhere but on me. The ones who made it a point of pride not to be understood by the old white guy with a pile of their ice money in his safe. At least until I made a call and the guy who'd made them the ice money showed up and I left the room and he 'splained things with a Taser. When I came back they were always a lot more respectful and well-spoken.

But this guy didn't irritate me. It was clear he was trying. It was also clear he could read the perplexity in my face, because his was starting to knot in frustration. Suddenly he reached across the table for my pen.

Okay. I jumped. Sue me.

His eyes locked on mine. I shrugged. His eyes stayed where they were, suspicious obsidian globes set in rhino hide. Then his basketball face split in a gap-toothed grin and he hee-hawed with laughter.

I joined in. At a much higher pitch.

Eventually my client settled back and assumed a serious expression. He unscrewed the cap from the pen. I started to wonder how a deformed barebershop janitor had acquired his easy familiarity with vintage writing implements.

But then his face contorted in a Maori mask of rage. He raised the pen like a dagger.

When I say I jumped, this time I mean jumped, as opposed to simply rising a little in my chair. I also squeaked like a chipmunk and narrowly avoided soiling myself.

Obviously he'd never seen anything funnier. And he got a lot of mileage out of the pen thing. A couple of feints and jabs followed by a none too flattering impression of a lawyer recoiling in terror. This was followed by more horse-laughs and thigh slappings. I sat there grinning and nodding, one hand feeling for the buzzer under the table and finding only fossilized gum and dried snot. Never a cop when you need one.

At length he sat down again and wiped his streaming eyes. He extended his hand and we shook again. Oh, good. All better. I'll just sit here with this comical killer between me and the door.

He picked up the pen again, this time with an elaborate flourish, and slowly pulled the legal pad towards himself. So as not to alarm me. Very funny, I thought.

He caught my eye and winked. It had already occurred to me that his act had been pretty sophisticated for a refugee from a diorama. At that moment I thought to myself Hmm. Idiot savant. Like one of those guys who can tell you the day of the week that any event in history fell on when he's not chewing on yesterday's Depends.

He bent over the pad, brow furrowed—and given that brow, that's saying something—and scribbled laboriously for five full minutes. At last he returned the pad.

I smiled indulgently. My files were full of letters from guys a lot smarter. YOO BETER HELP ME UR ELS!!!

The patronizing smirk was gone so fast I didn't feel it leave. In neat, almost school-teacherly script you wouldn't have thought those cartoon mitts capable of appeared the following:

Mr Raleigh--

Thank you very much for helping me. I understand that the consequences of being less than honest can be very dire. I also understand that if the government decides that I am a terrorist—and I assure you, I am anything but—you will have no alternative but to withdraw from the case and cooperate with whatever they want to do to me. Forgive my noticing, but I gather you've been a lawyer long enough to remember when things were different, and I would imagine that you find this all rather difficult.

After I read this twice I raised my eyes to his. Was it my imagination or was he smiling?

I put the pad back on the table between us and flipped to a clean page. With one of the other pens I began to write: *How did you learn--*

He immediately began to write on the same page.

No need; consider me mute, or effectively so for anything complex, but not deaf. I hear very well. Have you ever noticed that when two interlocutors rely on different media of communication, one instinctively adopts the other's? Even when it's entirely unnecessary?

"No," I said slowly. "No, I haven't."

This was not shaping up the way I expected.

Undisclosed location, two years later

I am *not* an animal.

Of course I'm not. Leave aside the dispositive evidence that I can read and write. Attainments I will presently explain.

I do not in the least resemble an animal. At least, no more than my distant cousin with the keys to my pen. I am just over five and a half feet tall. When last measured, at the time of my initial confinement, my weight was a hundred and seventy pounds. Very little fat, may I add with a pride that I no doubt acquired osmotically from my earliest readings—fashion magazines found in subway trashcans. My disproportionate weight is largely the product of bones somewhat thicker and muscle mass greater than yours.

Contrary to the few caricatures I was allowed to see before I was deprived even of tabloids, I do not lean forward any more than you do. Search my knuckles for telltale calluses if you like. Nor do my arms dangle like a baboon's. If anything, they are somewhat shorter than yours. While my legs are scarcely those of an Olympic sprinter, neither are they out of place on a wrestler. In short, if you were to find me sweating under a barbell at Gold's Gym or piling out of a landscaper's truck at a Hamptons palace, you would not look at me twice.

From the chin down, at least.

Our features are neither brutish nor simian. And I must point out that my cranial capacity is substantially larger than yours. Rather like that of the dolphins, another intelligent species whose continued survival is the product of their comparative isolation. From you.

I must admit, however, that my profile differs more radically. My forehead and chin both slope away from the rest of my face. My nose is large, suited for warming the air blown off a glacier. Our other principal difference, the bony bulge at the back of our heads, is covered by hair—which, incidentally, is thicker than yours. The remaining distinction is the ridge over my brows, a feature equally pronounced among your steroid users.

So, as you can see, our presence among you is partly explained by our superficial similarity, if not resemblance. It is further understandable in light of your ability to ignore your own people's suffering. Imagine a windswept, rainy November night. A Wednesday. On an abandoned Garment District cross street. You huddle into your Burberry and swing your briefcase. You barely notice the homeless man rooting through garbage. Just as you are about to pass he glances up and your eyes lock. You stare, startled, at a face that should have been dead twenty thousand years. But just for a moment. Some mongoloid, you think, and then he is gone from view and memory alike.

That is, if he registers at all. In my boyhood, when I took my turns at dumpsters and garbage cans, I could sit in the middle of the sidewalk and sort through my forage in an organized way, confident that busy executives and lawyers shrieking into cell phones would walk around or step over the little Neanderthal boy rooting through their leavings.

My boyhood. I was born after the Nest had made its move into SoHo. In those days it was possible to find large empty spaces, entire floors, in old industrial buildings partly or entirely abandoned. Because we sleep in piles regulated by kinship, and because we evolved in frozen Europe, only on the coldest nights did we need to light the Sterno cans or barrels filled with newspaper whose light might give us away on Mercer Street.

But Mercer Street would have been empty anyway. In those days, it was good to be a Neanderthal in SoHo.

I often pressed my father about the Nest's migrations. But he was not a very good historian. In fact, I am not at all sure that he was my father. Not that this matters. As I've said, we sleep in conjugal piles and descent is determined matrilineally. Thus we are without the dynastic impulse. More importantly, we are disinclined to the sexual jealousy that preys on you so cruelly. But perhaps this complaisance is not such a blessing after all: the jealousy that drives your murders also fires your art. There will never be a Neanderthal opera.

I digress. Of course I digress. Am I not a monkey man, unaccustomed to linear thought and the division of time into minutes and hours? How could I be trusted with the assembly line?

Well. In any event. My father told me that he had been born when the Nest was still in the basement of an abandoned munitions factory across the river in New Jersey. Hard times, he said. The factory, huge as it was, was centered among acres of parking lots, and the whole complex was a dozen miles from the nearest town. So that loose lips would not sink ships. As a result, my father explained, our people lived in a state of perpetual half-starvation, situated as they were a long night's walk from the suburban garbage cans from which we mined our half-eaten Swanson's TV dinners.

Dangerous work it was, too, my father said. Back then your people were far less inclined to avert their eyes from the misshapen. Thus if one of us was seen after dawn or caught at night in the headlights of a Ford V8 filled with Weehauken teenagers, the likely result was a mirthful beating from which the bleeding victim crawled into a drainage pipe, to expire alone, which would be reported as WINO DIES IN CULVERT. Thus our ranks, already thin, dwindled further during those Jersey days.

But difficult as those days were, said my father, there were good times too. We recovered a bit of our pride, however briefly, however much we were forced by circumstances. You see, we need protein. A lot of protein. I have read that before you forced us into the world's darkest corners, our diet was ninety per cent meat. Though we have adapted, a bit, to your world's leavings, we have to be very hungry indeed to eat just-discarded fries when there may be a Slim Jim at the bottom of the trash barrel.

In New Jersey, according to my father, we returned to the ways of the Great Hunt. In the tradition passed down from our uttermost ancestors— whose methods, developed for plains swept smooth by retreating glaciers, were uniquely well-suited for the square mile parking lots of New Jersey.

Regrettably, similar terrain did not harbor similar prey. To be sure, imagining themselves chasing down the mammoths on which we first cut our improbable incisors, the men of the Nest drove their quarry forward into a pit in which it would die under a hail of stones. Howling, raining down death, they were as one with the artists who commemorated their triumphs over giant deer and hippopotamus-sized bison on the walls of caves.

But my father and his brothers chased to their deaths stray dogs. Not even feral packs, good dogs gone bad. No, just setters named Rusty and shepherds called Rinny who followed the wrong raccoon up the wrong road. Nodding proudly my father described the night he had singlehandedly run down a golden retriever barely out of her latest puppyhood, tender enough to be eaten almost raw. Face set in the martial lines of a hunter victorious, he pointed to the ragged leather collar he wore around his neck like a toque, from whose middle hung a tarnished steel tag. "They gave me this to keep afterwards," he said. "From the dog. There are marks on it. Do the marks mean anything?" His voice was shy; he was the child and I the parent.

I bent forward. Tenderly I lifted the steel tag up to my eye. Just visible under the tarnish:

BRANDY.
IF YOU FIND ME, CALL MY MOMMY AND DADDY, LAKELAND 2-1209

"What does it mean?" he asked.

"Hero," I said. "It means you're a hero."

"It does?" he said.

"Oh, yes." I pointed to the dog's name. "This says 'hero'". "And here," I said, moving my finger to the next line, "it says, 'Through his skill and bravery fed the Nest.'"

My father nodded solemnly. His eyes welled with pride.

One would think that we were driven out of Jersey in cinematic black and white by peasants with torches and pitchforks, enraged at the monsters' decimation of their domestic pets. One would think that the last of our kind would have been hurled from the highest turret of Castle Frankenstein by a Basil Rathbone appalled by his own offenses against the Almighty. But no. We were exiled by forces both more and less dramatic.

Having not yet been born I cannot be sure of the truth. But history is not what happened; it is what is said to have happened. And because I have not only what my father and uncles and even mother and aunts have said but also what I learned in those long slow afternoons in front of a terminal at the New York Public Library, I think what I know may be close to reality.

Perhaps I should first give you the public record. The following appeared in Fate, December 1963. Because it is the only interaction between my people and yours documented in modern times—indeed, the only interaction that appears anywhere but myth and guilty nightmare—I pored over it so frequently as to commit it to memory.

The magazine, about the size of a paperback, bears on its cover a black and white rendering of heavily armed troops surrounding a huge and apparently busy industrial plant, their rifles leveled at what seem to be baboons in spacesuits. The astro-monkeys brandish menacing ray guns. Above the factory swooshes a flotilla of flying saucers, obviously intent on strafing the troops with futuristic weapons.

AS KENNEDY SLAIN, SAUCER APEMEN DRIVEN FROM DEFENSE COMPLEX--NATIONAL EMERGENCY LEAVES ALIENS "SAVED BY THE BELL."

Weehauken, NJ--*Special to* Fate

In a "coincidence" that will forever reverberate in the annals of state and ufology alike, the first pitched battle between man and saucerman took place just as the President who opened democracy's front on outer space fell to an assassin's bullet.

At 9:00 AM on November 22, combined elements of the Army, National Guard, and New Jersey State Patrol—monitored by Air Force flyboys from Project Blue Book—gathered to confront the first verified alien outpost on Planet Earth. For years, this part of New Jersey had been terrorized by night-crawling extraterrestrials. Readers of this magazine will be familiar with the January 1959 apparition of an ape-like semi-human in suburban Weehauken. Only the quick thinking—and swinging nine-iron—of orthodontist and family man Leo Weber prevented the alien from extending its toehold from garbage cans to family room. And this reporter still recalls the fear written across the face of Jersey teen Phil Osborne when he recounted the events of that night in October 1960 when he "came up for air" on Millburn's Lovers' Lane to find a simian face spread across his driver's side window.

But this morning the reign of terror—imposed from somewhere in the Pleiades—was going to end. Weeks of methodical intelligence gathering by local law enforcement had pinpointed the gunpowder factory as the saucermen's landing strip. Its huge parking lots offered plenty of room for the largest mothership to touch down, and the factory itself—empty since the end of the Korean police action—made for a jim-dandy barracks for the first wave of alien invaders. Thus, officers reasoned, the factory was the logical choice for a saucer beachhead.

Their suspicions increased when they checked their files for old reports from the powdermill. For years passing motorists had complained of "ghost lights" inside the abandoned factory. Those brave enough to approach reported eerie, otherworldly chanting. But the clincher came when officers prowled the perimeter and found an open pit filled with bones—dog bones—-freshly picked clean of every shred of flesh!

That was enough.

Well aware that it was Fido today and Cub Scout tomorrow, the Weehauken police swiftly contacted the Pentagon. The Garden State's

National Guard Adjutant General hand-picked his finest troops; the Army contributed reservists drilling for the jungles of Viet Nam.

On the morning of November 22nd, it looked like all systems were GO for the free world's first shots at the alien slavemasters. The State Police sealed off the entrances. Steely-eyed Guardsmen fed fresh clips into their carbines. Their commanders, peering through binoculars, could just see through the factory's filthy windows the shadowy outlines of apelike aliens preparing to make an outer-space Alamo.

But it was never to be. Just as the order was about to be given, the walkie-talkies crackled. The first shot had been fired, all right. But by the slavemasters—Kremlin slavemasters—against the free world. JFK was dead. All troops and police were needed to guard railways, harbors, and airports against civil war or Russki invasion.

Gritting his teeth, the Jersey State Police commander in charge of the alien extermination operation gave his men the order to turn back. But filled with the defiance that made Molly Pitcher's name worthy of a highway rest stop, he grabbed a weapon from a passing soldier and fired a single round—a rifle grenade—at the alien outpost.

"Damn you, you rats," he snarled. "We'll be back."

Surprisingly enough, there was a kernel of truth in that account. Relatives who had survived into my literacy were all remarkably consistent and employed our then-current vocabulary for those of your people we could classify. One day not long before we left New Jersey, in the late autumn, the Nest was startled by the sudden arrival of an official armada. Discounting for my people's general hysteria, and coordinating several versions, it seems as though there were two to three police cars (black and white long) and one jeep (green square). A police officer (blue black man with hat) addressed the tribe through a loudspeaker (hollercone) My best guess—after long and intimate exposure to your people—as to his words is as follows:

HEY YOU FUCKING WINOS! GET THE FUCK OUT OF THAT FUCKING PLACE! NOW! CAUSE WHEN WE COME BACK WE WON'T BE SO FUCKING NICE!

At that point, my informants agree, he threw something at the building that broke a window and filled a gallery with smoke that probably would have hurt anyone if they had been in it, because weeks later it still smelled bad enough to make you sneeze. He and his friends watched the toxic fog curl through the broken glass before heading back to the cars. Just before the blue-black man with the hollercone got into his black and white long he addressed us one last time.

AND LEAVE OUR FUCKING DOGS BE!

After that it was clear that New Jersey would cease to be our home.

I should tell you something about the Nest at this point. We were by then among the last—if not the last—representatives of our kind. Though I am sure many of us have said the same thing over the millennia and been proven wrong. It may yet be that Sasquatch or Yeti is one of ours, truer to our arboreal roots than my own clan, who will stay far enough from you to eke out a few more generations before dissolving into your genocide.

At our most robust we were fewer than two hundred, and as I have said, our years in the Garden State resulted in a net loss in population. By the time the saucer magazine had gone to print, our Nest was just over a hundred. Our last contact with another Nest having been generations before, we were as inbred as Hapsburgs, and almost half of our infrequent pregnancies produced unviable monsters. For that reason the Great Grandmother of each of our Descents was scrupulously careful to prevent incestuous intimacy. This was not difficult. As I have said, desire and its evil twin jealousy burn far less brightly for us than you. Thus it was each Great Grandmother's duty to arrange with her colleagues couplings likely to result in healthy offspring, occasions preceded by careful examination of each partner's scents and secretions and accompanied by chanted music composed by their own ultimate grandmothers in the days of the sabertooth.

Despite maternal rule on the family level, our governance, like our meat, was provided by men. The oldest man of each Descent met solemnly with his peers to mull over whatever issues of peril or justice confronted our little state—generally, the equitable division of what food we had, which was consumed communally anyway. Occasionally it was necessary to deal with a matter of genuine urgency, such as planning a midnight foraging run behind a McDonald's. Then the elders deferred to their senior member. Their senility was never problematic, because we never outlive our minds. And not, sadly, because our minds are so strong. Likewise committed to the men were the burden of forage and glory of the hunt— the latter, as I have told you, practiced exclusively on vermin and domestic pets in modern times.

27

Otherwise both genders shared equally in the activities that occupied the majority of our waking time. You have seen that despite their greater size, our brains are different—we lack almost entirely your capacity to manipulate symbols. I am one of our few who has learned to read. But this limitation, fatal though it has proven in a world of abstracters, does not extend to our other talents. As I have said, the atrophy of our abstract reasoning was commensurate with the hypertrophy of our visual discrimination. Though we cannot count, we can paint. The walls of our Nest glow with pigments passed down and improved upon in every generation since the last Ice Age, compounded from resources dug from the earth or pilfered from garbage, whirling in patterns abstract or representative. We live in abandoned industrial warrens not only for secrecy, but to give ourselves wallspace on which to work. Our youngest children, sooner than they can confidently walk, begin to seek out objects to fit into collages whose schemes they have only begun to see, and whose completion may be found only in their graves.

That we do so should scarcely surprise you. After all, you have seen the deer and wild horses on the cave walls and wondered how or why simian brutes on the edge of extinction found it within themselves to squander time and energy on mere decoration. But they did, as we do.

We no longer leave such traces to be found and wondered at. We have trouble enough as it is without exciting the curiosity of urban archaeologists or pop sociologists. Thus when we abandon a Nest we deface its walls and ceiling and floors so that our existence remains concealed. You may wonder how we can so easily extinguish a generation's work. But your own artists will tell you that it is the act of creation, not the thing created, that is the object of the enterprise.

I should add that we have recently deviated from our destructive secrecy. When we at last found ourselves in New York, some of our younger members—Iincluding me, in my boyhood—were intoxicated by the sudden freedom of anonymity. For the first time in generations, we were able to walk the streets, if only in the small hours, in weather that drove your people into hiding. Thus we employed overpasses and subway tunnel walls as our canvas. At first we used chalk; later, we discovered spray paint. Equipped with dozens of nearly empty cans liberated from trash barrels behind hardware stores and body shops, we rattled through pre-dawn streets barren of traffic to our alleyway easels. For a stolen hour we swirled and curlicued our designs over brick and steel. Our products naturally went unsigned. Their provenance, however, was assured by their similarity in style: busy fields of action crowded with balloon-animal figures.

I'm certain it is not the first time Neanderthal art inspired a trend. Our puffy cloudlike drawings were limited to concrete in obscure neighborhoods. Obscure, but not completely invisible. Especially from passing outer-borough trains.

Soon the young of your people, with readier access to paint and a better grasp of letters, began marking every surface with increasingly complex signatures and designs. Sprawling TAGGER16 competed with ragged JAJABOY on subway cars and Perrier billboards. Bodega storefronts crawled with spray paint filigrees as elaborate as Abbassid calligraphy. In our early morning forays into your world we studied the competition and, I like to think, improved on it.

The product of another weary evening at the terminal. The New York *Times*, Metro Section, September 17, 1977. Another surreptitious record of our presence and so etched in memory.

GRAFFITI , ONCE SPRAY-CAN VANDALISM, NOW AN "ART"

The initial paragraphs liltingly deride academia's endorsement of the defacement of the urban environment as a legitimiate expression of the creative impulse. Our reporter wanders through a West Village gallery, plastic cup of jug chablis in hand, archly cataloguing the bemused responses of celebrity visitors—including Mayor Koch's "Feh, what do I know from art?" These paragraphs are worthy of reproduction:

Keith Haring, the curator, was far more eloquent. Standing before one of his own works—which, ironically, he displayed at the Columbus Circle station last month in an arch commentary—he traced its crude animistic energy to graffiti. "Graffiti," he said, "is like jazz or blues. It's the visual equivalent of street music. It's part of our aesthetic environment, way outside the academy, and it drives what I'm doing now, what Basquiat's doing now, what Schnabel's doing now." He waved an arm at the piece behind him.

Half a dozen of his signature figures, outlines of people, almost stick figures, white on black, stand in a row. Their arms stretch upwards towards a giant hand that reaches from beyond the edge of the canvas, its huge finger pointed down.

Michelangelo's God and Adam? I ask. "Nah," says Haring. "Just like something I think I saw on the subway one day."

Something I think I saw on the subway one day. I'm afraid not.

The "signature" figures in Haring's work were, in fact, the product of another artist. Namely, me.

No, no, I don't suggest his work was stolen. Just that the inspiration was a little more direct than he would have liked to admit. I was very young, only just able to leave the Nest in the company of a few of the older, warier boys. But I was as well-known then for my painting as I would later become for my literary skills, so they soon arranged opportunities for me to show my work outside.

Though I started with stick figures ranged in static lines like pickets in a fence, I soon acquired the confidence to give the figures themselves width, and soon after, action. Nothing elaborate, of course. Just outstretched arms ending in little paw-like hands, all thumb and palm, like mittens. A few diagonal lines radiating from their heads to suggest excitement. And it will not have escaped your attention, your curiosity now alerted, that these "signature" creatures have wide bodies, stubby limbs, and round heads—rather like my people.

Again, I don't suggest for a moment that my work was stolen. It was for an artist of the dominant race to take my simple beginnings to the next level that I in my ignorance and evolutionary inadequacy could not attempt. Years later I saw the commercial expression of the inspiration we had provided. Your artist had become a cottage industry and set up a boutique on Lafayette Street. No Neanderthal would have conceived of the things I saw in its windows. T-shirts of sexless figures rubbing one another's crotches. On a coffee cup, in teal and scarlet, one figure violated another from behind. On a bookbag, another, on its knees, buried its face— that is, if it had one—between the legs of another, standing, whose paws rest on its fellator's head.

Clearly, you are far more advanced than we.

Charging conference. White Plains, mid-March.

Braunstein was already there when I got to the DA's office. Not a good sign.

I knew that he was going to be there as soon as I got to the courthouse. Usually there aren't a lot of white vans with uplink dishes and Frenchmen with sat phones parked across the street when someone's looking for a zoning variance. And guys like me aren't usually followed into the building by shrieking reporters when we're trying to make a deal that keeps our clients out of jail—and away from shrieking reporters.

But that's guys like me. Who are not, I guess, guys like Braunstein.

I was gratified to see that, for the moment at least, Braunstein was kept waiting in the outer office with a bunch of guys like me. Though there was still plenty of room for him to sit in one of the civil-service-issue burgundy herringbone armless chairs on the other side of the dentist's office window, Braunstein stood. Because to sit would have creased a bespoke silk-mohair suit with sleeve buttons left unbuttoned just so we could all be sure that he wasn't wearing something he'd found at the Barney's warehouse sale. Worse, sitting would have given hoi polloi the opportunity to see the bald spot lurking under the Frederic Fekkai styling of gray locks that fell to his shoulders. Worse still, they could have seen how small he was. I'm short, but Braunstein was even shorter. Unlike myself, who inexplicably hunches his five seven frame, Braunstein carried himself like a grenadier.

So when I got buzzed through, there he was, strutting back and forth in front of the window in a three foot circuit, his chest thrust out, screaming at a assistant through a cell phone in easy defiance of a NO CELLPHONES PLEASE Xerox that had been taped to the window sometime during the Clinton administration.

I dropped my briefcase, nodded to some of the guys who had so little self-esteem as to sit, and signed in. I tried to catch the great man's eye, but he was too busy rearranging the troops at Austerlitz. I thought for nearly a second about the message I might be sending before I sat down in a chair not good enough for Braunstein and took out the *Times*. Paper again, mind you. When it finally disappears, I thought, maybe I'll start doing the crossword on the iPad. Not until.

I wish I could tell you that One Across was a six-letter Greek word for excessive pride causing ultimate ruin, but sadly it wasn't. As I was struggling with "'power corrupts' peer" Braunstein finished the last clause of the Treaty of Versailles and had the leisure to notice me. Or more accurately my coat.

"Barbour, right?" said Braunstein.

"Right," I said.

"Hunt ducks or something?"

"No."

"Tell you what. Keep you a lot drier if you got it re-waxed. Take it to Orvis on Madison."

"Thanks."

"So you gonna plead that psycho retard killer and save us all a lot of trouble?"

I swear I was about to say something cutting and clever but oh darn the receptionist rapped on her window and bellowed "GALILEO AND BLINGBLING." I had just enough time to pencil in LORDACTON and stuff the *Times* into my briefcase, collecting the admiring stares of guys like me envious of my association with the likes of Newton Galileo and his exquisitely coiffed counsel.

Just before I met Thatcher Flemming for the first time, when we were both much much younger and both in the Manhattan DA's office, I took one look at his name on a roster and figured he was a chinless Harvard aristocrat putting in his time in the sewers before he could make a lateral transfer to the US Attorney for the Southern District, then the Justice Department, and finally his rightful place in the House of Lords. Imagine my surprise when I actually met his six foot four chiselled faced shaved headed African American self. Turns out I was almost right about everything, though. Having come from a Massachusetts family emancipated when the Bay State was still sending its Powerball profits to Charles I, he was a lot better born than I was. And he had gone to Harvard.

The years hadn't been cruel, but neither had they been all that kind, since he'd moved north and got into political lawyering. His eyes were pouched and his jawline a distant memory, and it was pretty clear that these days shaving his head took a lot less effort than it once had. I, on the other hand, was completely unchanged.

When we got into the DA's office, Flemming didn't get up from his extra-large civil service desk. "Nice," he said. "I got a major league ball-breaker and a minor league ball-breaker. Two ball-breakers."

Braunstein smirked contentedly. "Let me make your life easy," he said. "Dismiss against Galileo and you can play big league ball against the farm team here."

Flemming snorted. "Who says you're major league, Stretch? This asshole actually practices law. Reads cases, talks to witnesses, writes briefs. Breaks balls. You, on the other hand, so far as I know, just suck Laura Ingraham's dick."

Braunstein had paled with rage but pretended that he was just a regular guy breaking balls. "Women don't have dicks," he said.

"My point exactly," said Flemming. He turned to me. "Now, ordinarily I would ask what we are going to do with these shitbags you so regrettably represent, but all these camera trucks in the parking lot tell me that Lord Fauntleroy here has no percentage in talking sense."

Braunstein had gone from dead white to claret. His second chin was beginning to swell like some kind of giant poisonous South American toad's. Any second now he would open his mouth and spear Flemming with a yard-long tongue. He rose to his feet and raised a quivering finger to Flemming's face. "Now you listen to me, goddamn it--"

His tirade was cut short by Flemming's peals of laughter. Genuine merriment, nothing sarcastic about it. "Okay, Princess," he said. "I was just breaking your balls. Now sit down and let's talk about this crap."

Braunstein sat slowly. I decided to jump in as he struggled to return his complexion to its usual Caribbean tan. "I been framed," I said.

"Haven't we all," said Flemming. "Your man, I regret to say, was holding the weapon whose business end undoubtedly issued a high-speed mushrooming projectile that shredded the pulmonary artery of one Einstein Spinoza, resulting in an explosive exsanguination that not only caused his death within seconds but further really fucked up an expensive carpet in questionable taste.

"But wait, there's more. No fewer than seven witnesses, upon the arrival of the justly alarmed police, said as one, "He da man, He da man." And not in a good way." He raised a hand as I opened my mouth. "I grant you that the only thing their statements agree on is the actual shooting. And that all of them are completely at odds with the crap ass forensics we were able to get after the Bedford cops had a circle jerk at the scene. But be that as it may, I think you'll agree your man looks best for this, which is why he's down for murder two."

I raised my eyebrows. Flemming settled back in his chair and laced his fingers across his modest paunch, his own eyebrows raised attentively. "You forgot the powder," I said. "True. My boy's hands were all over the piece, but three successive chromatographs were negative for propellant. Or anything like evidence of firing. No metal. He didn't fire that gun."

"That is quite true," said Flemming, his hands still over his sternum. "Except maybe the last part. But let me now turn to our well-dressed friend. Not to suggest, Raleigh, that you are anything but. Always the best turned-out man in the room. Until today. Look at this guy, will you? Hey— do those sleeve buttons actually button?" He half rose and leaned over the desk. "My grandfather was a tailor, so I appreciate these things."

Braunstein started to answer but Flemming burst out laughing again and waved him off. "Just kidding, just kidding." He sat down. "Now, you my friend, have your own problems. In ascending order. One: for at least a year Newton Galileo and the decedent struggled verbally, and on at least two witnessed occasions, struggled physically, for control of Think We Dum Niggazz—Doctor King would've been so proud, by the way—giving him a pretty clear financial motive. Two: less than a month before the killing, Galileo discovered that the twins carried by his significant other, or rather, one of the significant others resident at the Bedford dojo—a Ms. Marie Curie Sontag—were the spawn not of himself but the late Mr. Spinoza.

"Hmm. Third, we have the fact that each and every witness' statement is entirely inconsistent with every other except for the critical fact of Blingbling's guilt, and oh, I forgot to mention, are entirely consistent in that the witnesses are demonstrably, legally, fucked up on a minimum of three Class B-and-above controlled substances at the time of the shooting.

"But fourth, and most importantly, we have a pair of Mr. Galileo's gloves in the upstairs fireplace. Where even a Bedford cop could find them. Because the burning cashmere lining smelled just like burning hair. And he was surprised anyway that Mr. Galileo would have a fire burning in an empty room with the windows closed on a March night when the temperature in these globally-warmed times was sixty degrees.

"Oh, yeah. The piece—which Mr. Galileo was too busy to register while discovering the moons of Jupiter or whatever—he bought hot from a felon four days earlier."

Flemming unlaced his fingers and leaned into Braunstein's face. "So tell me," he said, "why shouldn't I change my mind about who I like more for this?"

Braunstein seemed to have relaxed a lot during Flemming's exegesis. He actually chuckled and shook his head. "God," he said, "and I thought you guys out here in the burbs were all a bunch of sleepy hicks. Boy, was I wrong." He stood up and extended his hand to Flemming. "It's been a pleasure and an education."

Flemming, looking a little confused, stood as well and shook. "See you in court, tiger," said Braunstein.

"Yeah, you too," said Flemming.

Next, Braunstein extended his hand to me. "Hey, kick this guy's ass. Just don't get me in the shit too, okay?"

"Okay," I said, every bit as confused as Flemming but taking the hand anyway.

Braunstein clapped me on the shoulder. He strutted to the door like Napoleon but when he reached it turned and gave each of us an Elvis raised-thumb-and-extended-finger pistol shot and wink. Then he was gone.

Flemming and I sat silent for a minute. The DA was first to speak. "Huh," he said.

"I have to agree."

"I guess he didn't want to talk about a plea."

"I guess not," I said.

"He also didn't want to talk about his theory of the case."

"Not that either."

"You want to talk about a plea?" he asked.

"Not just yet."

"I don't blame you." Flemming extricated himself from the state-issued chair and looked out the window at the parking lot with the satellite trucks. I couldn't see him, but I knew that Braunstein was waving his arms and sticking out his jaw like Mussolini declaring war on Abyssinia. I also knew that Flemming was thinking about three kids who'd be hitting college in two, four, and six years, and how badly a media clubbing could hurt his chances of reelection.

After a minute Flemming turned away from the window. "I have a confession to make."

"What? It was you? Thatch, I didn't know you moved in those circles."

"Wish I did. But I don't. When I said that the Bedford cop found the

35

gloves in the fireplace because the cashmere lining smelled like burning hair, a reasonable person would've inferred that the lining was burning, right?"

"I did. Not that I'm reasonable."

"Hell, anything but. It was just the outer edges of the lining scorching. I guess whoever it was tossed the gloves in without making sure they landed in the center of the flames. Sloppy. Anyway the leather shells are too toasted for forensics to tell us whether there's powder on them beyond a reasonable doubt, but the left glove does bear a suspicion of a powder trace, and Mister Galileo is left-handed. Forensics tells me there's a chance they can match DNA in epithelial cells they found to a suspect. Any objection to a sample from your guy?"

"You could get it whether I objected or not."

"True enough, but it'd take another couple of days, and something tells me that Dame Edith down there is going to keep me busy. Listen," he said, settling back in his chair and lacing his fingers behind his head. "Another reason I want a sample. I won't lie to you. Homeland's been asking questions."

I'm pretty sure my dismissive shrug looked genuine. "Not enough that I think they want to file a notice or anything," he continued. "But they're a little, shall we say, nonplussed by a defendant in a high profile murder case with no Homeland passport, no driver's license, no social security number, and fuck, no last name. Or first name. He's really weird looking on top of it. You can blame them for a lot." He picked up his desk lamp and spoke to its base. "Just kidding! But you can't blame them for being a little suspicious about this one."

"I don't see why," I said. "Like I told you, he's an orphan. A Gypsy orphan. The tribe or whatever it is raised him. They squatted in an old factory in Jersey when he was a baby and then crossed the river into SoHo when he was still a kid. This was back before there was a Victoria's Secret in SoHo. Anyway, when things gentrified they moved into TriBeCa, and when that went high hat into the Lower East Side. By now most of them are dead. So he's a funny looking guy with no papers. There must be one of those washing dishes in every diner in America."

"Right," said Flemming. "But none of them is accused of shooting an entertainer. And Homeland does have an obvious interest in very public crimes by illegals—kind of their turf, right? But Raleigh—umm, Gypsy?"

"Gypsy. Check it out. When we were kids there were still Gypsy scam artists working Times Square and the Broadway camera shops. What they'd do, they'd have one of the Gypsy girls, looked like Cher but with great tits, walk up to the counter and pull up her shirt. While the Hassid at the register was popping his yammy one of the guys would drop a couple grand worth of cameras into a sack. Gypsy guy goes out into the night; Gypsy girl restores her modesty; Hassid goes into the back to choke the chicken. Or flick it, I guess. But yeah."

Flemming studied me with a careful suspension of disbelief. "So your guy makes a living reading Tarot cards?"

I snorted. "Guess you don't read the papers. Or your files."

"Why should I? They're both full of shit."

"Guess so. Anyway, he was doing your basic off-the-books sub-minimum wage gig sweeping up hair at a buzz cut palace in the Middle Village when his eponymous co-defendants paid a visit in-state and were amused by his antics. Seems he can dance. Especially likes hip-hop. So he used to pick up spare change at the barbershop by busting moves like Mr. Bojangles or something."

"Eponymous," said Flemming musingly. "I like that. We don't hear that often enough around here. I'm not sure it's apt, though."

"Whatever. So Archimedes Kafka or whatever he calls himself thinks he's funny and takes him along and gives him a bottle of Cristal and loads him down with bling and before you know it our little Gypsy is on stage with TWDN. And the rest, as they say, is history."

"I actually did read the report. I was just torturing you for sport. My cops say NYPD wasn't able to trace any of the mongoloids he says he was flopping with. Can he help?"

"How could he? I don't know if your boys have picked up on this yet but he's not the kind of guy for Skype. Or a prepaid calling card. Or smoke signals."

"He seems slow, I grant you that. Are you thinking diminished capacity?"

"If it looks like he did it, sure. But it looks like he didn't."

"Okay," said Flemming. "Maybe he didn't. I got other customers. For the record, you don't object to a DNA sample?" He started fishing through a drawer for a consent form.

"For the record I don't. And you could anyway if I did. But I should be there when it's taken. Not that I don't trust you, I just want to keep Blingbling calm."

"Fine. Can you hang around for an hour? I can get a tech down to the lockup pretty fast."

I nodded. He stood up and we shook. "I wonder why Prince Valiant left like that," he said as we walked towards the door.

"Sensitive, I guess."

"I guess. Except he didn't seem pissed. Oh well." We were at the doorway to the waiting area. "See you around. NEXT!"

That was late Friday morning. Naturally the evidence techs hadn't appeared in the next hour or the third hour after. By the time Blingbling had a barely-controlled eye-bulging panic attack as his inner cheek was swabbed, my plan for a wild boar ragu and half bottle of Barolo at Gustavino had faded to a wistful hope for a chef's salad at the Cheesecake Factory at the Westchester Mall. But because I found a Powerbar in my briefcase I toughed it out until I got to the City around ten o' clock.

There was an Iranian grad student I was helping work through her father issues with my special psychotherapy, but she was across the river visiting the folks in Newark. I thought about calling but decided I'd better not; however secular the family might have been before they fled the revolution, and however Westernized they'd become since, something told me they wouldn't exactly embrace their only daughter's hook-up with a shyster twice her age. However boyishly charming. And while there was clearly an expiration date somewhere on the box, things were good, and I didn't want to accelerate the inevitable.

A wise man would have sought an early bed and a bright Saturday morning. Not being one of those I took a four-pack of Sweet Action Ale to the office, where I drank it and thought about the case while smoking three cigars. Just to make sure I felt really bad the next day I lit another cigar on the way home, which I perched half-smoked on the window ledge of the Peculier Pub while I stopped for a last pint. It was still smoldering when I came back out, and I was just lit enough to finish it.

Somehow I got to the Equinox by ten the next morning. Acutely conscious of the sinful nicotine and hops reek leaching from my pores in a locker room populated exclusively by twenty-eight-year-old mesomorphs who might have just stepped down from the Parthenon frieze, I laced my

Asics as fast as I could and headed out to run. Somehow I managed not to hurl during six ugly, hungover middle-aged miles along the river. Ordinarily I would've given myself a pass on the weights but the last beer seemed to have edged me marginally closer to man boobs, so I tried at least to pretend I was lifting.

It was just after noon as I strode down West Fourth sucking a protein shake. My path took me past what had been, for fifty years, an arthouse movie theater but was now a rich kid club called Petronius Arbiter. There were police sawhorses at either end of the street and a couple of bored looking uniforms idling around the entrance. I was puzzled until I remembered a Page Six piece from the day before advising that one of the President's daughters—I couldn't remember whether it was the one who went to Yale or the really stupid one; whichever it was, the other was off in Iran with her mother, comforting the troops—had been celebrating her thirtieth birthday there. Petronius' crew was still hosing vomit and condoms off the sidewalk.

Nice, I thought. Interesting how even in the City, where seditious libel prosecutions are never brought—in the tacit deal that makes the Patriot Amendments work, the Administration doesn't try to enforce petty authoritarian statutes in Blue State hotspots—the press is too scared to show a Presidential child spewing down a Chippendale's jockstrap. Oh well.

I dropped the rest of the shake in a trash can and checked out the offerings at a news kiosk. The other thing about that deal is that the Feds don't try to enforce Red State social agendas here in Gomorrah. Not only because it wouldn't work, but because Mormon conventioneers need someplace to buy porn. The Red States now being constitutionally free to require mandatory decency filters on every ISP in their respective jurisdictions, whack-offs in half the country once more depend on ink-and-paper skin rags.

Even though I don't have a decency filter, I didn't tarry long at Juggs or Lesbian Leg Show. No kidding, I wanted to see if the New York Review of Books was out. I used to subscribe but it's just faster to buy it at the newsstand. Wouldn't want to wait. And here as well I still prefer paper.

Then I saw the *Post*. All of a sudden the day got a lot worse.

Undisclosed location, two years later

I have tried to piece together how my Nest, alone of our people, survived to meet what might be our species' end on an alley off the Bowery. Our legends—and if you are honest, the most cursory review of your own history— agree that you began to hunt us down as soon as you realized how nicely certain rocks fit your hands. We had abandoned Africa long before you came out of it; our bodies are not well-suited to heat. Neither adventurous nor numerous, we remained in Western Europe. Your first waves of slaughter drove us from the Mediterranean basin, where memories of us became the basis of your demonology. We lived longer, and in greater numbers, in Gothic forests. Some tribes of your people, oddly enough, maintained us to be holy, having lived so long and deeply in the forest that we had shed human attributes to merge with the earth. But the Roman blitzkrieg, ripping through the sacred wald, had little patience for the amusing superstitions of the Teutons, and so burned out or sealed off the caves in which the German barbarians concealed their deformed useless eaters.

And so with each passing generation fewer and fewer survivors were driven deeper and deeper into the wilderness, until at last there were hardly any survivors and no wilderness at all. I conjecture, with the confidence of utter ignorance, that in Roman times we managed to survive by somehow making our way across the Danube where we could once again gull the Germans into leaving offerings at cave mouths. And after Rome fell, was it not fourteen hundred years before the villagers of Europe's wooded middle ceased to fear the dark outside of their farmsteads? Fourteen centuries in which the remaining Nests could live on the slowest hens and oldest goats on the poorest farms in the most remote villages. Fueling all the while legends of werewolf, warlock, and golem.

But it was also fourteen centuries in which your people had at the oldest, slowest, poorest, and most remote of us. We were already few. At what I guess, from what I have heard, was our high-water mark around the time of the Second Crusade—at which point, coincidentally, gargoyles began to sprout from your cathedrals, their apeish forms commemorating the friction between our peoples—there can have been no more than five thousand of us, scattered among two dozen Nests. But as your people grew more numerous mine grew less; well-organized burghers, and lords back from the wars, made short shrift of our smaller colonies at the borders of civilization. Thus, we fell back into central Europe. There, physical isolation and the multicultural tolerance of successive Ottomans and Habsburgs allowed for the odd-looking subjects who scrounged around the edges of market towns.

According to my father, when his forebears—the Nest's leaders at the time—decided to leave Croatia, they knew of only three other Nests in Europe, one of which, contrary to our few laws, had inbred itself to the point of extinction; another had not been heard from in almost a decade. The elders therefore assumed themselves and the Black Forest colony to be the last of our kind. Thus, one night in 1911, an embassy from that Nest, composed of their most fertile young women and virile men, met my ancestors for one last frantic exchange of genetic material before we were forever separated by the Atlantic.

You will ask first, why, and second, how.

As to the first question, it is difficult to imagine how anyone with a spark of sentience could have failed to be impressed by the progressive extinction from one century to the next of our fellows and family as your people took up more and more of the earth. Or the rate at which your occupation was increasing.

And the last vestiges of the world we so tenuously inhabited were soon to be split asunder by war. I don't pretend that we enjoyed a prescience that escaped Lord Kitchener; we had no idea that the continent to which we clung would shortly be bisected by trenches stinking of cordite and squishing with blood. But we did know, even if you didn't, that what was soon to happen would be very big and very bad. Because, of course, we knew you better than you did yourselves. And not only through our generally violent collisions. As I've told you, I am not the first of my people to read, but the generation that orchestrated our diaspora was that which allowed the gift to die. Until me.

So my great grandfathers decided that it would be a good idea to go. Where? Asia was out of the question. Already too dense with yours. Why exchange one starvation for another? Similarly, Africa was unsuited for a people who had thrived in the last Ice Age. We toyed, I am told, with Argentina, which offered vast spaces into which we could readily disappear, and the southernmost extremes were cold and full of game. Transportation, however, proved an issue; there was little direct shipping between Split and

Buenos Aires in 1911. And my ancestors soon recognized that their flight would be difficult enough without transshipping in Hamburg, where even the most lax definition of human would probably exclude us.

So it was decided that our future lay somewhere west of Ellis Island.

Which brings us to the second question: How? My great grandfathers spent nearly a year poring over castaway newspapers and studying the Imperial Habsburg docks. I am proud to say that it was a direct lineal ancestor of my Descent—a genius, can you doubt it?—who posed as a brain-injured veteran of the Balkan Wars to negotiate the Nest's passage with the factor of a Pennsylvania coal mine. Early one morning they shuffled aboard in filched woolen overcoats and shawls, sloped foreheads covered by peaked caps or babushkas, to huddle miserably in the lowest levels of steerage.

Our histories, with the exception of that which I now write, are oral and are usually sung or chanted. The story of our passage to America is punctuated with the sounds of seasickness, each bard outdoing the last in his graphic rendering of miserable upheavals. Worse still, our people were easy prey to diseases from which we had long been isolated. And prey as well to our fellow passengers, some of whom had lived long enough in cities to recognize easy marks. Fully a third of our original number did not reach these shores.

Those who made it off the boat were afforded special treatment at Ellis Island. Apparently the coal mine's agent in Zagreb had cabled Pittsburgh to advise that however cheap the latest coffle came, its obvious genetic defects would not survive medical inspection. Unquestionably, money changed hands. How my ancestors must have been envied by recent arrivals from County Tyrone and Calabria as they shuffled to the head of every line and finally to a line all their own! Next, hustled out a side door into a truck all their own and into a cattle car all their own. The bards' songs from this leg of the trip are again punctuated by retching; five hundred miles by swaying train is a lot for Neanderthals bred to birth and death in the same dozen acres.

But we arrived in Pennsylvania, in the very southwest corner of the state, where it seems my jailer Captain Graner also was raised.

Captain Graner likes to tell me about himself, for reasons I do not quite understand. Why, for example, should it concern me that he was wrongfully persecuted as a result of heroic acts in the last war of the old system, before the Patriot Amendments set everything right? Perhaps he thinks that by telling me that he was once a prisoner himself I will see him as a fellow sufferer and tell him more than I actually know. Perhaps that would work if his hours-long monologues did not take place with his boot upon my neck and my face pressed to the floor. Sometimes, when I dare to roll my eyes upwards, I think he touches himself as he recites his struggle against malevolent superiors.

But I digress. Ape men will. I warned you.

Our people fared surprisingly well in Fayette County. Surprising because it was, after all, our first prolonged cheek-by-jowl exposure to your people since Gilgamesh. But we were good workers. Short and muscular, there was little we could not achieve in the slanting galleries of bitumen. And our irregular appearance—to the extent it could be detected in the feeble glow of carbide helmet lights a thousand feet down—shortly meant nothing. Within a week Carpathian, Sicilian, and Neanderthal were equally black. And stayed that way. Only the most fastidious showed up at six o' clock on Monday morning much cleaner than he had left at six o' clock on Saturday night. After just a few months even the freshest of your youth sloped his shoulders like one of us, and after a year he was so joint-sprung and over-muscled that his bones might have been slipped into a Smithsonian exhibit case without exciting comment. Physically we were among our own.

And of course you wonder: *But none of you spoke English?*

Neither did anyone else. Whenever a Migacz would try us in Polish or a Jurich in Serbo-Croat we would answer in our own language. Our interlocutor would shrug and according to his temper return to his work thinking nothing more, or else that Saturday night, sitting at the kitchen table, ask his wife's grandmother, who had come over from the Old Country with them, whether she knew the language of *k'thik-k'shree-k'thik*?

Unlike our co-workers, we were never forced by circumstance to learn the common language. They eventually earned their way out of boarding houses and into tar-papered two-families in the little patch towns around the mines. We, however, because of the dispensation that had brought us to America, were housed communally and fed in a disused machine barn. After a few years of relative prosperity, even our slow passions produced children. A few Descents moved out of the barn and set up housekeeping in a worked out gallery. Because we never had to handle money, our inabilities in that respect were never discovered and never taken advantage

43

of. Working hard at the dirtiest jobs, we were even afforded a degree of respect. Thus my people, the Slopeheads, thrived for a generation among the Polacks and Hunkies and Dagoes.

Sadly, it was only a generation. One evening just after Pearl Harbor, when the mines worked triple shifts to accommodate the needs of democracy militant, no one saw the canary swoon. Seconds later the earth trembled and coal dust belched from the shafts, followed by the roar of collapsing galleries. Hundreds died in the third worst mining disaster in Pennsylvania history, nearly a hundred of whom were men of the Nest. As I told you, we were hard workers, eager for the extra kielbasa we would earn on a double night shift. Worse than the loss of our men, however, was the carnage in the galleries that housed their Descents; naturally, over years of disuse, many of their supporting timbers had been pressed into service as building materials or firewood. As a result, the shock of the first and weakest subterranean explosion brought the ceiling down on nearly half our breeding women and more than half our children

I will say this for your people. Just this once. This once you embraced us. When that mining town awoke to screaming sirens we were one people. Your widows keened alongside ours; your grandmothers picked up our babies and wrapped them in their shawls. When the terrible news spread that not only Slopehead miners, but their wives and kids as well, had perished in the disaster, the hardest Slovak pit boss put his arm around a Neanderthal's heaving shoulders and led him back to the office shed for cigarettes and whiskey. And most movingly, during the terrible few days that followed, when the local funeral home was displaying bodies for half an hour before interment—all the time possible given the press of other business—our fellow miners saw to it that the few Neanderthal bodies recovered were given Christian burials as well. And at their expense, as it was widely known that the Slopeheads had neither facility with nor use for money.

I smile as I write this. Just think: But for my misfortune the world would never have known of our life among you. Imagine, then, a hundred or a thousand years from now, the uproar in the anthropological community over the discovery of Neanderthal bones in a Pennsylvania cemetery.

Once our elders recovered from the immediate shock, they were confronted with a number of unpalatable truths. First, so far as they knew, not just half of our tribe, but half of our species, had perished in the disaster, for our tenuous contact with Europe had broken before the war began. (It is inconceivable, of course, that our people survived Hitler. Speaking of anomalous bones, I can't help but wonder whether my own cousins may be found in the charnel pits of Belsen-Bergen or Treblinka.) Thus, as they regarded the survivors—too few female and far too few children—they regarded the future of our entire race. Second, and worse, the mine that had been their home and livelihood was gone. And however warmly the community had embraced us in the heady aftermath of catastrophe, the mine had taken with it more jobs than lives, and the harsh arithmetic of scarcity left little surplus sympathy for us. Thus it was decided that it was time to head back in the direction from which we had come.

Had things gone otherwise, perhaps I would have grown up aspiring to a UMW card—like Captain Graner's brother-in-law, who he has told me in his moments of intimacy works in one of the county's few surviving mines. Stockpiling coal against the day when there is no more oil to be stolen. Perhaps we would have traded sandwiches at lunchtime.

But no. That other universe ended when the mine exploded, just as the universe of landwhales died when the cetaceans lumbered back into the sea. We could no more live again as equals—or more accurately, tolerated inferiors—among your people than we could sport among dolphins and blow spume from blowholes in the backs of our heads.

And so we went to New Jersey.

Change of venue. Manhattan, late March.

I kept telling myself it could have been worse. But how I couldn't imagine. Maybe it was a slow news day.

Most of the *Post's* cover was a split photograph. On the left an African American with exclusively gold teeth in a Savile Row suit, whom I had lately learned was Newton Galileo; on the right, a Hebrew American with teeth concealed by a scowl, also in a Savile Row suit, whom I had long known to be Ronald Braunstein.

HIP-HOP KILL DEFENSE DOUBLE WHAMMY

Ron "the Ram" Braunstein, high profile criminal lawyer QB'ing the defense of the foul-mouthed self-proclaimed "street poets" Think We Dum Niggazz, dropped two bombs today. Only time will tell whether they were smart bombs or dum—pardon, dumb.

Just before the clerk's office closed, the Queens-born mouthpiece filed a motion for change of venue, asking for the case to be moved to Manhattan because his clients, "men of color, could not expect a fair trial in suburb—(contd p 3)

Stunned, I opened the paper and was about to walk off with it before the guy in the kiosk reminded me, first in Urdu then in English, of the obligations of capitalism. I reaffirmed his faith in the system with a wave of my phone at the reader and leaned against a lamppost to finish the article.

Not content to change venues, Braunstein had made sure that it would be impossible for Homeland to forget about Bling. Through the simple expedient of pointing out that his client had come up the hard way—the American way—from Bed Stuy to Bed Fly through his own talent and efforts. Unlike the funny-looking terror suspect cowering in a minimum security Westchester jail. Okay, he didn't actually say funny looking. But he did say terror suspect. Which until yesterday only four people outside Homeland knew. That is, if you counted Bling, which I wasn't too sure about. Oh Christ, I thought. Perfect.

Not that the venue issue was a huge problem. I'd probably be better off defending a blatant freak in front of a Manhattan jury anyway. Except the objective here was to avoid a trial. I'd had a much better shot at that with a career prosecutor like Flemming who wanted to be home by six than some hard-on who'd see me as a step to Albany, Washington, and finally, who knows, Buckingham Palace. Flemming probably wouldn't oppose it—why shouldn't he get a pain in the ass off his docket?—so my doing so probably wouldn't do much good.

No, the real problem was the T word. Or more accurately, the H word. Not terror, but Homeland. The Men in Black were, shall we say, not exactly insensitive to the shifts and nuances of public opinion. Witness the detention of most American Baha'is when AmeriFoxFacts pointed out that the religion had been born in Jesus-hating Iran. So there was a reasonably good chance that some black-uniformed community college man in the windowless office on Foley Square would say *Hmm, maybe the Iranians are using deformed hairsweepers to slip under our radar.*

I went home and showered. There were fourteen messages on the voicemail that hadn't been there when I left. All from media outlets. I redialed each, let it ring twice, and hung up, defeating the "calls to his attorney were not immediately returned" line that features so frequently in death row habeas petitions. I thought briefly about a cigar but decided to capitalize instead on my freshly re-oxygenated mental processes. I hiked back to the office.

Much to my surprise there was nothing of note waiting other than Braunstein's motion for change of venue. Good but not great; usually when the Homeland cops filed a motion to intervene, to maximize delay they served defense counsel by snailmail, typically sent from the most distant of the contiguous forty-eight states and sometimes with insufficient postage.

There was, however, a voicemail from Flemming. I wasn't surprised. "Hey," he said. "I'm jumping into the tank on this one. You and the Princess need a more sophisticated milieu. Good luck with it, sport."

Well, that was nice. But it didn't make me any happier about what I had to do next. Namely, catch a train to White Plains to explain all of this to Blingbling.

A week later I was in the Manhattan DA's office on Centre Street. Somehow Braunstein had been persuaded that publicity, just this once, was not to his benefit. Instead of sliding between coiffed and tailored press baronets with murmured 'scuse me's, I elbowed aside ice dealers in reeking snorkel coats and ice whores who'd run their fetuses through public housing garbage disposals.

Centre Street's a funny place. Once you get past the cinderblock and metal detectors and scratched bulletproof plastic of the new annex and go through another set of metal detectors and sniffer dogs, you find yourself in a Tammany Hall palace of marble and oak and civic murals. Which nevertheless still stinks of greed, ambition, and fear, as though Gentleman Jim Walker kicked over his spittoon and ground its contents into the shabby crimson courtroom carpets.

Two turns of an art nouveau stairway took me through a gilded double door into a waiting room much different from Flemming's. The swirly plastered ceiling was about fifteen feet above a fitted blue carpet worked with the seal of the Empire State. The oak-paneled walls, smoke-stained from a time generations ago when nervous supplicants were permitted to indulge, were lined with sepia-toned photographs of mustached cops and double-breasted DA's who'd built careers smashing bootleggers' kegs and deporting first-generation Mafiosi. Two heavy tufted leather couches faced one another on either side of an incongruous gray metal desk at which sat a receptionist so old that she might have begun her career as an elevator operator. Behind her was an enormous picture of the Twin Towers belching smoke, and below them, a list of the police and court personnel who had died on 9/11.

There was one other person in the room. Braunstein, carefully arranged across one of the couches. Legs crossed, arm stretched across the back. The picture of confidence. "Hey," he said, "nice of you to show up. Subway strike or something?'

"I'm early."

"So you are," he said, glancing languidly at his Patek. "My driver was a little worried about traffic so I said hey, err on the side of caution. I spent my time talking to this nice lady—"the former elevator operator simpered—"about Queens. Did you know she's from Queens?"

"I did not know that," I said.

"I went to Queens College," he said. The elevator lady looked as though her private parts were moistening for the first time since prom night. "You, I think, went to Yale."

The elevator lady apparently considered this to be tantamount to membership in the North American Man Boy Love Association. "I did," I admitted, floundering with my briefcase as I tried to settle on the opposite

48

couch.

"You must tell us what that was like," he said, affecting a William F. Buckley drawl. "Us peons," he grinned at the receptionist. She giggled back. "Tell us, did you know President Bush?"

"No. I'm old but not that old. Not nearly." As the elevator lady stiffened I added, "And I drink a lot, but not *that* much."

I suddenly realized while it wasn't illegal—yet—to ridicule a former president, it may not have been the best idea to pick that one. Bush, after all, was a patron saint for the Men in Black, the founder of the War on Terror that gave them reason to exist. And this lady probably talked to them every day. Her console bleeped. "Hey," I said, "saved by the bell, huh? I'm always at my dumbest when I try to be funny."

The elevator lady rose from her desk and opened the door to the inner sanctum. My suddenly damp shirt unstuck from my back as I scrambled to follow Braunstein, who strolled forward, hands clasped behind his back and head thrust forward, as though he were about to inspect a regiment of dragoons. I leaned to his ear and whispered, "Usual bullshit, right?"

"Maybe yes," he said, "but maybe no."

Torrington's office had the splendor befitting the youngest full deputy and the shabbiness appropriate to a civil service gangbuster. His aircraft-carrier-sized desk looked as though it had been hand-carved from a single chunk of fumed oak by Irish nuns who'd fled the Famine. But those few square feet of paneled wall-space not covered with photographs of Torrington, or front pages about Torrington, or the hey-I'm-a-family-man kiddie drawings that I assume Torrington bought online, were taken up with battered battleship gray filing cabinets with hand-lettered labels.

Torrington was standing behind his Celtic Baroque desk as we walked in. He wasn't wearing a jacket. His tie was loosened, his collar unbuttoned, and the cuffs of his white shirt were carefully rolled halfway up his thick forearms. His hands were planted on his hips. His tanned face was set in hard lines under a thick head of salt-and-pepper hair that had never been cut for more than twenty bucks including tip.

It was such an obvious pose that I almost burst out laughing, but I figured that would be a bad idea. Then I thought about pretending that he was Bobby Kennedy or Rudy Giuliani but decided that would be an even worse idea. Instead I just nodded and reached out to shake, but when I saw he wasn't going to reciprocate I turned the gesture into a nervous hair

49

smoothing.

This was not looking good. Torrington was young enough to be ambitious and old enough to be dangerous. And while he was always an arrogant prick he usually didn't look like he was posing for Mt. Rushmore, either. Plainly he saw us bent over with our pants to our ankles and himself on the front page of the *Post*. Not good at all.

Braunstein hadn't bothered to try to shake. Instead he just stopped in front of the desk and jerked his head at a chair in the corner. "Who's your friend?" he said.

It was then that I realized that Torrington was playing to an audience, and it wasn't us. In the corner was a colorless middle-aged middle-sized guy in a gray Jos. A. Bank suit, white button-down shirt, and red and blue striped tie. "A representative of another government agency," said Torrington. "You'll know which, if and when."

My stomach tightened. For the first second I'd hoped that our friend with the strip mall wardrobe came from DSI. After all, the President had recently been grumbling about the corrupting influence of urban music on the nation's rural heartland, so maybe the Department of Social Integrity would be weighing in against TWDN. Not that there was much that they could do; even the Amended First Amendment left artists a fair amount of room. But an administrative decency injunction could result in royalties being escrowed for up to a year, a financial death sentence for most musicians. Particularly free-spending rappers.

But another covert glance at the man in the corner—who, alarmingly, hadn't acknowledged our arrival with so much as a nod—made clear that he would have been a lot more comfortable in a black Homeland Police uniform. Actually, he would have looked a lot better in another uniform altogether; it was easy to imagine him in field gray with a swastika armband.

"Okay," said Braunstein. "So why are we here?" He looked directly at the Homeland cop, something I wouldn't have done for fear of turning to stone. "Let's see the DA tell us while you're drinking a glass of water."

I was starting to like Braunstein.

The Homeland cop didn't react, but I thought I saw one corner of Torrington's mouth twitch upwards. Just for a second. "After you're all finished fucking yourselves," he said, "sit down."

We did. Sit down, that is. The chairs were nice. Comfortable battered leather. Comfortable, at least, when your anus isn't clenched against Federal intrusion.

Torrington made a big production of sitting down himself. He pressed his fingers into a steeple and heaved a sigh that I'm sure they heard in Yonkers. "You guys have problems."

"No," said Braunstein. "Our clients have a problem. You. We're here to fix that. At least I am."

"I think you said we," I said, so as not to seem completely like a potted plant.

"I did," said Torrington. "Excellent point. Actually a plural 'you.' I chose my words carefully." He inclined his shaggy head towards Braunstein. "Maybe *both* of you should pay attention."

Braunstein snorted. "So talk."

"Okay," said Torrington, unsteepling his fingers and folding his hands on his immaculate blotter. He looked straight at Braunstein. "You have a problem. Singular. Forget Galileo's witnesses. When the cops showed up they were all so high that crossing the street with the light was a felony. And speaking of felonies, they've all enjoyed the hospitality of the Empire State on at least two occasions. And we found enough drugs and guns so that if we want we can make sure their parole officers haven't been conceived yet. And if we forget that, we just kind of remember that all of them kind of depend on the inexplicable success of TWDN—Newt Galileo, proprietor—for livelihoods that would otherwise have been earned from ice sales and twenty-dollar blowjobs. So all your witnesses are felons in possession of drugs and firearms with a clear pecuniary bias in favor of your client."

"But that's not your problem."

"Oh," said Braunstein. "I didn't think it was. 'Cause I've had much worse. As better men in this office know."

"Good idea, pissing me off," said Torrington. "But you get a pass. Because I want to watch you deal with this one. We got the forensics back on the glove. Sad to say, the DNA's Galileo's. Or more accurately, Sovereign Shawmut Snopes'. Wonder why he needed a stage name."

"Big fucking deal," said Braunstein. "That's easy. The demented deformed retard that this mope—" he inclined his head towards me—"no offense, has the honor to represent—wait, the demented, deformed *paperless* retard, grabbed one of Newt's gloves and threw it into the fire.

Nicely framing this innocent upstanding pillar of renascent urban African American culture."

"Renascent," I said. "Nice."

"I thought being a Yale man and all that you'd like that," said Braunstein, not breaking stride. "Especially coming from a Queens College dumbfuck like myself. But anyway, forget the DNA, I can explain that. I can explain it in a way that makes things even worse for this scheming retard."

"Except," I said, "for the fact that he is, as you so insensitively put it, a retard."

Suddenly I was holding the talking stick. Braunstein stopped himself halfway into settling back in his chair in smug satisfaction; even the Homeland guy raised his eyebrows, though I didn't like the little smile that was starting to play around the corners of his mouth. Why was he starting to look more and more like Major Strasser? Any minute now I'd be telling him I came to *Casablanca* for the waters.

"So to make this work," I said, "a guy who looks like a runaway from a sideshow, a guy who's so dysfunctional he has no Homeland Passport, no social, no fucking birth certificate, has to first say hmm, for reasons still unknown I'd better fatally shoot this guy, and then say hmm, maybe I'd better grab Newt's glove and throw it into the fire because it'll look bad for Newt and there's this thing called DNA that I never heard of and even if I heard of it I couldn't possibly know what it is."

I looked around the room. Braunstein remained stiffly frozen in his interrupted trajectory to reclining. Torrington was likewise still. The Homeland cop, however, stirred.

"That's all correct," he said, in a flat Midwestern accent. I thought I saw the glint of a monocle, but of course it was just my imagination. "And if that were all, I wouldn't be here. But that, unfortunately, is *not* all.

"It's the DNA that's the problem. *Your* problem, Mr. Raleigh. We have little doubt of Mister, erm, Galileo's guilt. It doesn't matter to us, one way or the other. One animal killing another is scarcely an issue of Homeland security."

My bowels froze. Not just because of what he said, but because he had said it. Granted TWDN weren't the nicest people, but they were human. And more to the point: black. Which Strasser was not. Even by the somewhat elastic standards of modern racial sensitivity, for a white federal law enforcement officer to refer to black defendants as animals was not cool.

That it had been done deliberately, in our faces, was clearly intended to remind us that he had the power to make sure this case never saw daylight. And not coincidentally, in the interests of national security, with the merest nod to due process, make sure that no one involved with it did again, either.

I risked a glance around. Even Torrington seemed shaken. If it seemed expedient, even a promising young DA could join the rest of us in Undefined Administrative Sequestration.

The Man in Black continued in his nasal monotone. "You understand, Mr. Raleigh, that your colleague's attempt at his press conference to embarrass us into taking action against your client had no effect. It's the DNA. Your problem with the DNA, Mr. Raleigh, is not the glove, but your client. The sample he provided—and I trust, Mr. Raleigh, this comes as a surprise to you—is consistent with no known ethnic group. Not Albanian, not Iranian, not Chechen, not Somalian. Nor further. He is not Caucasian, he is not Negroid, he is not Polynesian. My agency, Mr. Raleigh, has the largest database of genotypes in the world, not even limited to those now walking the earth, because it includes samples from the sailors Sir John Franklin buried in the permafrost when his sailing ships were caught in ice while seeking the Northwest Passage. Your client, Mr. Raleigh, seems to belong to no one, living or dead. Hence our interest."

Everyone was very quiet. The three of us who didn't report to the Homeland Czar were acutely aware of having received extremely sensitive information, as a result of which we might leave the room heavily sedated to awaken in a secure facility on Diego Garcia. The one of us who did report was silent out of habit.

I had to say something, so I did. "Makes sense," I said, hoping that I was the only one hearing the quiver in my voice. "He's an abandoned child of third-generation inbred Gypsy alcoholics. His parents were first cousins and at least one pair of grandparents were brother and sister. So far as he knows he's the only kid in the family with ten fingers, five on each hand. He tells me that in his caravan or whatever snipping off vestigial tails was a coming of age thing. I'm surprised he doesn't have gills."

The Homeland cop chuckled. "Nice try, Mr. Raleigh. Or perhaps I should say, nice try Blingbling. Because again, Mr. Raleigh, I give you the benefit of the doubt and assume that you simply put the best face on what your client has told you."

Funny how a nondescript guy in a gray suit can command attention when he has the power to make you disappear. "So what is it you know that I don't know?" I said.

"Yeah," said Braunstein. "And remember, he's a Yale man."

Nobody laughed, but I was now sure I liked Braunstein. I stole a glance his way but he was looking at the Homeland guy like a cobra who'd just spotted a giant mongoose.

The Homeland guy settled back in his corner chair and spread his hands on his gray flannel thighs. "Well," he said. "First of all, Mr. Raleigh, I'm sure that once you have an opportunity to collect yourself you'll remember everything you've learned about DNA in twenty-six years as a criminal lawyer." I swallowed hard. It was twenty-six years. Of course, any chimp with a laptop could have found that out in half a dozen keystrokes, but it was not reassuring that Major Strasser had taken the trouble to remember it—or worse, let me know that he remembered it.

He went on. "While there are many genetic accidents or environmental mutagens that damage DNA, they do nothing to alter the comparatively few, and very well known, molecular markers of ethnicity. Forget alcohol, drugs, inbreeding, and cosmic rays—the mitochondrial DNA tells us who you are and where you came from better than any family bible.

"So, Mr. Raleigh, I'm sorry to tell you that if your client says he's a Gypsy he's not telling you the truth. As I said, we think that you believe him. That means that you don't have any information to the contrary that you're obliged to give us." Just for a moment he met my eye. "I don't need to tell you what the consequences would be if things were otherwise."

I was, of course, scared to death, but this little bastard was starting to piss me off. Not because he was trying to scare me with things he could really do, but because he was talking like a villain in an airport paperback. Conduct unbecoming a federal officer, in my book.

"Thank you for reminding me of my obligations under the Patriot Amendments and the enabling legislation," I said, "and please take no offense when I tell you that I can read the law. That said, what the hell are you talking about?"

"Just this, Mr. Raleigh," said the Man in Black who this time just happened to be wearing gray, "we've referred this matter to a genetic anthropologist who will tell us with certainty where your client comes from. And Mr. Raleigh," he said, leaning forward, lowering his voice to a confidential whisper, "you might want to tell us first."

I was leaning forward myself, and I was starting to tell him to fuck himself in something other than a confidential whisper, when Braunstein broke in.

"Mars."

The Homeland cop jerked like a hooked carp.

"Yeah, that's it. Mars. Hey, Raleigh, think these guys need us any more?"

"I can't imagine why," I said.

"'I can't imagine why'," said Braunstein. "Now, see, if it was me, I would've said something like fuck no, but that's an Ivy League education for you. Anyway, you got us so scared we have to go slip our tampons back in. Scuse us." He nodded to Torrington. "Here's a tip: don't have the golem here sitting next to you in front of the jury."

Braunstein had a hard little smile from the moment we left Torrington's office. It was clear that he'd taken genuine pleasure in jeopardizing our careers and maybe our lives by tormenting the Man in Black.

I didn't say anything until we were outside. "So," I said as we drew up to a bathwater hotdog guy, "thanks for jumping in. I guess."

"You guess?" His eyebrows crawled up his forehead like furry caterpillars. "You *guess*? Those cocksuckers were about two seconds away from taking out the Vaseline and giving you the cellblock lovelock." He got the hotdog guy's attention with a snap of his head.

"Don't take this the wrong way," I said, "but I didn't have you pegged as the altruistic type."

"Two with kraut and mustard. You want one?"

"No thanks. Like I said, I didn't have you--"

"I heard. I'm not. Very perceptive. You're a smart man. Boolah boolah. If your guy goes down as a terror risk my guys are all of a sudden not just looking at state time for maybe getting a little careless with firearms, which is something I not only do not admit but strongly deny as a fucking lie, but maybe Federal charges for negligent harboring or, even worse, Homeland charges for complicity. And if *that* happens Homeland and the IRS go up the ass of TWDN, Big Pimp Bonah Records, and finally Sony/Disney/Toyota Tunes. Stripping them and their stockholders of every penny attributable to the work of a hip-hop act foolish enough to adopt a circus geek who turned out to be an Iranian plant."

What amazed me was not that he got this out in a fast Queens Bugs Bunny rap while eating a hot dog swimming in condiments, but that he did so without getting a shred of kraut or speck of mustard on his tie. "A *what*?"

"Iranian plant. What else could he be?"

"You don't believe that."

"Of course not. But maybe *they* do. And, even if they don't, they're going to act like they do and hey, that works for me."

Okay," I said, "so why piss them off? Remembering, most especially, that once a D notice hits the record our own asses are on the line."

"Most especially," he said, his words somehow coming out clearly through a churning mass of masticated food of which I unfortunately had a pretty good view. He was halfway through the second dog. "I do bear that in mind most especially. See, this is where you and me are different. I know, I know, you and I. If Homeland screws you, maybe gets you suspended, maybe sends you to Gitmo. Whatever. You go down easy. Not a trace. No offense, but that's the way it is. I go, it's Anderson Cooper. No way Homeland sends me down unless they have to. They just needed to be reminded, that's all."

A stretch SUV with blacked out windows rolled slowly up the street and beeped once. "My ride," said Braunstein. It pulled up at the curb opposite and parked under a giant Homeland recruiting billboard featuring a square-jawed hometrooper in dress black. It was so big I could read the motto under the eye-and-thunderbolts patch on his shoulder. SEMPER VIGILO. Always Watching. Guess that semester of Latin came in handy.

Braunstein mopped up mustard with a napkin and dropped the results in a trash can. "Want a lift?" he asked.

I shook my head. "See you in court," he said as the car swallowed him up.

"Right," I said. "Boolah boolah."

Perhaps I should be alarmed. Captain Graner has been unusually kind to me.

But perhaps not. Perhaps I exaggerate. But then again, perhaps I don't.

I know that I will not leave here alive and that sooner or later there will come an order from Washington or some acronymous military command and that will be that. I do not imagine that I will be given even the minimal warning that I understand my Iranian, Indonesian, and Albanian fellow prisoners receive.

My, how busy you have been. Those are just the ones I know about from the newspapers. Though many of the voices I can just barely hear in the night beg for death in Arabic and what I think is Farsi, many others plead in dialects so obscure that I doubt there are even desk officers who can read them. The Homeland Police cast a wide net.

Again, I digress. How clearly I now understand why your powers of concentration entitled you to the world's dominion.

In any event, Captain Graner has been, if not kind, noticeably less threatening. Naturally I assume the worst—which, of course, given his history would be the best; that his soul has healed overnight so as to permit him to leave a condemned man in some degree of peace.

Ah. I reassure myself. If Graner is incapable of mercy then his apparent mercy means nothing. Yes, I will die of old age wherever it is they have taken me.

Nonsense. I am dying soon. But the previous fifty words afforded me a minute's relief from that certainty.

So I have told you how we came to America, how we came to New York, how I came to paint the streets with memes that would replicate like viruses through your postmodern world. But, you ask Blingbling, how did you learn to write? How did you learn so *much*?

Not so much as that. If I had learned all I should, I would not be here.

I should tell you first where here is. Not that I know. Before my ignorance brought me to this place I had read, as I'm sure you did, that the current administration established facilities for the interrogation, trial, and summary execution of terrorism suspects in addition to that founded by its predecessors at Guantanamo. Assuming that I am at one of the acknowledged facilities, I believe it is Gitmo. For these reasons: First, when I was frogmarched from one interrogation room to another without a blindfold I saw not only tropical palms but the watchtowers and faded green-trimmed whitewashed barracks of a military base long in place. Second, and more important, some months ago as I cowered in his office, Captain Graner, frustrated with the failure of an air conditioner, threw open the window to admit the molasses scent of burning sugar cane.

Ah, I thought. Cuba.

But third, and most important, is this: Guantanamo, being the oldest and largest and most public of the holding facilities, as well as that closest to the American mainland, is the place where those whose deaths are least likely to cause trouble are sent to die. And my death will cause no trouble at all.

Wait, wait. The scent of burning sugarcane. Perhaps I am in Louisiana. No, better, Hawaii. Yes, that's it, Hawaii. That explains everything! Tropical foliage, Captain Graner's sudden kindness. I am not being interrogated, simply debriefed. Shortly I will be given an aloha shirt and a camera and a hundred dollars and a chit for Mai Tais at the Royal Hawaiian. Apologies all around, thank you for your assistance in the War on Terror, the President will call you to offer congratulations on your hundredth birthday.

Another minute of hope. Crashing to pieces on rational examination.

Enough.

By the time Keith Haring had incorporated our artistic efforts into his own, SoHo was becoming inhospitable to Neanderthals. The artists who moved into freezing lofts little different from ours were shortly followed by Birkenstock boutiques and wine spritzer bars catering to uptown patrons. Though J Crew and Victoria's Secret and sweaty German tourists were still decades away, even at night there were too many slumming stockbrokers for us to move about in comfort.

While still a boy—my people do not reach puberty until well into our teens—I moved with the Nest—now reduced to just over forty—east to the Bowery. A narrow building whose first floor was occupied by a long-bankrupt Chinese restaurant supply company afforded plenty of space and an almost limitless supply of cockroaches and rats with which to satisfy our unending need for protein. Late at night our bolder youth, myself among them, crept around the corner and into an alleyway behind CBGB to hop and gyrate to the bass lines coming through the walls. Once we took our act to the street in front of the bar itself, where queued-up club-goers, apparently under the delusion that we were Bronx-born moonwalkers, stuffed with dollars a Dunkin Donuts coffee cup that I had the foresight to bring. My enterprise brought me a rare and reluctant beating from the elders; our performance had jeopardized the Nest's secrecy.

Strange. Just now I wish they had beaten me harder and not wept with pity as they did. Had they, perhaps I would not find myself where I am.

Though our move afforded us food and space, we found security only within our walls. My father died some years after we settled off the Bowery. At least, I'm almost certain he did. One night he went out and just didn't come back. Among your people, I know, this is not an uncommon occurrence. My father, however, did not have the option of starting a new life with his assistant in a Trenton suburb, if only because he was one of thirty surviving members of another species. No, I think I actually read my father's obituary, a few paragraphs in a back issue of the News that I stumbled across years later, dated a week or so after his disappearance A brief description of the battered body of a deformed and presumably homeless man found in a Mott Street dumpster. His assailants presumed to be the crackheads who then overran the neighborhood. Why my father? Because the medical examiner, in describing the pathetic corpse, casually mentioned that it wore an old dog tag—not military, but canine—around its neck.

I wish I knew where my father was buried, and under what name. His own—I've never been able convincingly to transliterate our language to yours, and so I won't attempt it now—translated roughly as Hunter and Provider, Son of Plentiful Milk, Daughter of Comforter in Sorrow.

I suppose you're curious as to my name. Remain so. It is my last privacy. I move my bowels facing the unblinking red eye of a video camera.

I wonder, were my father's nameless remains eventually removed from a refrigerated drawer in the coroner's office for a solitary unmourned disposition in potter's field? Or was he given to medical students for dissection, misinforming a generation of doctors as to the thickness of skull and configuration of the brain? I doubt he was cremated; your multi-ethnic City would never permit the accidental desecration of a Muslim or Catholic body.

As I consider my father's ashes I wonder about my own. I know that the interrogators have on occasion burned a Muslim corpse before Muslim prisoners, hoping that abomination would loosen tongues. What will they do with what's left of me?

I wish I could stop thinking about death. Especially mine.

Enough.

How I learned to read:

It would be wrong to imagine that I am the first literate Neanderthal, though in all modesty I concede that it is entirely possible that I am among the most. As I told you earlier, my ancestors in Croatia had among them readers sufficiently avid to anticipate a European catastrophe to which King-Emperor, Czar, and Kaiser were equally blind. Nor am I the only reader in my generation. In fact, all of us can read to some degree, at least to the extent that we can recognize whole words like DANGER or STOP. Otherwise the last of us would have died on the third rail shortly after our arrival in the City. And the Mothers kept alive their limited knowledge of the relationship between some letters, whole words, and their related sounds for the education of the particularly adept.

That, however, was not enough. What the Mothers taught was not literacy but cryptography. Certain shapes equaled certain sounds. As I approached maturity it became frustratingly clear that my great grandfathers' knowledge had not survived them; rather, the last reader had died in that Pennsylvania mine blast and his grandchildren were as ignorant of his secrets as Rosicrucians of their founders' alchemy.

Thus I approached manhood seething with schemes. Your lordship over nature, it seemed to me, sprang from the enormous stockpiles of knowledge that literacy enabled you to transmit across generations, whereas bardic memory limited our ability to do the same. I reasoned, then, that if only we could learn to read, my grandchildren could emerge from hiding as your equals.

But, as I say, I soon exhausted the Mothers' ability to teach. I tried to learn more on my own, mumbling over traffic signs, comic strips, magazine covers. All of which stubbornly kept their secrets. True, I could tease out a sound or two, but Dilbert might as well have been written in hieroglyphics.

But then I found the Rosetta Stone.

One November midnight thirty years ago I was given dumpster duty on East Fourth Street. Usually slim pickings at best—the neighborhood in those days consisted of actors struggling against the bus ticket home to Minnesota, upscale heroin addicts, and the cheap ethnic restaurants that catered to both. So I was disappointed, but not embarrassed, by the lightness of my backpack as I ducked down an alley between Cucina di Pesce and Ali's Albanian.

I tripped over it. Literally.

It was a Seagram's box, the kind people beg from liquor stores when they move. I picked myself up off the slimy pavement and dragged the box—it was surprisingly heavy—to a fire exit with an overhead light.

It was full of books. Not just any books. Books for the youngest readers. "Brown Bear Brown Bear." "Pat the Bunny." As I pawed frantically through them I almost wept; if only I had someone to read to me, how much I could have learned!

But there was more than just books. There was an object a little bigger than a computer keyboard, cheerful red plastic, with rows of big square toddler and Neanderthal-friendly buttons. Each bearing a letter of the alphabet. I pressed A.

I nearly soiled myself when the toy spoke. "A," it said. The letter glowed.

I pressed again. "ah."

A third time. "A."

Fourth. "ah."

I tried the next letter. "B," said the same sunny voice.

I pressed again. "Buh."

My hands shook. Inspired I pressed A, and keeping it depressed, B. "Ab," it said.

B first, then A.

"Ba."

Sobbing and laughing I stuffed my Precious into my backpack. Should I press my luck no further, or should I take more? Suddenly struck with fear—what if I should make myself too conspicuous with an overstuffed bindle and lose it all to a couple of addicts?—I decided to limit myself to half a dozen books. Desperate to get out of the alleyway and back to the Nest I picked my Alexandrine library almost at random.

Seconds later I was back on Fourth, as inconspicuous as a caveman in the East Village could be. Which, at four in the morning, was very. I moved as fast as I could without running, and as alertly as I could without seeming furtive—though the police were not yet formally invested with arbitrary lethality, all the street people, even Neanderthals, knew that one wrong move could result in a punitive rape or a shallow grave in the

Meadowlands.

However fast I traveled, my emotions ran faster. First I was exultant—Prometheus bringing fire to his benighted people. Rapidly, though, my joy deteriorated into anxiety. What if I stepped in front of a cab? What if those staggering Jersey boys in their fog of beer and Drakkar Noir decided to round off their New York night by stealing my pack? What if I had left the power switch on and the Rosetta Stone was draining its life away? *What if I had left it behind in my haste?* Twice I ducked into deep doorways to assure myself that the keyboard was both present and alive. On the second occasion I was so relieved that I burst into hysterical tears and clutched it to my chest, settling to the stoop and rocking it back and forth as though it were an infant snatched from a burning building. Finally, crooning terms of endearment, I secured it again in my pack and crossed the last few blocks to the Nest.

Despite the noise two padlocks and their chains must have made when I violated the Bankruptcy Trustee's seal, no one except the Oldest Mother was awake when I made it to the fourth floor. We sleep long and deeply. Another reason we will die with me.

After we cradled and sniffed and licked, she carefully emptied the contents of my pack. After a long study she said, "Forgive me. But I don't think we can eat any of this." But because she was not only the Oldest Mother, but the Oldest Mother of my Descent, she knew me for who I was. Thus a smile played around the edges of her eyes, if not her lips.

"No, Great Grandmother, we can't."

"Then, Great Grandson, of what use is it?"

"Great Grandmother, I cannot tell you yet."

"And why is that?"

I leaned forward confidentially. The smile had migrated, just barely, to the corners of her mouth. She gave me her ear.

"Because, Great Grandmother," I said, "I don't think we have enough batteries."

Expert witness. New Haven, late May.

The seasons have sharp edges in a college town. Summer begins in a single weekend of double-parked Volvos and sweaty dads floundering under futons. By six o' clock on graduation day the young scholars are all gone, nursing the sick suspicion that maybe their best days really are all of sudden behind them.

Braunstein's methodical ball-breaking had given me an idea. While, in my circles, a Yale diploma is the equivalent of a KICK ME sign between the shoulderblades, it's not always without use. I made some calls and signed some papers, and the defense copy of Blingbling's DNA assay was on its way to New Haven. A few days later I got a snail-mail from the Yale Anthropology Department. Apparently Weiss figured that Homeland thought someone who actually used paper mail was too backward and slow-witted to be dangerous. Anyway, he had something to tell me. So the next Saturday morning I was in New Haven.

I'd missed graduation. Instead I got to town just as the alumni were gimping back for reunion weekend. Luckily it wasn't my year or I'd've had to stare through all the people I hadn't kept in touch with for the very good reason that I couldn't stand them. But I still got to see my future bleakly mapped out in five year increments of older classes. Each looking worse than the last. What was scarier, some of the younger guys weren't looking so great either.

New Haven had changed a lot since I first arrived, more than thirty years before, a terrified refugee from a Pennsylvania coal town. Back then the Elm City was still given over to hookers and winos at sunset, and a stoned midnight run to Mr. Donut was a life-threatening adventure. But a generation of gentrification had turned the area around campus, at least, into a pretty credible impression of a college town, and more than one doorway into which I'd once blissfully urinated now opened into a trendy boutique or tapas bar.

Campus, of course, had changed much less. It was supposed to look as though it had remained the same since the fifteenth century. Which, of course, was just before white men washed up on these shores. In fact, the Gothic piles that housed the undergraduates were copies of Oxford colleges, built in the 1930's by immigrant Italian craftsmen happy to work for Depression wages. They had gone so far as to sand the marble staircases so that the steps bowed in the middle, as though worn down by centuries of scholarly tread.

Even though the summer session hadn't officially begun, there were still plenty of kids around. Including young ladies happy to have sun and breeze kiss their skin. Naturally they brought the Iranian to mind. A near contemporary of theirs, though she'd have been offended to hear herself so described. And she seemed to have been getting offended a lot lately. Up until a few weeks before we'd hook up for dinner or a night with no more preliminary than a text. Then blammo. Her nights were suddenly filled with undefined business, and the messaging balance of trade had gone lopsided the wrong way. I'd been down this road often enough to know that it was short and dead-ended. But we'd both—I think—been enjoying the ride. And even though I knew that the outcome was not in doubt, my throat tightened just a bit as I realized that I would miss her.

As I eyed her younger sisters swanning around campus, I tried to console myself with the thought that if I'd had a shot at her, they were still on the table too. Kind of an intergenerational geometry. If A equals B and B equals C, then A equals C. Not surprisingly, it didn't work.

Weiss was in the Peabody Museum at the other end of campus. Halfway there I cut through the Woolsey Rotunda, a circular pavilion joining the Commons with the concert hall. Its walls were carved with the names of Yale's dead from every war from the Revolution on. I noticed that they hadn't gotten around to Afghanistan or Iraq, much less Iran or Indonesia. Maybe they had to wait for the wars to end. Just so they'd know how much space they'd need. The way things were going they were going to have to build an addition. Voluntary Conscription reached deep, even in the Ivies.

His office was in the museum annex so I didn't get to see the dinosaurs. Instead I went up one flight and through an archway that said ANTHROPOLOGY. His door was open and he was at his desk. "Hey, asshole," I said.

"Hey, dick," he said, not looking up.

Nice to be able to pick up right where you left off. Weiss had been my roommate for all four years.

I sat down in the visitor's chair, one of those collegiate colonial Windsors intended to make you think that Cotton Mather just might drop by. "So," I said.

"So," he said, turning away from the potsherds or whatever it was he'd

64

been studying. "Who else knows I've seen this?"

Weiss had been scary intense at eighteen, and time hadn't mellowed him. Even so, his edge shook me a little. "Nobody except the FedEx guy. If he opened the package. I didn't have to disclose you as a witness, if that's what you mean. Anyway, what do you care? Sure, it's a high profile case and Homeland's looking at it, but you're just a respected academic who'll no doubt confirm the government's concerns."

"I'll explain later. Over a beer. Which you're buying."

"Sport. I like the way you think. But it's ten thirty."

"Rudy's opens at noon. See you there."

He'd warned me that Rudy's had not only moved, but changed. When we were undergraduates it was the kind of dive that attracted bikers and grad students in equal numbers. Even though we were then already years into a statewide smoking ban it still reeked, and it looked as though neither it nor half its patrons had ever seen direct sunlight. And while it had a kitchen, if I had to choose between eating its offerings versus something I'd found on the men's room floor, I'd've had to toss a coin. But the beer was cheap enough that we could afford an occasional shot as well.

Not so now. Apparently it had moved around the corner when it lost its lease years before. The owners had taken the opportunity to turn it into something that looked suspiciously like a gastropub—white tile walls, retro light fixtures, and a couple of dozen microbrews and imports on tap. As I waited for Weiss I actually looked at a menu.

At twelve fifteen he slid onto the stool next to me. Blinking in the transition from midday June to barroom dusk he studied the specials chalked on the board. "I keep forgetting they sell food here."

"Yeah. Mussels? *Really?*"

"Yeah. And not only will they not kill you, they're actually pretty good."

"Wow. Everything changes."

"Not everything. I see you've started without me. What a surprise."

"Still my first," I said.

"Wow. Your sponsor must be proud." He caught the eye of the big guy on the tap. "Jeff. Sea Hag for me and give my grandfather another of what he's having." He glanced at the guys at the other end of the bar. "Kind of early for fresh-faced lads, don't you think?"

"Probably just back from their croquet game."

"They look like Rudy's types to you?" He sounded anxious.

"No, but so what? What the *fuck* has crawled up your ass?"

"Your gerbil. I just don't want to be overheard. Especially by guys wired for sound. I guess I'm just paranoid, but let's sit in the back anyway. I may need to spread out a bit." I had just noticed his messenger bag.

We took our beers to a booth. He opened up his laptop. "Okay, Sparky," he said. "You asked what crawled up my ass?"

"Yes."

"I'll be happy to answer that. But first let me ask you some questions. Number one—your client ever look kind of, oh I don't know, *funny* to you?"

"He's deformed," I said. "Inbreeding and fetal alcohol."

"Ah yes," said Weiss, nodding sagaciously. "Inbreeding and fetal alcohol. I see. Let me ask another question. Does he look *familiar* in any way?"

"Like how?"

"As though you might have seen his picture somewhere. We know textbooks are out of the question. In fact, books of any kind. Cartoons? Comics?"

"Well, shit. Of course. He looks like a fucking Neanderthal."

Weiss drained half his glass. "And there, my friend, you have put your finger on the cause of my discomfiture."

"The gerbil up your ass?

"No."

"Then you've lost me."

Weiss drank the other half. He folded his hands on the sticky table, the model of academic reason. "He *is* a fucking Neanderthal."

It was still twilight when I walked out of Grand Central. Somewhat unsteadily; Weiss had done a lot of explaining, and it needed lubrication.

I blinked at the Terror Alert billboard opposite the Lexington Avenue entrance. Brilliant tangerine letters two stories tall ran across its base. RISK IS HIGH TODAY! REPORT ANYTHING OR ANYONE SUSPICIOUS! Above the crawl stood a hundred foot image of the Homeland Czar, her arms crossed, elegant in the black uniform that looked like an SS pantsuit.

Earlier, at Rudy's, just before I'd stumbled into daylight and a cab, Weiss had sat at our table with his head in his hands. He never had much tolerance for drink, and he'd sunk eight IPAs. "How did this happen?" he said. How the *fuck* did this happen?"

"How did what happen?" I asked.

"This shit. All this shit. Dirty bombs that aren't there. Secret police. State media. How the *fuck* did this happen? "

"Beats me," I said. "Maybe if we'd watched more public TV." I glanced at the bar. One of the fresh-faced boys was still there. The beer in front of him looked pretty flat. Maybe Weiss was right to be anxious. I decided it was time to go. Before we drank ourselves into Gitmo.

I looked at the line of cabs and then at my watch. Seven thirty. I hadn't called the Iranian yet. Maybe she was free.

But maybe not. I got into a cab and told the driver to take me to Central Park West and Seventy-Sixth. There was somebody there I needed to see even more than her. At least for now.

Despite fuel costs and the international situation, the steps of the Museum of Natural History were dense with tourists. Twenty minutes in the security line and I was on my way to the Hall of Human Biology and Evolution.

I hadn't been for over fifteen years. It must have been a rainy Sunday afternoon with somebody I still liked enough for that kind of thing to be fun. It hadn't changed much from what I remembered—evolution, after all, is a slow process—except for a couple of additions. First was the big wall panel added after the Patriot Amendments:

"EVOLUTION" IS JUST A THEORY!

Many respected scientists believe that the fossil record has been misinterpreted. They, like all the world's faiths, believe that we were created by a Supreme Being in our present form without passing through any of the stages you see here. To get a better understanding of these competing theories, be sure to visit the Halls of Intelligent Design and Creation Science. (This statement certified Fair to Faith by the Department of Social Integrity.)

The other new thing was something Weiss had told me about. It was a glass-fronted diorama about the size of a Manhattan kitchen. Inside was a slender brown figure about three feet tall. The figure could've been mistaken for a young boy except for its face, chinless and broad-nosed, with no forehead to speak of and its eyes almost invisible under an overhanging brow. Beside it was a rat the size of a springer spaniel. Over the glass it said:

HOMO FLORESIENSIS: THE HOBBIT PEOPLE.

There were panels at the foot of the display.

The people of Flores, a remote island in the Indonesian archipelago, have long told tales of a "Little People" that lived in caves, isolated from the rest of humanity, until they were exterminated by the Dutch in the seventeenth century. Anthropologists had long believed these stories to be folklore similar to the myth of the leprechaun. In 2004, however, Australian paleoanthropologists made an astonishing discovery. Working at a dig reliably dated as thirteen thousand years old, they found skeletons whose tiny size and misshapen skulls led them to conclude that they had come upon the burial site of deformed children. Soon, however, they realized that despite their size the bones were those of full-grown adults. More importantly, the "deformities" in the skulls were characteristics found in Homo erectus. (Previous display) DNA proved what the excited scientists had already guessed: they had discovered a new and entirely different human species. Unlike most other finds you see displayed here, this species did not go extinct before the rise of modern man. Instead, it was certain that H. Floresiensis had survived as recently as thirteen thousand years ago, when our ancestors were already building their first cities. Isolated in Indonesia, they thrived among the Komodo dragons, midget elephants, and giant rats represented here.

And—who knows?—maybe the legends were right, and this primitive species survived into comparatively modern times to meet its end at the hands of the Dutch.

Or us, Weiss had said. The stories didn't end with seventeenth-century explorers. As recently as the start of the Mahdist rebellion there were occasional reports of little people spotted deep in the Flores rainforests. If they were smart enough to survive the archipelago's separation from the mainland, said Weiss, they were smart enough to recognize the Dutch for the threat they were and hide in the interior. But now, he added, Chemical Counterterror's made the whole jungle toxic, and the bunker busters we've been dropping in the mountains must've destroyed whatever shelter they had. So even if they survived the Dutch, they hadn't survived us.

I passed the equally hapless Denisovans. Their replicas were pretty hypothetical. All their DNA had been found east of the Urals, and the Russians weren't all that crazy about swapping science with us these days.

I was standing in front of the Homo erectus diorama. Not a pretty sight, and I have cousins in West Virginia. In the painted background were low mountains; in the foreground, scrub. There were three figures. A sullen-looking male who resembled nothing so much as a half-shaved ape dragged a carrion antelope by its antlers towards his little family circle. Wifey held a skin in her teeth while flensing it with a sharp stone. Granny, whose bowling-pin boobs actually reached below her waist, was even hairier than her son-in-law. I thought the reconstructionists had gone a bit far with the horseflies clinging to each figure. I got the idea without them. They stank.

The figures you see here are the common ancestors of every species in this exhibit—including the people looking at it. Modern man, Neanderthals, Denisovans, and H. Floresiensis all descended from Erectus. But it is important to remember that they descended separately—despite a common misunderstanding, we did not "evolve" from Neanderthals. Rather, each species sprang from this common ancestor, like cousins with a common grandparent. But unlike cousins, the separate species—which developed over tens of thousands of years—could never interbreed. DNA tests have shown that each species inherited different and distinct characteristics from Erectus, so much so that they are as different as horses and cows. And while the discovery of what was thought to be Neanderthal DNA in modern humans demonstrated interbreeding in the distant past, that has since been shown to be mistaken. In fact, the "Neanderthal" genetic material was a legacy from Erectus that Neanderthals shared with us.

Sadly for our distant cousins, Floresiensis and Neanderthal, their evolutionary road proved a dead end.

Oh yeah?

I was standing in front of the Neanderthal exhibit. Even after my day with Weiss, my jaw dropped. If you had dressed the young male in the foreground in an orange prison jumpsuit he would have been Blingbling. How no one had seen it before was incredible. Except, of course, for the fact that it was impossible.

Or so, Weiss said, he would have thought—until the discovery of

Floresiensis. Back in the day he would have tossed the DNA as junk, no matter how many times it came back the same way. In fact, that's what he was inclined to do when he first saw Blingbling's. No human being could have had those genetic markers. So he sat down to send me an email telling me that I could keep the DNA out of evidence as fatally flawed and completely unreliable. But just before he did so he googled Blingbling. Not being a big TV guy he'd never seen him outside a grainy *Times* photo on page three of the Metro section. When Weiss saw the full color, high-res mugshot he swallowed hard. Couldn't be. But he was a scientist so he had to do what he did. Ten minutes later he knew that Blingbling's DNA was a one hundred per cent match with H. Neanderthalis.

"So," Weiss had said, a couple of hours before in Rudy's. "A Neanderthal. Living among us. Before Flores I would have said it was preposterous. But now—well, how can I doubt the evidence? But here's the problem. Your man had a Neanderthal Daddy and a Neanderthal Mommy. He had four Neanderthal grandparents. He may have Neanderthal brothers and sisters. And lots of Neanderthal cousins, aunts, and uncles. So let me ask you this, sport, because at some point the Homeland cops are going to figure this out and ask you the same thing.

"Where are the rest of them?"

Good question.

Undisclosed location, two years later

You can, perhaps, appreciate my amusement at your people's reaction to proof of our coexistence. Even if you believed it to have been only in mist-shrouded antiquity, instead of our having persisted cheek-by-jowl, hidden in plain sight, until the present.

Initially, carbon dating that demonstrated our short-lived contemporaneity seemed to make little impression beyond a few articles in popular science journals. It was assumed, apparently, that our communities lived apart, isolated by sparse numbers on a still-untamed planet, until ours dwindled and died. Without your help.

How I smiled at your willful disregard of your own nature! How I laughed when you explained away the subsequent discovery of our genetic material in your own as mere junk left over from a common ancestor— still clung to by your state religion—or evidence of tender couplings that ultimately resulted in our species' absorption by yours.

Nonsense. I would refer you to your own history, but your capacity to edit it has now gone from the generational to the hourly, from the effacement of monuments to former emperors to the cybernetic forgery of congressional candidates spouting obscenities and treason. Our bardic memories, transmitted orally from generation to generation, have thus become more reliable than the streamable fantasies of ones and zeros floating numinously in a cyberspace not a ten-thousandth of you begins to understand.

But if you did refer to ink on paper, your own epics would inform you that you treated us no differently than any conquered people. Our end was no different than Troy's at the hands of the Achaeans—you killed the men and raped the women.

The killing, of course, didn't stop at the moment of victory. Nor was it limited to the men. The older and less appealing women died at once. The young and attractive—comparatively few—were enslaved. Their male children were killed at birth; the weaker and smaller girls as soon as their deficiencies became known. Their mothers perished as soon as their sexual utility staled.

Each successive generation saw fewer of my people and more of yours, so that our genocidal skirmishes, and subsequent genetic merger, became less frequent and finally ended. By that time our few survivors had learned how to hide.

Until me.

I had hoped to be the Neanderthal Prometheus. Instead, I am Ahab, dead already, my extended arm pointing the way forward to extinction as I precede my fellows into the depths.

Literacy took me like a drug. The initial heady rush was followed by a craving for more, then more still. My dumpster duty now had a new purpose, for I searched for newspapers and magazines as well as food. And as I was learning to read, New York's alternative tabloids began to distribute in the city without charge; thus, in addition to coffee-stained issues of the *Post* and *Vogue*, I had pristine editions of the Voice and the Press. Whose advertisements, I have to say, were a great deal more instructive in your ways than *Brown Bear Brown Bear or Pat the Bunny*.

Writing was far less difficult to acquire. As I've told you, we are all artists. Once I had learned to convert symbol to sound, sound to symbol was almost second nature. My penmanship is almost calligraphic.

At last I felt ready to beard the lion in its very lair. So to speak. What I wanted—all your knowledge—was guarded by the stone lions on Fifth Avenue. Many times I had shuffled past the New York Public Library longing for the day when I could somehow enter its bowels and decrypt its secret entrails. But illiteracy and my obvious otherness promised to keep the doors locked forever.

Fortune, however, had thrown the key to literacy at my feet. How could I fail to trust my luck? One weekday autumn evening, when the streets were dark and I knew from long surveillance that traffic at the library would be light, I readied myself in the men's room of a midtown Starbucks. Oblivious to the pounding on the door, I used up a dozen yards of paper towel and a pint of hand soap in a sink bath. Next I trimmed my brows and beard with a child's blunt-tipped scissors. Finally I pulled from my Food Emporium plastic bag the best and best-fitting clothes we had ever liberated from a Goodwill drop box: Dockers khakis, a pair of size 14 black wing tips, and an XXL Lakers sweatshirt.

The beating on the door sounded like a battering ram as I cleaned up the stray hair and paper and puddles. I picked up my bag and shot the bolt, prepared to dodge an outraged executive with espresso-charged bladder.

But instead of a hyper-caffeinated stockbroker I saw one of your people less fortunate even than myself. I, after all, had a home to go to and family who would worry if I did not. We were face to face, noses a foot apart. He reeked of alcohol and madness and the street. His eyes were afire and his face contorted with aggrievement. But what was before him appeared to be another larger and somewhat cleaner man. For an instant he struggled visibly with the dilemma that he must have confronted a dozen times a day: whether this was the final indignity he could not let pass or a minor affront not worth a weekend in four-point restraints.

Apparently the latter. He dropped his gaze. "Scuse me, man," he said, standing aside to let me pass. Stunned, I nodded my thanks and made for the door.

I walked down Fifth Avenue with my head held high. Not because I—first of my people?—had received the deference of one of yours. But because one of yours had called me "man."

Perhaps I could pass after all.

"You haven't been honest with me," said Raleigh.

I stared at my hands, folded atop the fresh legal pad he always gave me at the beginning of one of our meetings. When I didn't answer, he tapped my hands lightly with his elegant fountain pen, so that I met his eyes.

He looks like many of the men I used to see in your city. Neither old nor young, with thinning gray hair artfully cropped to disguise its scarcity and his vanity. Still slender and athletic from careful eating and long hours streaming sweat under giant televisions in fitness clubs. But his eyes were pouched and watery from years of worry and alcohol. At every meeting his smell betrayed my prospects—when the odor of cigar was a faint memory, things were going well; when it thrust itself between us, my life was in jeopardy. And today the heady reek of tobacco had grabbed me by the throat the moment he entered the interview room.

He tapped my hand again. "Blingbling," he said. "Look at me, please." I did. His face was harder than I had ever seen it, his thin-lipped mouth a geometer's line. "You didn't tell me the truth."

I picked up my felt-tipped pen to respond. He stopped me with a hand around my wrist. "Speak. Please."

Startled, I dropped the pen. Over the months he'd grown able to understand my simple spoken pleasantries, but anything of substance was still committed to writing. "About what?" I blurted.

For a long moment he didn't speak, and I was genuinely afraid. What would become of me if I lost him?

But at last he barked a laugh and I relaxed a little. "Well, Bling," he said, leaning forward, "over the years I've had occasion to question some of my clients' humanity. Because they've engaged in conduct unbecoming of the species. How is it, I've said, that a *human being* could club his senile mother and disabled sister to death and then live with their rotting corpses just so he could continue to collect their social security checks? How is it that a *human being* could punish an unproductive ice dealer by throwing his twelve-year-old sister into a dumpster with five starved pit bulls?

"Good questions," he said, nodding sagely. "Excellent questions. But until very recently, philosophical questions. *Rhetorical* questions. Because, you see, everyone I represented was a featherless biped. Which I used to think was the definition of a human. Plato, right?"

I couldn't help myself. "Aristotle."

"Right," he said. "Right. You are so right. Aristotle. Boy. What an asshole I am. To be corrected on a point of classical philosophy by a Neanderthal."

While your people disputed carrion with jackals on the veldt, mine hunted big game on the glaciers. An injured spearman might wait a long time on the ice until the hunt could return to him. As a result we developed the ability, if not to hibernate, then to slow ourselves down in response to stress. As Raleigh spoke my heart fluttered so furiously against my ribs that I thought it would shatter its boney cage and fly away. But then my terror crossed some boundary laid down in my genes and suddenly I was at sleepy peace, my pulse barely in the double digits, staring again at my folded hands while my lawyer droned incomprehensibly in the distance.

My trance was broken by the heavy tap-tap-tap of his pen on my skull.

"Sorry to interrupt, Mahatma," he said, "but we really have to deal with this. As I was saying just before you crawled down the rabbit hole to Wonderland, a Neanderthal corrected my knowledge of the classics. The Neanderthal being you. And as I said a few minutes before that, I've wondered in the past whether some of my clients were human. Their crimes notwithstanding, they were. You, on the other hand, are not." He settled

back in his chair. "Care to explain?"

Defendant's family. Manhattan, early June.

When I woke up I was alone. Which didn't disturb me because I often do. But as early-summer late-morning light pushed its way through blinds I thought I'd closed completely, I was sure I hadn't gone to sleep that way.

I rolled over. The sheets puffed up a pretty good scent of sex sweat. Aha. I was right. But, as I rolled, something crackled on the pillow next to me.

A yellow sticky captioned with the art deco logo I'd commissioned in a brief burst of positive equity. WWW.RALEIGHLAW.COM The logo took up nearly a quarter of the sticky, but the message was pretty succinct. *I can't do this anymore.*

Of course you can't, I thought. I'm one year short of twice your age. So plainly we can't do this forever. Which explains why this is the third time you've left in the past six weeks. Then again, I can reliably find your clitoris without causing a lot of collateral damage. Which is why you've come back twice.

I rolled onto my side and studied the parallelograms that the windows cast on the hardwood floor. That's right, parallelograms. Windows. Plural. I have three windows in my bedroom. And it's not the only bedroom, two floors over Charles Street. I'd bought the place cheap during the last crash when over-leveraged stockbrokers were coughing up assets like tubercular lungs.

For a while I wondered whether this time she would call me, or I would email her. Or whether neither of us would do anything and the sticky note would stay on the pillow until the cleaning woman came by on Wednesday. I lay there with my hands folded beneath my head, remembering the night before.

My hand was on the small of her back, just above the coccyx, rolling her pubic bone forward and down onto mine, upthrust. Her brown nipples were nearly black with erection, hard as bullets, her hands cradling my head as she thrust first one, then the other, into my mouth, crooning Farsi words of love. As I ground her pelvis into mine she rolled her eyes and said, "I'm not ready to come yet; it's too early." But seconds later she gave herself the lie as she planted the heels of her hands on my chest and drove herself down on me, breaking into shuddering sobs.

And as I remembered, I stirred. My choices seemed to be limited to picking up the phone or the bottle of baby oil in the bathroom cabinet.

But then through the half-open door I heard a click, followed almost immediately by a cheery burble. After which came the rich odor of Porto Rico Coffee's Brazilian Espresso Blend. Somehow I had remembered to fill and set the Krups the night before.

As the poet says, Malt does more than Milton can/ To justify God's Ways to man. Coffee's pretty good too.

I threw off the covers and limped into the kitchen, my half-mast boner bouncing like a dowsing rod. I drew a cup of coffee and was about to sit down on a stool until I remembered I was naked. Even alone, it's something I won't do, if only because of the sucking sound that accompanies standing up. So I stood at the counter and tried to figure out what to do about A. my Iranian and B. my Neanderthal.

The first part was easy. The usual half-life of a hissy fit was thirty-six hours. So I'd give her till Monday night to decide whether she meant it and then make the call. Thus giving her ample opportunity to assess her prospects in a city in which reasonably athletic unmarried heterosexuals, even those just over fifty, were in short supply. And I'd be assuaging her Persian pride by making the first step. Of course, she could decide she meant it after all, in which event all I'd lose would be a little dignity. Which was also in short supply.

Now the hard part. My boy Bling had put me in something of a bind. I'd call it a dilemma but a dilemma has but two horns; this was more like being impaled on a sea urchin. Life was tough enough when he was just a minimum wage killer freak that the highest-priced legal talent in the City was trying to turn into a piñata. That was now officially the good old days. Before I found out that my client was an evolutionary impossibility.

Let's see. On the one hand his rather surprising status was the greatest single scientific development of the past two hundred years. Proving as it did Darwinian evolution, as though evolution needed further proof. Which you would think would be a good thing. Except that the Constitution of the United States As Patriotically Amended permanently cast evolution in doubt, thanks to the red-state knuckle-draggers in the Senate and their blue-state quisling colleagues. Who apparently thought hey, while we're setting up a dictatorship, let's make it a dumb dictatorship. Hence the Fair to Faith clauses in the Amended First Amendment. While Scientific Creationism wasn't exactly the state religion—how could it be a religion if it had science in the name, right?—it was close enough that conclusively and permanently exploding it would not be looked upon kindly in official circles. Including the circles that could make me disappear.

Therefrom arose my problem. Or problems. Obviously, the fact that my client was not a, umm, person, strictly speaking, raised a genuine issue as to whether he was answerable to a criminal code exclusively applicable to human beings capable of conforming their conduct to it. A category which, however liberally the Supreme Court had applied it to nine- year- old fetal alcohol victims with ready access to mommy's gun, probably didn't reach evolutionary false starts long thought extinct. So his diminished capacity was a defense I was obligated to raise.

Aha. But if he wasn't a human within the reach of the criminal law, what was he? Obviously an animal. Animals are property. And Bling was an animal without an owner. And animals have neither procedural due process rights to trial nor substantive due process rights to life. Thus, if I succeeded in a motion to dismiss on the basis of his non-humanity, I might well be buying Bling a quick blast of phenobarbital at the pound and a mass cremation with all the Christmas puppies. A course which would sweep an embarrassment to the state non-religion under the carpet.

And while I left aside the obvious repercussions of revealing Bling's provenance to consider the immediate tactical issue, I could not long ignore them. Maybe fifteen minutes, tops, after the filing of any motion disclosing the fact that I represented Alley Oop, every media outlet in America and the civilized world as well would be up my ass and his without the aid of a colonoscope. Not such a bad thing, perhaps. Though it refused to pay UN dues "on principle," the Administration seemed to recognize that it pissed off the rest of the world on so many big things that it should throw it a bone sometimes on the smaller ones. So if the world media were alerted to the scientific wonder I happened to represent, Homeland might be much less inclined to make him and his lawyer disappear. A course that the Just-Down-out-of the-Trees Full Gospel Baptist mega-churches in the red states would surely be urging once this unclean insult to true religion became publicly known.

But I was getting ahead of myself. I couldn't do what I had to do next with Bling until well after dark. And it wasn't yet noon. The coffee was almost gone. I sipped what was left in my cup and decided that there was no real loss of face if I called the Iranian a little early.

Maybe I didn't lose face, but I didn't gain a dirty afternoon, either. She didn't pick up. I spent the balance of the daylight hours returning client voicemails suggesting I was ignoring them in favor of my newfound deformed hip-hop carriage trade. After three hours of abasing myself to mid-level ice mules illiterate in their own languages, I felt I had to do something to restore my pride. So I headed over to the Apogee.

A mistake, at least in the self-esteem department. It was still earliest June, so the waiter-actor-models hadn't yet abandoned weekending New York for the Hamptons. And though I'd finally accepted the fact that no one in his fifties can pummel and Pilates himself into the shape of a brokerage trainee fresh from Princeton's lacrosse field, it is nevertheless painful to confront a locker room full of Michelangelo's wet dreams.

But the workout silenced the gremlins, at least for the moment. I did an hour of intervals on the stationary bike and five sets of everything in a chest and triceps routine. Leaving me pleasantly exhausted and convinced that if I hadn't reversed the decline, I'd at least slowed it.

It was almost dark when I left the gym. I had time to kill and it was one of those early summer Sunday nights when the air is sweet and every girl realizes that maybe she's beautiful after all. So I walked. Since I was going to wind up on the Lower East Side anyway I thought I could do worse than a quiet pint at DBA, which to my surprise was actually quiet, and where to my greater surprise I actually had just one pint. I thought about going into the garden in the back with the merry smokers, but a quick peek through the door revealed a few too many young ladies with exposed rock-hard abdomens for the comfort of a man wrestling with the possibility that he might have just doinked his last woman under thirty. So instead I nursed my microbrewery pale ale in the long, dark, narrow, yeasty bar and thought about calling her again.

But no. Pride and an empty glass propelled me into the street. It was ten o'clock and a dozen blocks to Bar Veloce. Which is also narrow but bright and clean-lined in that natural Italian style that suggests that sometime in the first century Augustus decreed that there would be no ugly doorknobs. It was almost empty. I had a very nice glass of aglianico with a prosciutto, asiago, and sundried tomato panino and an insalata misto, a meal which at the diner down the street would've been called a grilled cheese bacon and tomato sandwich with a house salad. The witching hour yet to arrive, I nursed a series of decaf espressos—contradiction in terms if ever there was one—and worked the crossword while every now and again glancing up at the continuous play of Fellini's Roma on the big screen at the end of the bar.

After the third pointless coffee I decided to get down to business. I'd bought a pair of cargo pants at J. Crew the day before to hide my tools. I clanked a little bit as I got off the stool and made my way to the street.

On a summer Sunday after midnight, the lower east Side was almost empty. There was a time when money was beginning to trickle into the Bowery because the ground everywhere else in Manhattan was pretty much soaked with it. So CBGB got gutted to make way for a boutique mall, and a dozen wino SRO's went co-op. But then the FBI lost the dirty bombs and Queda turned into Mahdists and started blowing up oilfields and the Patriot Amendments passed. The next thing you know we were at war in every country beginning with a vowel, except England, Ireland, and Italy. And then gas cost more than crack and whaddayuh know, China stopped being all that interested in dollars. And then things got really bad.

The consequence of which, so far as my immediate surroundings were concerned, was that a lot of architecturally distinctive restorations of nineteenth century shitholes had stopped mid-stream a couple of years ago. So that corner bodegas inherited their painstakingly resurrected tile floors and LED pin-lights. And ice was being dealt from half-finished home theaters in brownstones wrapped in shreds of the blue tarp that had surrounded them when their developers went bankrupt in the crash.

But it could have been worse. Though I cringed to admit it, the Patriot Amendments had provided the current city administration with some useful loopholes in the civil rights of the arrested. So if the cops really didn't have to worry too much when iceheads died in custody, I could walk through the Lower East Side without a laser. I guess if you're going to plunge a country into despotism and poverty it helps to keep the drug-crazed underclass invisible. Just so it looks as though you've done *something* good.

The address Bling had given me was, in fact, a boarded up commercial tenement just off the Bowery whose most recent use had been a Chinese restaurant supply store. Just as he'd said. Good. Maybe a client was telling the truth. First time for everything. Probably because he was a caveman. And as he'd also said, there was a heavy chain and padlock securing the front door, to which had long ago been taped a very impressive looking BY ORDER OF THE TRUSTEE IN BANKRUPTCY FOR THE SOUTHERN DISTRICT OF

NEW YORK. Which, by its terms, if you read the faded script—as I did in the beam of my brand new Paragon Sports Tek-Lite—had expired when I was still in the DA's office. I loitered in the doorway for a few minutes, hoping that I'd pass for a real estate mogul out for a midnight stroll, researching foreclosed properties. Certain that instead I looked like an old white guy trying to score a blowjob from a chickenhead ice whore before limo-ing back to wife and kiddies in Bedford. Though the Bowery was half a block away, I saw about as much foot traffic as I would have on a dirt road in the Catskills at the same hour of day and day of tweek. Reassured, I thrust my hands into the pockets of my cargo pants and ambled towards the alleyway between the building and its neighbor, doing my best to look casual. Whistling, if you can believe that.

The alleyway was barely twice as wide as I was. Naturally it stank from generations of drunken defecations; there just aren't that many passageways like that in this part of the City. I took out my Tek-Lite and twisted the beam-width ring until the flash was as focused as a laser. With the tight circle of light just ahead of my feet I made my way down the alley. Underfoot I heard vials and needles crunch, and I was glad that I had worn shoes rather than flip flops. The walls on either side crawled with graffiti, some of which, I was startled to notice, actually looked more like art than vandalism.

At the end of the alley was a doorway. Over the door was a light fixture with a bird's nest in place of a bulb. Just as Bling had said. So far, so good. The door was steel, also chained and padlocked. The chain, however, was barely enough to secure a bike, and the padlock was bright around the keyhole with recent use. Also as my client had suggested.

I took out the bolt-cutters. For a moment I thought to start whistling again to conceal the metallic snap and rattle of a disbarment-grade felony, but decided against it. One quick squeeze and I was through the chain. I took out a slim jim, which for those of you who don't drive tow trucks or break into buildings is a slender flexible metal strip. I slipped it into the narrow space between door and frame, worked it up to the bolt, and popped it in less than thirty seconds. I probably could have done it faster with a credit card.

I stood there for nearly a minute wondering whether I really wanted to do this. I decided I really didn't but I had to do it anyway. I pushed the door open.

I had turned the light all the way down to allow my eyes to adjust. The first thing that struck me, though, when I stepped over the threshold into the Neolithic was not what I saw, but what I smelled. Somewhere in the back of my head I expected the wet newspaper moldy bread dirty clothes reek of a street person's flop. Instead it smelled like woodsmoke and musk. Oddly pleasant. Maybe the Body Shop could market it as a shower gel. Caveman Nights.

I pulled the door shut behind me. Directly ahead was a stairway. From the top of which I could hear rustlings and chitterings, like a nest of squirrels in a brownstone's crawlspace. With the door shut I twisted the Tek-Lite's ring and spread the broad beam over the stairwell.

It was like nothing I'd ever seen. Imagine that the Warner Brothers had hired Michelangelo to decorate the Sistine Chapel with allegories of Bugs Bunny come again in glory to judge the living and the dead.

The walls were covered with painted images. All executed with the kind of Old Master precision you see at the Met, in wild Matisse colors from MoMA. A faithful reproduction of the Last Supper took up most of one wall. Faithful except for the fact that it included Spongebob Squarepants and Homer Simpson among the celebrants. And hovering behind the table were a couple of female figures I didn't remember from the original who suspiciously resembled a Gaga Madonna and Beyonce Magdalene.

On another wall were voudou demigods and Santeria saints who looked like they'd just jumped off Dominican votary candles and grown twice life size. Gutshot Lee Harvey Oswald cringed at the foot of a Salvador Dali cross on which Malcolm X looked to heaven for release. Which probably would have really pissed him off. All on a background of autumnal blue, depth on celestial depth, that Giotto would have envied. It was as though every crazy SoHo sidewalk artist had been kidnapped by aliens, given an MFA, and dropped back here with a commission.

The thought of aliens made me look up. The ceiling was the color of midnight, darker and deeper than the October afternoon of the stairway walls. Across it was the Milky Way, chased in silver. Not in planetarium precision, but as the heart-stopping starfog stretching from horizon to horizon that I had seen lying on my back on a blanket in a Pennsylvania field with my first girlfriend curled beside me, smoking my father's Chesterfields, wondering how much further we could cheat curfew.

I dropped the beam to the stairs themselves. I laughed out loud. Each riser was decorated with a row of Keith Haring figures, supporting the step above them with paw-like hands. Or, standing on those hands, with their feet. Or once or twice, forming human pyramids so that the uppermost figure bore the weight on its back. Like caryatids.

As I started up the stairs I happened to glance down. Old *Post* and News front pages had been varnished onto the treads. My heels struck the yellowing features of Presidents, Homeland generals, proconsuls from all our far-flung protectorates. Something I'd always wanted to do.

I got to the landing at the top of the stairs. There was a large steel door that looked impervious except for a lock no better than the one downstairs. Which I could barely find among the dancing rats twining over the door and across the jamb and onto the walls. They glowed in the colors you find only in the deluxe hundred and twenty eight-piece Crayola box. I couldn't decide whether they looked more like city rats or the giants who'd shared Flores with Bling's cousins. Probably city; they looked tough, and I swear one had an earring.

I slipped the slim jim through the jamb and over the bolt. The door clicked and sprang forward a quarter of an inch.

I stood there quite a long time. The woodsy smell was very strong now. From inside I could hear squirrely rustling and behind it a soft frantic chatter.

My hesitation really doesn't require a lot of explanation. All I had to do at this point was close the door, turn around, and call the Eichmann clone at Homeland, and I'd be out of it. Next thing you know Bling would be getting waterboarded at some undisclosed location and every hint of his existence would be expunged. I wouldn't be at the center of a gospel-singing mouth-breathing firestorm over evolution because there wouldn't be one. My increasingly flabby ass would be covered and I'd still have the quarter mil fee because I'd been such a loyal citizen. And I wouldn't be spending the odd philosophical moment wondering how the fuck all this happened.

Ah, yes. The odd philosophical moment. Even if the Bar had amended the Rules of Professional Responsibility to comport with the Patriot Amendments, I grew up under the old school. A client's a client. Even if he's subhuman. In fact, especially if he's a subhuman. Because that's what lawyers are for. Anyway, I liked the guy.

I pushed the door all the way open. The chirruping reached a terrified crescendo. I stepped through. Beyond was a large commercial loft, probably five thousand square feet. Between my little flashlight and the streetlight streaming through filthy windows I could make out only the glitter of however they'd decorated the walls and about twenty thick shapes huddled in a corner on the street side, as far away from me as they could get. I resisted the temptation to beam the light at the base of my chin for my famous Boris Karloff impression and instead pointed it at the floor.

I reached into a cargo pocket. The huddled pile pulled together even tighter and I thought I heard a couple of muffled screams and sobs. I guess they'd been around us long enough to know about the things we carried.

But they didn't have to worry about what I had in my pocket. It was my phone. I opened the recorder app and raised it so the speaker was pointed towards them and turned the volume all the way up. I took a deep breath and hit Play.

The Neanderthals fell silent as Blingbling addressed his people.

The door just closed behind Captain Graner. In my hand is a slab of beef jerky. "Here," he had said, passing it to me just as he left. "Knock yourself out."

My fingers curl around the leathery anonymous meat. No longer can I imagine his generosity a recognition of our common humanity, or at least, our mutual sapience. Rather, this may be my last meal.

I fight the urge to weep. An unequal battle. I disintegrate into shuddering sobs, and as though in obedience to his parting words I pound my fist into my forehead again and again and curl tighter and tighter. At last I lie on my side on the floor, wrapped in a ball as I was in the sweet sea beneath my mother's heart before she expelled me into your world. I lie for a time I cannot measure, exhausted, nuzzling Graner's gift, the leather slick and soaked with tears and mucous.

Finally I relax. Comforted perhaps by the certainty of death, the freedom of utter hopelessness. It is your nature to flail and struggle towards the light as it flees; ours, to sink gratefully into the warm embrace of the dark. My ancestors, after all, invented afterlife and burial long before yours. Hugging the spears and tools they had used in this life and would need in the next, garlanded with flowers, my remotest grandfathers melted back into the earth in graves we had dug for them, over which we planted the skulls of the great bears we dreaded and worshipped and occasionally, reverently, slew.

I rise to sit on the edge of my bunk, head nearly to my knees. I breathe deeply and sit up. I slip my last meal into the breast pocket of my orange nylon jumpsuit.

I must tell you how I came to be here. While I still can.

As I said, I had expected that having brought literacy like Prometheus with stolen fire I would have been greeted with adulation. Or at least gratitude. But no. Like Prometheus I was to be chained to a rock.

The Nest was far less interested in my discovery than I hoped. Great Grandmother, of course, appreciated its significance; she cuddled me for hours crooning my praises, nodding sagely as I detailed my plans for the education of our race. Only after a dozen siblings and cousins had expressed only so much attention as politeness required did I realize that my newfound knowledge was not universally admired.

Crestfallen, I sat night after night in a filthy window, silently mouthing the advertisements for personal injury lawyers and laser eye surgery on the sides of passing busses. One night, when the rest of the Nest snored in its conjugal piles, Great Grandmother crept up behind me and opened her arms. Gratefully I crawled into her embrace. She cradled me within her creaking joints and whispered the truth she had earlier withheld: they really did not care. Exhausted by the hundreds of generations in which the effort of survival—that is, surviving you—had consumed all our intellectual energy, there was nothing left, in these latter days, for scholarship or simple curiosity. True, enough of the fire remained for us to decorate our successive surrogate caves, swirl spraypaint on alleyway walls, chant the old epics, tread the old dances. But after that there was nothing. Nothing for anything new. If my sons, Great Grandmother said--whoever they were among the Nest's few cubs—had not inherited my spark, we were done.

We lay curled in silence for a few moments. My head pressed against her withered dugs. "So," I said, "what shall I do?"

Her reply was so long delayed that I thought she had fallen asleep. At last, though, her lips sought my ear. I stopped breathing, thinking that she would speak some great secret of our race formerly reserved for the eldest matriarchs, that I would be the first of my gender to hear, or that I would be sent on some great quest like Parsifal, perhaps to find another Nest surviving in secret, whose existence was the subject of millennial myth and quotidian gossip; or that she would command me to take my secret and myself to the streets, to die alone frozen in an alley or shattered under drunken boots, so that the Nest could placidly drowse and mumble away our species' last days like a dreaming dog suckling in its sleep.

My heart fluttered as she cleared her throat. But her words were nothing I'd imagined.

"Great Grandson," she said. "Great Grandson. You have to get a job."

However poorly we understood your people, we understood that you valued money. Why was sometimes unclear; that you did was never in doubt. Living as we did on the remotest edge of your commercial world, somewhere between the homeless and domestic pets, we were able to exist almost entirely without it. In our Lower East Side home every alleyway teemed with fresh meat on the paw, rats too stupefied by their long symbiosis with you to remember their days as prey, at least of bipeds. Even the slowest of our young men could bag a dozen in an hour. Whatever our wild diet lacked was easily supplemented from trashcans and dumpsters, which also provided us with the raw materials for our art. Clothing came from unattended Salvation Army drop-offs.

But even if we survived without money we needed it to sweeten our lives. Which, like yours, are a brief burst of light between two infinite darknesses; like you, we long to enrich the intermission between endless nothings. Our tastes, however, are much simpler than yours. Not for us the vacation houses and enormous cars and vast buildings with which to cheat eternity's emptiness.

We needed money for hot chocolate.

Your civilization's addictions otherwise held nothing for us. True, every generation of our young drained the last drops from discarded Popov bottles to discover anew that liquor made us sick and nothing else. Each of us once drew deep from a long Marlboro butt and wondered after the retching subsided why you persist in your self-inflicted injury.

But give us a castaway mocha latte and we'll tongue the cup dry like German shepherds and then chew the paper to suck out every last trace of sweet richness. Chocolate—liquid chocolate, especially hot, though some heretics among my brethren favor chocolate malts—strikes the same center in our brains as opiates in yours. A Hershey bar will do in a moment of desperation; hot coffee with cream and four sugars quiets the craving for a day or so. But a Starbucks Venti with whipped cream strikes us like a truffle before a starving hog. In our time in Manhattan hot chocolate had become part of our religious observances, a single cup if that was all our panhandlers could obtain, passed from hand to hand sipped sparingly as we called on the spirits of our ancestors to guide us through another day. But, if favored by fortune and your generosity, they would return with cardboard carriers full of sweet steaming elixir, still warm despite their circuitous routes, the change they could not comprehend dumped into tip jars as offerings to the charity gods, and it was Mardi Gras.

Of course that was not the only thing for which cash was needed. The increasingly antiquated boomboxes to which we danced needed power, and live batteries were never to be found in dumpsters. And sometimes our children, on the infrequent occasions they were permitted daylight, would squall—like yours--for a street vendor's balloon. And like you, what could we do but thrust money into the seller's hands. But you knew whether it was enough, and if it were too much, what to expect back; we could only hope the immigrant merchant would take pity on a buyer from much farther away than he. Your children's castaway toys are buried in the swollen landfills that circle your cities. Ours, however, are enshrined in our art, so that Styrofoam lizards that miraculously grow into neon alligators after a night soaking in water are now part of the collage winding across a central pillar in our home.

My eyes well up as I write. *Our* home. Are you still there, any of you? Have I destroyed you all? I hope I have not. But I know I will never see you or our home again.

Enough.

Great Grandmother, in consultation with the other matriarchs, had decided that literacy afforded me access to your world and its good things on a scale denied us for generations. One morning, then, I dressed in the clothes with which I had previously assaulted the Public Library. In my pocket was a carefully printed entreaty: I AM RETARDED AND MUTE. I AM HONEST AND WORK HARD. PLEASE, DO YOU HAVE WORK FOR ME? Thus armed, I set out to conquer your world.

Unfortunately, the Lower East Side of Manhattan is not known for early rising. Even on a Saturday spring morning. The only unshuttered establishments were coffee shops whose customers were painfully hung over and whose staffs had less command of your language than I. At each I met different degrees of rejection. At best a sad shake of the head and a cookie slipped into my hand along with the returned note; at worst, and more typically, no, no, you go now, a finger pointed at the door to which I stumbled, humiliated, as bleary patrons tried to focus on their lattes.

The morning toiled towards noon as I reached St. Mark's Place. The t-shirt shops had begun to roll back their steel barricades. At each, however, the hiring decision seemed to lie in the hands of a Mr. Wu; at each, Mr. Wu, he no here.

Mid-day found me at the intersection of Lafayette, Astor Place, and despair. The weekend city had at last stirred itself. I stood in front of the big Starbucks, battered carelessly by brunch-bound New Yorkers and sight-struck tourists. Every few minutes the shop's door opened to tickle my brainstem with the scent of coffee and cocoa, and my heart broke because my pockets were empty of anything but my sweaty crumpled supplication. I

87

thought briefly to enter the mothership, to thrust my plea into a barrista's hand, certain of rejection but hopeful of a sweet steaming tub on the cuff.

But no. A fragment of dignity asserted itself. I would not beg. I squared my shoulders and walked across the street to the just awakened Astor Place Liquors. Which apparently did not need a non-speaking stockboy to sort the single malts. Nor did Kate's Organic World, and even less so the narrow Barnes and Noble outpost

I had earlier decided that if I reached Broadway without a job the whole enterprise was pointless. SoHo boutiques would not find me an attractive management trainee.

My last stop was the corner of Astor Place and Broadway. The sidewalk was dense with commerce. The Russian émigrés had already set up tables with reproduction Leninist posters. The air, heavy with Broadway exhaust, was further burdened by the incense and essential oils the Nigerian vendors hawked. An obvious Arab, beard bristling proudly but otherwise somehow shrunken with fear, manned a Nuts-4-Nuts cart. I threaded my way between merchants and gawking tourists to my destination.

A big sign over the basement entrance, almost at eye level for passing pedestrians. ASTOR PLACE HAIRSTYLISTS. As I walked down the short flight of stairs from the sidewalk the double glass doors swung open and three Latino teenagers bounded out, yoked with gold chains as heavy as Tudor chancellors', their hair cropped painfully close. I saw as they passed that each had a design shaved down to his scalp: one lightning bolts; another, a cross; the third a Yankees logo.

I stepped inside. I'd expected darkness. It was, after all, a cellar. But this basement blazed. Dozens of fluorescent strips hung from the low ceiling, their light reflecting from whitewashed walls and a hundred barbers' mirrors and what looked like an acre of shiny worn linoleum. Stretching back as far as I could see was a maze of sinks and revolving chairs, densely peopled by shearers and those about to be shorn. From it all rose the buzz of razors, rush of water, whine of vacuums, but most of all speech: English a mere plurality fighting for position against Spanish, Chinese, Korean, but most of all the eccentric Italian of Sicily. (Because we do not read, we listen, and because we do not understand the words, we understand the rhythm.)

On my right was a bulletin board behind glass. Push-pinned to it were Polaroids of celebrities in these very chairs, their names and dates of tonsure recorded in magic marker scrawl. I was impressed. Mets and Yankees; Jets and Knicks; Kennedy and Clooney. All of whom, I blush to say now, I immediately recognized; my earliest reading, after children's books, had been People and Us. Many pictures and easy words.

The doors behind opened again. "Watch your back, bro." A young man in the expensive dishevelment of a weekending banker brushed past me. I took a deep breath and walked down the remaining steps to the main floor. Directly in front of me was a desk at which sat a very fat middle-aged man with a cigarette behind his ear and a teenaged boy with a trucker hat on sideways. They stared at me as though I had escaped from an entomologist's specimen bottle. As I fumbled with my placard another man, a barber I assumed—reasonably, I think, because he was covered with other people's hair and had a pair of scissors in his hand—arrived at the desk and began a heated exchange with both.

I waited politely. At last the fat one held his hand up, palm out, to the barber and turned to me. "Yeah?"

I stepped forward and extended my plea. As the fat man reached for it the barber tore it from my hand and scowled vendetta at his colleagues.

He studied it closely for far longer than he had to, lips pursed, brows knit, nodding sagely. He was a tall man with a big belly straining a green, white, and red Italian soccer shirt. His thinning hair was teased into gelled ringlets. His jowls were decorated with a fashionable two day scruff just a little thicker than his mustache. "You want a job, eh? How you gonna get a job looking like that?" He dropped a heavy paw on my shoulder and spun me to face another branch of the tonsorial maze. "You come with me, I make you look good." He gave me a shove between the shoulder blades and spat something at the desk that I can only guess had something to do with mothers.

"This way, this way," he said from behind, nudging me along. "You don't speak, you understand right?" I nodded. "See, right, some people speak, they don't understand. Like some guys I know. Talk alla time, don't know shit. Like hey, Mario make us lots of money, let's break his balls. Hey, here. Sit."

I half fell into a chair as he swept a cloth around me and fastened it around my neck. His station was wreathed with pinups: nearly naked B-grade actresses falling out of lacey push-up bras, lips wet and eyes glazed; soccer stars punching in goals; grinning actors with cropped hair;

aerial views of Sicily. He spun me to face the mirror. Terrified, I confronted myself.

Even allowing for the startled eyes and white lips of an anxiety not usually associated with a little off the top, I was appalled at how little I resembled my fellow customers. How had I ever thought I would pass in this world? Who else had the heavy shelf of brow under which my eyes popped? The sloping chin and forehead? The leathery rufous skin, so thick it creased rather than wrinkled? What would Mario say when he found my hair coarser than anything he'd yet encountered, or worse, when his flying clippers found the bun of bone at the base of my skull? Was this, at last, the end? Would my people be discovered and undone by a haircut?

My face was screwed shut in panic; my breath shallow. "Hey, don worry, I ain't gonna poke your eye," said Mario. Certain that this caveman interloper was about to be found out, I forced my lids up and risked a glance to the side.

I needn't have worried. This was New York.

Other barbers clipped and gossiped; other customers, waiting, bent their attention to Maxim or the *Times*. Those who met my stare largely did so with indifference. One actually nodded. However strange I looked each had seen something stranger that day. *And nobody cared*.

I gusted relief and sagged into the chair. "Hey," said Mario, his scissors crunching through my pelt, "what are you, anyway? Some kind of Indian? Not like a cabdriver, you know, but like a Cherokee or something?" He stopped cutting and faced my reflection in the mirror. His hand went to his mouth and patted it rhythmically. "Woo-woo-woo. You know, Indian? Like cowboys and Indians?"

I was prepared for this. Carefully I articulated the ethnicity I had chosen for my people.

"What? Heshe? *Heshe*? What the *fuck*?" His face contorted with contempt and I suddenly feared the scissors.

I shook my head violently and tried again.

Mario took a long moment before he erupted with laughter and put both hands on my shoulders. "Oh, okay, *Gypsy*. You okay then, man!"

He lifted his hands to his not inconsequential breasts and bounced them up and down, grinning. "I know this Gypsy girl once back in Naples, hoo boy she had big tits. Crazy too. Too crazy for me, big tits, whatever fuggedaboudit. Your Gypsy girls have big tits?"

90

I nodded.

Mario considered. "Crazy?"

I nodded again.

"Too crazy for you?"

Inspired, I shook my head.

He roared again and pinched my earlobe. "See, I know I like you!"

For the next quarter hour he buzzed and clipped and shaved and compared his Gypsy and other conquests to the girls surrounding his mirror. At one point he stopped and pointed his scissors at Maria-Gracia Cucinotta. "Any Gypsy girls look like her?"

Forming my response carefully, I said, "Lots."

He laughed again and slapped either side of my head, gently, and said, "Hey. You have me over for Sunday dinner, right? I meet your cousins. Okay, we done. You like?" He held a mirror to the back of my head.

Stunned, I murmured, "Yes."

"You come in looking like some kinda retard, now look, you sell stocks and bonds, right? Right!"

I nodded dumbly. He was right. Cropped and trimmed I was still a Neanderthal. Yet a Neanderthal transformed. Though I scarcely resembled one of the GQ models on the mirror, I could easily imagine an Upper East Side nanny instructing her charge not to stare at the poor man. Instead of calling the police.

"You come with me," said Mario. He whipped the black cloth from around my neck, scattering bristly clippings. I followed silently as he worked his way among his fellow barbers, clapping backs and hurling good-natured insults, occasionally calling attention to his handiwork. "You see this guy when he come in? Ape man, right?" At this my bowels shriveled in fear; had I always been that obvious? "Hey, look at him now, movie star, right?"

We had reached the front desk. The fat man and the teenager were as they had been. Both stared incuriously, first at Mario, then me. At last the fat man spoke. "So?"

"So this, you fat fuck," said Mario reasonably. "You remember this guy when he come in? No? Right, sorry, I forget how stupid you are. Here, this remind you, eh?" He waved my employment application in the fat man's face. "Oh yeah, now you get it, crazy homeless retarded guy. *Now* you look at him, eh?" He threw a heavy arm over my shoulders and drew me forward.

91

"Movie star, right?"

I was almost incontinent with fear. The fat man was reddening with anger and neighboring barbers were chortling and nudging their clients. A dispute between your people with a Neanderthal in the middle would not end well for me and mine.

The fat man spoke through a sneer. "Movie star? Fuck you."

"Oh, fuck me? Okay, fat man, get up, I show you. I show everybody. Come on," he said, waving his free arm with the other still draped over my cringing back. "You guys, laugh now, take a look, you see who's a barber here." Taking me with him he shambled to the foot of the stairs. He planted us both in front of the bulletin board touting buzzcut celebrities. "Come on, funny guys, you look."

Several barbers, clippers in hand, had formed a circle around us. My eyes were fixed on the floor, which despite my prayers to my ancestors stubbornly refused to split and swallow me up in sheltering earth. I could hear wheezing Sicilian curses that heralded the fat man's approach. When at last Mario was satisfied of an adequate audience he turned to the bulletin board and pulled out a pushpin supporting the aging Polaroid of a famous client. Still hoping for divine deliverance I did not dare look.

"*See what I mean? Movie star!*" Triumphantly he held the photograph next to my face.

My ancestors heard an hour's worth of frantic supplication in what could not have been a minute of ensuing silence. At last it was broken. "Holy shit," someone murmured.

"Hope his agent don't see this," said one.

"Wow," said another. "Separated at birth, maybe. Except Malkovitch has a chin." He paused for a moment. "Forehead too."

"Yeah," said Mario, "you see now, eh? You see who the real barber is, right?"

The fat man spoke. "Show's over, ladies. Back to work. And you," he said to Mario, "in the office."

"You wait here," said Mario. "I get you job. You see."

Naturally, my first impulse—like the second, third, and fourth—was to bolt the instant he was gone. But two things held me back. First and most pressing was the constant surreptitious scrutiny in which the other barbers kept me, glancing every minute or so to the corner in which I shuffled and cowered. Their attention was not unfriendly; one even winked when I inadvertently allowed him to catch my eye. Yet I imagined that if I ran I would thereby confess the crime of my anachronistic existence, and that as I fled down Astor place, ricocheting off pretzel vendors and Ghanian watch merchants, hot on my heels would follow a pack of baying barbers, scissors held high as cavalry sabers, behind them their customers, shaving cream flying from their jowls, barber's capes fluttering at their shoulders. Second, and surprising, was something I believe my people have never felt towards yours: gratitude. Probably because there had never previously been a reason for it. Though I won't pretend that had I been discovered, I would have fled like a felon, my flight burdened with shame at having betrayed a man who had tried to do me a kindness.

And so I stayed where I had been told, shifting nervously from foot to foot, ducking my head whenever a new customer popped through the double doors. Mumbling hopelessly first to the ancestors, then the bears and mammoths they had slain, and at last in desperation to the secret Great Mother who had given birth to the world of ice and tundra in which we had long ago been happy.

Religion presently failed me. I hunched in a corner near the bulletin board, arms crossed, head bowed, rocking and crooning no louder than comfort required. Perhaps perplexed customers would think me a davening Hassid, head inexplicably uncovered.

Suddenly the door through which my new friend had long ago disappeared burst open. Mario emerged, beaming triumphantly. Behind him was the fat man, sullen, his wattles almost puce. Despite my patron's buoyancy I feared the worst and started to edge towards the door.

But the door was too far away and suddenly filled with half a dozen teenagers shoving each other aside in their eagerness to be clipped. The fat man settled into his perch. Mario extended his hand, which the fat man grudgingly took; eyes averted, he gusted, "Yeah, whatever."

And then Mario was upon me, face bisected with a grin, his hand out. "So, Gypsy man," he said, "when can you start?"

Defense witnesses. Manhattan, late October.

This close to midnight the air was pretty cool despite China's new one-child-two-cars-per-family policy. Cool enough so that I took pleasure in the warmth from the Starbucks carrier in my hands. A carrier which I deftly took up in my left while I knocked shave-and-a-haircut-two-bits—our crafty code—with my right on the cavemen's door. This time I got in without committing a burglary.

In his message Blingbling had told the rest of the sideshow to trust the nice man. Though hesitant—actually, petrified—at first, his fellow throwbacks had gradually warmed to me and my weekly visits. At each of which I relayed a speech from Bling to which I recorded a communal reply. Maybe not the smartest thing I'd ever done; if he really were a terror suspect I'd've been buying myself a needle to the next world, without regard to his actual guilt, for aiding and abetting. But the one bright spot in Bling's evolutionary mess was that whatever else he was, a Mahdist in a dynamite waistcoat he was not. So I felt reasonably safe.

Reasonably. But just in case I came at a different time and by a different route at each visit. These days usually by two or three different cabs with a subway ride in between. Something a sixteen year-old who'd read a lot of John LeCarre could have seen through, so the net effect was probably to advertise my guilty knowledge to whoever was watching. But hey, I had to try, didn't I?

Today I'd come bearing something in addition to a fireside chat. Even though I'd given up my feeble efforts to piece together their language after the first couple of weeks—their whistles, pops, and clicks predated anything Indo-Aryan by about a hundred thousand years—I 'd been able to figure a few things out from their surroundings. And judging from the reverently cleaned and stacked cups, boy, they loved their Starbucks.

I knew I was right the second the door creaked open. Behind it was a Neanderthal who could've been Bling's younger brother—in fact, he probably was. There weren't many of them, as far as I could tell, and their bloodlines must have been as tangled as my West Virginia cousins'. Unfortunately he hadn't had his sibling's sartorial advantages; he was wearing old sweatpants and a fifty-pound rice sack from which holes for head and arms had been cut, and his very large feet were bare. Nor had the coarse thick hair that covered much of his big round head ever seen a

Middle Village buzzcut palace. But when he smelled the creamy goodness of half a dozen extra Venti mochachinos his face split in Bling's innocent, goofy—and these days, increasingly rare—grin.

Bobbing his head he waved me inside and locked the door behind us. He almost scampered up the stairs, now lit only by the dim rectangular glow of the open door above. I followed more slowly. Still grinning, he waited at the top of the stairs. With a pretty good impression of a bow and a sweep of the hand—where the hell had he learned that, watching doormen?—he urged me into the Nest.

My hours and days in interview rooms with Bling had pretty much prepared me for his male relatives. But despite that, and the experience of earlier visits, the whole clan at home was still overwhelming. There were about twenty of them, at least something like that present at most visits; the building was big and I'd only seen this single room. So far as I could tell they were evenly divided between the genders, and to the extent I could judge—Bling had told me they rarely lived much past sixty—the youngest looked to be just out of his teens and the oldest sixty-one.

I said I was prepared for the males. When I'd first seen a Neanderthal woman I was taken back to my freshman year. Art history, at the very beginning of a very big book. A crudely carved fertility goddess, fat and faceless, that had been found in a cave painted by our earliest ancestors twenty thousand years ago. Apparently Bling's brothers liked the ladies thick. Though substantially shorter than the men—five feet max—they shared their broad builds, coarse hair, and muscularity. Unfortunately they padded it with what I guessed to be at least fifty additional pounds, evenly distributed fore and aft between huge sagging boobs and wobbly melon buttocks.

As usual they were waiting in their story-time circle, squatting on their haunches, their big black eyes gleaming in the streetlight that forced its way through the filthy windows. But their solemn silence broke the second they scented what I carried. Giggling like children they leaped to their feet and executed an elaborate pantomime happy dance. But unlike the master race I happened to represent, they didn't kick, gouge, and elbow their way over one another to get at the goods. No, instead they maintained a respectful distance, beaming and nodding, trying hard not to stare at the cardboard tray still in my hands.

After a moment they drew aside to allow a very old woman—the apparent sixty-one year old—to approach me at an arthritic pace. She was hunched and by Neolithic standards skinny. Her features reminded me of a shrunken head, if you can imagine a shrunken head the size and shape of a regulation bowling ball. But even though it revealed nothing but withered gum and a few blackened stubs of tooth, the warmth of her spreading grin made me sure that this was the one Bling called Oldest Grandmother. That and the fact that she was a very old woman, of course.

She bobbed her head and clasped her hands in what I took to be gratitude, rocking back and forth. Taking my cue I extended the carrier, my head bowed in deference. She took it from me delicately and handed it off to another old woman. The rest of the tribe gathered again in its circle, quiet now, with an expectant gravity out of proportion with the prospect of high-calorie caffeine consumption. Oldest Grandmother took the first cup and presented it to me in both hands, her head inclined.

I was about to take it with a gee thanks but something about the way she was standing struck a chord from my now distant boyhood. A summer Sunday morning in a church stubbornly without air conditioning, the air close and heavy with incense. My mother is next to me. Old ladies drone the rosary in Slovak. A bell rings; the priest elevates the chalice towards Heaven, lowers it, and then bends to drink.

I had to equal the reverence of the congregation and kneeling acolyte. I took the vessel, lifted it skyward, then brought it to my inclined head to drink from the communion cup. I passed it back to the celebrant. Without drinking herself she offered it first to her elderly altar girl, who took a single modest swallow, and then to the first man in the circle. He took his own decorous sip, took the paper chalice in his own hands, and held it as the woman to his left had a drink. And so it went, hand to hand and mouth to mouth, each helping the next, none taking much.

It takes a long time to drink an extra Venti that way, let me tell you. It went around the circle twice. On each orbit it was offered to me again but I managed to turn it down without visibly hurting feelings; after all, I could bathe in it if I wanted, and I'd done the right thing by sharing the first sip. Finally the last celebrant killed it with a deep reverential tonguing that made me really glad that they didn't recycle, for the sake of the public at large.

I was starting to think about gently nudging them back to the business at hand and had gone so far as to ostentatiously fumble with the digital recorder. At that point the Oldest Grandmother launched the second of six cups, having first offered it to me. Slipping the recorder back into a pocket I congratulated myself for having taken a leak right before I arrived. However clean the Clan of the Cave Bear appeared, I really didn't want to find out about their sanitary arrangements.

As this cup began its rounds, the silence began to give way to something else. At first it was a rhythmic hum that flirted with the edge of perception. But it got gradually louder, gaining in intensity until it filled the big room, empty of all but the parishioners, without once rising in volume much above a murmur.

It wasn't the rosary. Or the drone of Tibetan monks. Or the call to prayer from a minaret, or a Gregorian chant. It was all of those things. The hair stirred at the back of my neck as I realized that I was seeing something that was already old when we were chipping our first spearheads. Something from which all of our music, and maybe all of our religion, had been imperfectly derived.

We were down to the last cup. Oldest Grandmother turned to face the circle and raised a hand. The chanting stopped as suddenly as if it had never been. She spoke in her hoarse whisper. The Neanderthals looked at one another with surprise. Or at least that's what it looked like to me, and Bling's body language had always been a lot easier to understand than his speech. After their initial reaction, the tribe appeared to endorse whatever it was the Oldest Grandmother had said. Nodding they rose to their feet and shambled to surround the matriarch and me.

I won't pretend that it didn't occur to me that I'd made damn sure that nobody knew where I was and that I was A, alone, and B, surrounded by not-exactly—humans—any one of whom, except Oldest Grandmother and maybe even her, could have taken me apart. God knew they were cute, in their lumpish way, but so's that irresistible pit bull puppy at the pound who's later responsible for your five year-old's eleven plastic surgeries.

As they gathered around I relaxed. Intellectually I knew that a genetic gulf separated me from these near-people so that I could never truly know them as my own. But had they been capable of any kind of organized mayhem they wouldn't be down to something smaller than an NFL franchise. And leaving reason altogether aside, on some other level—maybe a racial memory bubbling up to the surface—I was sufficiently assured of their harmlessness that I was able to tell that big knot on the top of my spinal column to shut up.

Oldest Grandmother took me by the hand. Hers was as leathery as Bling's mitt but somehow delicate. As she led me forward her younger relatives murmured and bowed and got out of our way. Accompanied only by her aged assistant—who I guess was called Pretty Old Grandmother—we shuffled to a big doorway in the far wall.

So far I'd only been in the one large room at the head of the stairs. Judging from the building's dimensions there had to be more space, but for all I knew it was padlocked or boarded up.

But apparently not. There was still a little light behind us available from the streetlights shining into the main room. Ahead was a long hallway that appeared to end in another door, with a few doorways on either side. All closed. I tapped Oldest Grandmother on the shoulder and held up my light. I had learned at my first visit that lights were prohibited inside. The reason was not far to seek, as we lawyers say; should an agent of the bankruptcy trustee, or the responsible realtor, or just some random buttinski be wandering around on the street one night, a light in the piazza would inevitably lead to unwelcome inquiry and abrupt relocation.

Oldest Grandmother nodded; apparently she thought we were in the clear. I turned the light onto a low wide beam and pointed it towards the floor just to be safe. The decorations I'd seen in the stairwell and outer room hadn't prepared me for what the tribe had done in the hall.

At first I thought they'd somehow gotten hold of a half-truckload of the glass tile you see in high-end designer bathrooms, one inch squares of intense color or shimmery opalescence. But when I cautiously tilted the flash upwards for a closer look I saw that it wasn't tile at all. No, this was all natural. Walls, ceiling, and floor were entirely covered with tens of thousands of tiny bits of oyster and mussel shell, little geometrically perfect pieces of smooth white and mother of pearl. They had somehow been cleaned and trimmed and fit together with fragments of polished colored stone to form loose spirals that looped across walls and floor and ceiling, swirling towards the open door at the end of the hall. The shells must have been filched from the Fulton Street Market before it moved to the Bronx decades ago, or maybe the dumpsters of downtown seafood houses. I wondered whether it had taken longer to gather the materials or assemble the work. I also wondered how a project of such sophisticated design and precise execution could have been carried out by missing links

98

wearing burlap bags.

As we shuffled along, the spiraling walls made me feel as though I was spinning down a rabbit hole. "Wow," I said. Oldest Grandmother smiled and nodded modestly.

The doorway at the end of the hall opened into a room much smaller than the main area, no more than twenty by twenty. Its single window seemed to face an airshaft so there was no light from the street. With my light still dimmed and pointed at the floor I could make out three shapes, two of them much smaller than any Neanderthal I'd seen before. The musky smell of the tribe was stronger here, more concentrated, but also somehow sweeter. The anxious chittering that usually greeted the arrival of Raleigh, ubermensch, was not only surprisingly loud for so few, but high-pitched as well. Oldest Grandmother clicked and popped, and it stopped.

Or most of it. In place of multiple voices there was now just one. Subdued but still there, a resentful whine that somehow sounded hungry. Oldest Grandmother tapped me on the arm and pointed first at the Tek-Lite and then upwards. Proving our species' intellectual superiority I wondered for a minute whether she wanted me to throw the flashlight at the ceiling. A quick reassessment divined her hidden meaning and I pointed the light up and broadened and brightened the beam, creating a nice indirect lighting effect.

The largest of the three shapes turned out to be a young Neanderthal woman. Despite what I assumed to have been reassurances from Oldest Grandmother, she hovered anxiously over the other, smaller, shapes I had seen. The larger was about the size of a bulky ten-year-old boy, but judging from the breastbuds poking the front of her Knicks t-shirt, she was plainly an adolescent girl of the tribe. She met my eyes once and quickly looked away, smiling shyly. Or at least that's what I thought. Raleigh, ever the charmer.

The smaller I was pretty sure was male. He was about three feet tall and somewhere around eighty pounds, thick-set and already sprouting his people's coarse pelt, premature muscle straining the Scooby Doo pajamas someone had found for him. As I met his curious gaze I was struck by his resemblance to Bling, and then struck harder by the possibility that I was looking at my client's son. And whatever else, quite possibly the last of his kind, final iteration of an intelligent species that had somehow dodged extinction for half a million years.

Oldest Grandmother laid a hand on my arm. She extended the still-warm Starbucks first towards me, then to each of the children. After each of the kids she held the cup to her own lips in a sipping gesture.

Okay, I'm going on record with this: I can be slower than an elderly cavewoman. It took me a minute to figure out where she was going. Finally I pointed at myself, then at the cup, then at the kids. She smiled and nodded.

Taking the cup from her I walked to the corner where the kids huddled around what I guess I'd have to call their nanny. The girl showed a little less self-restraint than the adults in the big room; she barely waited for the cup to be offered before she belted back three loud swallows. But she returned it more readily than any human child, without being prompted, and giggled and dropped her eyes when I made an exaggerated show of wiping my lips on my sleeve.

The boy was more decorous. When I passed him the cup he politely offered it to me. When I smiled and shook my head, he took his own noisy gulps and passed it back to his sister. It was gone in three circuits. If I remembered the drill correctly from my boyhood at St. Mary's Nativity, Oldest Grandmother was in charge of draining the last sacred drops and wiping the chalice clean.

But I guess I was pressing the analogy a little harder than circumstances would bear. I'd forgotten that what I'd brought was not only a sacrament but a tasty snack as well. The boy handed the cup back to me without ceremony. As I was about to turn away he threw his arms around my waist and pressed his head against my belly. Just for an instant.

Comfortably into my second half-century I had just been hugged by a happy child for the first time. But not by a child of my own species.

I was on the cab ride leg of my zigzag home. BamBam's sudden gratitude had affected me more than I would have expected. I'd managed to lead my life without any significant emotional entanglements that didn't involve an exchange of bodily fluids, and those, however frequent, weren't exactly grist for the troubadours. I'd been separate from the beginning; a smart bookish kid in a blue-collar family from East Buttfuck doesn't really find a lot of connection with the future heavy equipment operators at school, and the folks at home don't have any idea of what to make of him. And it wasn't much different at Yale. Though money alone didn't get you in, it didn't keep you out, either, as demonstrated by the percentage of my classmates who came back from Christmas break with Caribbean tans or ski slope windburns. I, on the other hand, was usually still trying to get the last of the grime off my hands from a two-week gig on the line at Perma-Kote Plastics, where I also worked summers instead of going to Europe. So while I wasn't the only working class kid from the sticks by a long shot, the princes and princesses reminded me daily that there was a big world that I wasn't part of.

The funny thing is that the smaller world I'd been so eager to escape kept me from ever becoming fully a part of the larger. At every rich kid's party there was a portion of me that felt sweaty and small. Which, sadly, I was. The sense of fraudulence followed me through law school and out into practice; who was I to be wearing a suit for anything but a wedding or a funeral, and where the hell did this briefcase come from?

Together with the fraud came betrayal. Inflicted, not received. I had, after all, turned my back on my family by escaping. Once, when I'd been in practice just a year or two, I was walking down Seventh Avenue near the basketball cages on Fourth Street. An older guy, sixtyish, in work clothes, stopped me for directions. I gave them and he walked off. I stood there a moment. He was my father's age and he'd called me sir. If my father saw me, a thirty-something snark in a Barney's suit and Bumble and Bumble haircut, and if we were strangers, he'd call me sir as well. I was now part of the world that told his part of the world what to do.

I guess the sense of separateness determined my career choices as well. I could've made the break completely: a white-shoe corporate litigation practice, grinding ambulance chasers and their drug deformed baby clients down to gravel with week-long depositions and an endless stream of pleadings they lacked the resources to answer. Not unappealing—- the hours sucked, true, but owning a house in the Hamptons rather than fighting for a weekend summer share didn't seem so bad. But when it came down to it and I had to choose sides, I picked where I had come from rather than where I'd wanted to go. Counsel to the downtrodden. And now counsel to the ultimate outsiders. Outsiders with whom I was inexplicably forming a warm and cuddly bond. What was next— weekends volunteering at the pound?

The cab turned onto Charles just as I finished up this decade's ration of introspection. Not a moment too soon.

She was waiting for me when I got back.

"Hey," I said, "unexpected pleasure." And that it was. Over the past couple of weeks getting her home had usually involved a second bottle of Barolo. I was starting to wonder whether she'd finally got a good look at a calendar. Or the slackness that was starting to set in just above my beltline no matter how many crunches I did. Anyway, because I'm basically kind of stupid I assumed this was a surprise booty call and leaned forward to kiss her cheek, cagily intending all the while to miss just a little bit and brush her neck with my lips.

Somehow my wily scheme didn't work. She turned aside so slightly that the movement was almost imperceptible, but still enough to have the same effect as a face full of pepper spray. "Don't," she said. "Not now."

Something about her tone prevented me from babbling *Ohboyohboy, later then right?* I took a half step back. "What's the matter?"

"Why do you see me?"

"Uhh. . .why do you ask?"

"Isn't it difficult for you? Doesn't it make problems? Don't people talk?"

I didn't immediately see past my own obsessions. "Well, I guess women my age give me shit about it sometimes, and I get jealous when you talk to men closer to yours, but--"

"That's not what I meant. Because I'm an Iranian. Because I'm the enemy."

Hmm. Maybe if I responded just right she'd be so overpowered by my sensitivity and warmth that we'd spend the balance of the night coupling like monkeys. Not that it had ever worked that way before, but what the hell, if you don't play you can't win.

"It can't be easy," I said. "But you're not the enemy. You're an American. And this is New York."

"You're right," she said. "About something, anyway. It isn't easy. But even if I'm a citizen I still have to register every year as Of Hostile Background. And my parents and brothers still have to wear ankle bracelets. And even if this is New York, today on the subway someone called me a towel-head."

For an instant I thought to hold her. But this was about Persian pride, not girlish hurt. She was seething at having been mistaken for an Arab. "See?" I said. "What'd I tell you about going north of Fourteenth Street?"

She jumped as if I'd slapped her. For a second I thought she was going to slap me. But then the smile began and even though she was fighting hard the laughter finally won.

I let it go for a minute. Then I stepped forward and without pretending to aim for the cheek started to work my way down her neck. Her hands went from my back to cradle my head as I nuzzled the hollow of her throat above her sweater's v-neck. There was nothing on underneath; as my hands traced her firm flanks my thumbs found stiffening nipples. I slipped my hands beneath the cashmere and pulled it off over her head. Our tongues met for an instant, but she pressed my head down onto a breast. I suckled like a starving infant as she unzipped me and wrapped her fingers around my erection, which was throbbing as though it had its own heart that beat only for her. She dropped to her knees and took me into her mouth, her eyes holding mine. Just before the inevitable became the imminent I raised her to her feet and pushed her towards the couch. Jeans that had seemed sprayed on came off surprisingly easily. Kneeling, I returned the favor until she pulled me up and into her.

Afterwards the only thing that kept me from falling asleep was the weird angle of my head wedged into the couch's leather armrest. "That's why," I said.

Stretched out full length on her back, nothing had kept her from slumberland. "Oh...ah, what?"

"You asked me a question. Why I see you. That. That's why."

It took her a little while to understand. "Oh. Is that all?"

"Isn't that enough?"

"Would that be enough for you?"

"Oh, hell yes. Ask any man whether he'd be okay with a woman saying You're a nice guy and everything but the only reason I'm with you is that you're a great fuck. Of course he would. In fact he wouldn't be able to imagine anything better. But it's probably never happened. Well, maybe it has. I mean, Boston won the Series, right? In our lifetime. And it was the very same night Kerry lost the election. And it was during a full eclipse of the moon. Let the scoffers say there's nothing beyond the grave." I was getting thirsty. I'd dripped a lot of electrolytes into that couch. "Want a beer?"

She had propped herself up on an elbow. I'd rearranged my own posture in order to avoid a ruptured cervical disc. As a result of our reconfiguration, her left nipple—which depending on circumstances resembled a small Oreo

103

or a large Hershey's kiss, but in any event something really tasty—was positioned about an inch from my mouth and her hair was spilling over my face. Creating a tent effect so that when our eyes met there was nothing else I could see. "Is that really all?" Her lips barely moved, an inch from mine.

"No. It's not."

"I didn't think so." The tip of her nose grazed my eyebrow; her lips brushed the corner of my eye.

"But it would be enough." I ran my tongue across her lower lip and took it gently between my teeth. I freed it to allow her tongue to find my ear.

"But it isn't all," she breathed.

My hand slipped down her spine and her back obediently arched. Lifting her breast to exactly where it should have been. I filled my mouth with chocolate.

Undisclosed location, two years later

Captain Graner gave me a candy bar today.

In my months—or is it years now?—at this place, our afternoon interrogation sessions have followed an almost Darwinian devolution. At least, I think they were afternoon sessions. Now I wonder. Perhaps the narrow window I passed as the Hometroopers in their black helmets and body armor frog-marched me down the corridor was no window at all. Perhaps it only seemed to be a window. Perhaps it was a screen. What a remarkable coincidence that it was the last thing I was allowed to see before my eye sockets were filled with putty and my face covered with a mask that allowed me to breathe just enough to hover at the edge of lucidity, which also happened to be the edge of suffocation panic.

Yes, now I see it. My keepers intended to persuade me that I was being interrogated but once a day, after I had slept and eaten and passed the results in the unending fluorescence of my cell. When, perhaps, I was being questioned five times a day or once a week, and that brief glimpse of tropical afternoon was intended to gull me into a false sense of regularity and order. That I had, in fact, slept eight hours rather than two. That I had eaten recently enough to sustain reason. That I could therefore trust my own judgment.

The early days--if that is what they were—of your interrogation were the most highly evolved. Neither the black uniforms who took me from my cell, nor whoever whispered questions through cigarette smoke wherever I was taken, indulged in the slightest hint of physical coercion. For that they had Graner. And even he was kept within close constraints. Then, occasionally, a belt thwacked against the back of a chair to make me jump and whimper, or a boot kicked my ankle to make me stumble and cry.

After the first few dozen sessions—what I then thought of as the first month—my captors decided to introduce clever psychological stressors to induce my cooperation. In this they were doubly misled: First, I had told them everything I knew or could ever imagine knowing within the first forty-eight hours of my captivity; and second, the inner recesses of my mind were apparently beyond the imagination of the Homeland Police.

It seems that because I had been apprehended in the company of African American musicians I was a hip-hop caveman—notwithstanding the fact that even during my brief turn on local television was my ethnicity the subject of speculation. I can only imagine that somewhere in the windowless fastnesses of Homeland Security there was a protocol for the interrogation of a rapper gone bad. Based, apparently, on a decades-old racial profile that, if articulated on a morning AM show, even today, would have led to an abrupt cancellation.

Thus, one day I awakened to the scent of a bucket of KFC wafting through the air conditioning. That afternoon one of the hometroopers lit a Newport. At any moment, I was sure, one of my civilian interrogators would emerge in Timberlands and a Phat Pharm hoodie. As I was dragged back from interrogation, I heard through an open door—the first time any door in that long hallway had been left ajar—TWDN's Pimp Kulcha Killa.

Ya we dum niggazz
Think we don know shit
But my whip got the spinnaz
An you gonna take the hit

Startled, I looked at my guards. For the first time in my captivity both were black. Until that moment I hadn't noticed the incongruity of being guarded almost exclusively by white men in a military drawn largely from your minority underclass. I imagine all your undisclosed locations are protected by white soldiers; the Homeland mandarins no doubt fear that soldiers of color will communicate telepathically with their prisoners, throw down their arms, and storm the fences with their dusky brethren.

Incredibly enough, my interrogators' strategy failed to compel the disclosure of things I did not know. Even after I awoke to find slipped under the cell door salacious prints from websites like Big Booty Hoes I somehow managed not to crack. I should tell you, incidentally, that the closest I've seen to an image arousing to men of my people is the Venus of Wittenburg, breasts and belly and thighs drooping earthwards in the proof of past fertility and promise of future generations. Your men, on the other hand, festoon every magazine with the images of what appear to be athletic boys with absurdly huge and impossibly firm mammaries. How often my cousins and I would chortle over discarded erotica I culled from your trash! To their disbelief I explained that not only did your men find these boy-women arousing, but that your women—and understand that I had pored over the plastic surgery ads in the back of the Voice and New York Magazine as carefully as any archeologist desperate to grasp the essence of Ur—willingly risked their lives to be sculpted into something that never existed in nature. I wonder, has it never occurred to any of you that breast implants are every bit as mad as foot binding? Or, for that matter, that stomach stapling is a surgical version of the Roman vomitorium? Both allowing the beneficiaries of Imperial abundance to avoid the consequences of their gluttony?

I will say, however, that the largest of the Big Booty Hoes weren't so bad.

Once again I digress. And improperly so. How can a monkey presume to understand, much less judge, Evolution's more favored children?

After the assault on my rapper psyche failed, attention was directed to my body. Nothing so direct as to produce the bubbling screams and choked sobbing appeals to Allah that punctuate my nights. Not for me the waterboardings and electrodes and blowtorches with which your freedom is protected in undisclosed locations. I can only presume that my keepers were directed to maintain me intact for eventual experimentation. So instead I was subjected to the subtler persuasions of searing heat and freezing cold—the latter of which, being suited by nature for the glacier rather than the veldt, I silently laughed at. When that failed I was confined in a box too short for me to stand and too narrow to sit, so that I was forced to squat with my back against the wall until my thighs quivered and I screamed and banged my head bloody and was dragged out with my limp legs scissoring wildly like a decapitated frog's. Other times masked men pummeled me with rubber sticks on pressure points that must have appeared on an acupuncturist's dummy, too lightly to raise a bruise but with a percussive precision that resulted in exquisite spasms of agony.

Having already told all I knew, I struggled to make things up. Desperate, I tied Astor Place Hair to a worldwide conspiracy of Mahdist barbers. For a time the beatings stopped. But then—I imagine after a raid had left a hundred chairs unattended—they renewed with doubled force, no doubt after Homeland's inquiries failed to produce a single Arabic-speaking Sicilian. I can only hope that Mario's time on the cross was briefer than mine.

Other frantically imagined leads proving equally false, I was turned over to Captain Graner. I am certain that my captors intended in doing so that my torment grow more intense and imaginative. In this they were not disappointed; in the years since his release, Graner had a working knowledge of anatomic tolerances and surgical technique worthy of a third-year resident. Many were the afternoons we spent with my eyelids retracted and my corneas menaced with the coal of his cigarette. First one, then the other, so close that the whole world was swallowed up in a glowing red ember like a dying sun, each time a little closer so that I whimpered and blubbered at the approach of blindness. Other days he snaked a hose into my intestines and filled me full of water until my belly bulged like a term pregnancy. He commanded me to stand at attention, naked, in front of a crowd of laughing soldiers until at last my sphincter gave up the unequal fight and I exploded, spraying the floor with reeking tan liquid. I doubled over with cramps and shame until Graner stepped forward and with a rifle butt knocked me backwards into a puddle of my own filth and held me down with a boot on my neck while my struggle to free myself drove dung into my hair and skin.

Other days still he simply beat me. But humiliation, particularly of a homoerotic nature, he appeared to find more effective. Or perhaps he simply enjoyed it more. Once I was led into an interrogation room in which Graner and his female assistant sat on one side of a long folding table. In front of them—facing me—was a spread of pornography. Dozens of magazines folded open to the most explicit labial displays and viscous splatterings. Because the photographs were without power to distract me, I couldn't help but notice that the pages were stained and waterlogged, as though the magazines had been harvested from my guards' latrine floors.

The room was small and four Marlboros had preceded the one Graner was smoking in the tin ashtray at his elbow. My sinuses had swollen shut before the guards closed the door behind me.

Graner stared at me for quite a while after the latch clicked. At least I think he did; he was wearing mirror aviator sunglasses that covered a quarter of his face. "Like any of this, monkey?" he said, pushing Juggs forward with a riding crop he had no doubt ordered on eBay.

I shook my head and looked anywhere but at him or the fleshbags on the page below.

"Huh," he said. "Reason I ask is we pretty much keep our eyes on you twenty-four-seven. Cameras all over the place. And you pretty much been a good little boy scout all these months. Hands on top the blankets all the time, know what I mean? Right, you shake your head, but you know what I mean. You're a healthy guy, God knows what species but a healthy guy, still young as near as we can figure. Thought to myself, hell, this boy must be just about ready to bust, give him a little help here. So I ask, you like any of this, monkey boy?"

My eyes were fixed on my feet. Thus I saw the tip of the riding crop slip between my legs. Disbelieving, I did not react until Graner lifted my genitals appraisingly.

He laughed as I yelped and jumped backwards. "Sure don't seem like you like it," he said. "Maybe you need it in three dee." He nodded towards his assistant. "Help him out, honey."

The assistant could not have been twenty, a girl of mixed ethnicity, café au lait skin dusted with cinnamon freckles under mirror shades the mirror image of Graner's, her face set in a caricature of military stoicism. She wore a camouflage t-shirt. Suddenly I became uncomfortably aware that she didn't appear to be wearing anything beneath it.

Graner tapped her belly with his riding crop. "Come on, honey, give the caveman a thrill."

Without changing her soldierly expression, the assistant grabbed the bottom of her t-shirt and pulled it up to expose her surprisingly pendulous breasts. "Wow," said Graner, "get a load of those. Hey, monkey, either it's cold in here or she really likes you. You like her?" Again he prodded my crotch with his crop. "Jeez, I guess not. You queer or something? What do I have to do, show you pictures of Fred Flintstone blowing Barney Rubble? Okay, honey. Cover 'em up. You're Ranger all the way."

Her features still stony, she restored her modesty. "Get the next thing set up, okay?" She nodded and left the room.

As I stood wondering what the next thing might be, Graner rocked his chair back on two legs and folded his hands behind his head. "I don't know about you, monkey. Hard case. In a manner of speaking." He inclined his head in the general direction of my crotch. "Hope the young lady wasn't offended. You know how sensitive they can be. Or maybe you don't. See, when I was over in Iraq, we showed a guy a rack like that it made him crazy. See they wanted to grab 'em, being red-blooded men before they got to be crazy motherfuckers, but then they got their heads full of this terrorist paradise shit and it was oh no no titty for me. Not unless I'm married to it and it stays at home covered up under a pup tent. So like I said we showed 'em a good pair of honkers and it was like watching a starved dog on a chain trying to get to get to a big bowl of Alpo just a little too far away. Except there wasn't no chain. Just the bin Ladin shit. All that was holding them back. Good as any chain, though. Eyes bugging out, panting, spit flying everywhere. God, there ain't nothing uglier than a horny Arab." The phone at his belt bleeped and he spoke to his earpiece. "Yeah? Good. Well, monkey, speaking of horny Arabs, time for you to strip down."

I froze. But just for a moment. Rape is infinitely preferable to death, if only because the latter is permanent. As I unzipped my orange jumpsuit the stone-faced assistant re-entered, carrying a coil of studded leather. Involuntarily I whimpered and flinched at the imagined first blow of the beating to come.

Graner snickered. "Hey, nothing to be scared of, monkey man." The leather was coiled around his right hand. With the left he spun me around and pushed me forward and down. "Hands and knees, retard. I know what you're thinking," he said as I did as commanded. "Don't get your hopes up. This soldier don't swing that way."

What I'd thought a whip was a leash tightening around my throat. Graner gave it a jerk. "Come on, Bonzo," he said. "We're going for a walk."

Motion to dismiss. Manhattan, early November.

I was surprised when she asked to go to a bumfight. But maybe I shouldn't have been. What else is Iranian politics, anyway?

It didn't take long to find out when the next bout was scheduled. Bumfighting is illegal, but illegal the way whiskey was in 1924. And I make my living off the kind of people who in the Coolidge administration would have been meeting trawlers full of booze at midnight on the North Fork. Well, kind of like them. Just worse. In any event, one phone call got me a text back with the equivalent of "Joe sent me" and we were off to the races. As it were.

We got there late, which was fortunate. Otherwise we would have had to hang around and chitchat with our fellow degenerates as we waited for the doors to open. Tonight's venue, I was surprised and saddened to learn, was a Garment District basement that in happier days, when the Twin Towers were still the North Star for drunks trying to get their bearings, had been one of the many homes of the Pleasure Barge. The Barge was a floating music party that charged ten bucks at the door and gave space to young musicians who would have been performing in garages in any city where real estate was cheaper. No longer, apparently.

On the cab ride over she'd been more excited than I'd seen her in months. As we waited on the sidewalk in the kind of drizzle that's just a little heavier than a fog she actually took my arm. We stood a little apart from the crowd, the only people on the streets at this hour. Everyplace else was a shuttered sari shop or Korean tailor. "These people seem nice, don't they?"

I smiled. "Nice enough, I guess." Around us were thirty or forty people, Jersey orthodontists and their botoxed wives and a smattering of slumming hipsters. "Wait till we get inside."

At that moment the doors clanked and opened. Out stepped two very large African Americans in hoodies that somehow didn't manage to conceal gold chains just a little smaller than the Lord Mayor of London's. One stepped out to the curb and into the street to scan for po-po's. The other stood in the entrance with his arms folded across his chest and regarded us with Olympian contempt.

"A'ight," said the bouncer, in a voice that would have set off the alarms in every car on the street, if there were any. "You know how we do. Show me the phone and the money." One by one the evening's culture vultures presented their cells and a wad of cash, the former to display the appropriate text, the latter to be jammed into the doorman's hoodie pocket.

We were last in line. As I got closer the bouncer looked at me curiously. Why I couldn't imagine; it's not like I was the only old white guy with a young woman on his arm out for an evening's sport. As I held up the phone and four fifties he suddenly grinned, displaying a grille composed of alternating silver and gold caps. "No man," he said, "money no good. You took care of my brother Dookie. Back in the day."

"Dookie?" I said. "Dookie—wait, not Duqwan Little?"

The bouncer was laughing. "True—but you the only one who ever called him Duqwan. And he appreciated that."

I burst out laughing as well. Duqwan was a relic of my earlier days, back when I'd left the DA's office and was starting to build a practice around hopeless chooches at the fringes of the drug trade. Even though his defense was the usual "some nigger I don't know said hold this for me for a minute and he run down the alley," I had managed to convince a former colleague that his large, loving, and supportive family justified probation.

"No shit," I said. "So wait—your older brother, right?"

He nodded. "I remember sitting in that courtroom waiting and waiting and waiting and how nice you was to our momma. I remember when you went out and got her a bottle of water."

At last, a good deed unpunished. "How is she?"

"She great. She a great grandma now."

"And Duqwan?"

He dropped his head. "Caught a stray. A stray, you believe it?" He looked up and shrugged. "The game, you know?" He clapped me on the shoulder, which somehow stayed in its socket. "Hey peace, man. I gotta close up. Enjoy the show."

The Iranian and I headed in. Her eyes glowed when they met mine. My hero.

On the cab ride I'd tried to explain some of the history of our latest spectator sport. Her interest had been piqued by a couple of grad school pals who said they had friends who'd seen bumfights. And she was, after all, planning to make documentaries when she grew up. So apparently, she thought, why go out with an old guy with ties to a dirty world if it didn't get her access to this slice-o-life?

What I didn't tell her was that bumfights were the product of our society's most recent couple of spirals down history's drain since purely hypothetical terror had prompted us to amend our rights out of existence and recoil from the rest of the world. That it had started with the dogfights to the death on which ghetto drug barons used to stake a hundred large, which had then turned into gangsta wannabees throwing pit bulls into empty South Bronx dumpsters to the same end. Nor did I tell her about its evolution into casual pickups in which a dozen guys paid two winos twenty bucks and a couple of forty-watts to beat the shit out of each other under an overpass.

But I did tell her that once the idea had taken off, the ice lords and what was left of the mafia had combined to promote it as a cross between the bare-knuckle days of Olde New York boxing and Gladiator. All, of course, with the allure of illegality and shameful joy of another's humiliation. So that now while the combatants were no more homeless after than before the fights, they walked away with a couple of hundred for the night's battery. And the technique had developed, if that's the right world, from simple all-in pummeling to include non-lethal arms and crude padding.

Tonight's site was not the ideal venue for anything, much less a spectator sport. Because it was a fairly cramped low-ceilinged basement there was no room for a ring, and of the seats—maybe fifty metal folding chairs—were arranged in a couple of concentric circles around the fighting floor, itself a circle no more than fifteen feet across. Propped in a corner was a whiteboard on an easel announcing that night's card. Three fights: Jihad Joe from Baltimo vs. Aryan Menace; the Black Scorpion vs. the extremely imaginative Terminator; and Kabul Killah vs. Semper Fi.

The seats were already pretty full, but Dukie's brother intervened to get us two in the first circle through the simple expedient of telling their occupants to sit someplace else. This provoked a heady blend of admiration and resentment from our fellow patrons of the sweet science. And of course the Iranian was almost dripping as we took our places amid the who's-that-guy buzz.

She took my hand between the seats of our high school cafeteria chairs. This was an exceptionally emotional display. I got all fuzzy. With the hand not occupied I pointed to the whiteboard. "You can tell from the stage names that most of these guys are vets," I said. "Though why they have stage names I don't know. It's not like bumfight results get printed in the *Post*. Give it time, though. Anyway they're homeless, so it's not like their reputations would be ruined or something. They all have PTSD or something worse, and they're all self medicating with whatever they can get."

The VIP glow dimmed momentarily. "That's terrible," she said.

"Guess so. But some of them like it. Or so I'm told."

"So what are the rules?"

I was a little startled. I'd assumed her friends would have told her. And of course there's this internet thing the kids seem to like. "There aren't any," I said. "The organizers try to match guys up more or less evenly. They don't want it over too fast. They come out and fight until one of them goes down. When he can't get up it's over."

The glow faded a little more. "So that's when the referee ends it?"

I snorted. "No referee, darling. No count. By and large these guys stop before they kill each other. And if it looks as though someone's getting killed, one of the bouncers pulls off the killer."

There were fine beads of sweat on her upper lip. It was warm in a basement room packed with bloodthirsty hipsters but not that warm. "Do they get killed?"

"Not often," I said. "Causes problems. But when it does, well, that's why these things are always close to the river."

Her hand slipped out of mine at the pretense of smoothing her hair. I'd had high hopes that the ease with which I'd got her entrée into the underworld and a display of blood and testosterone would have her horny as a bonobo. But suddenly we were no longer Nick and Nora Charles at an art deco prizefight, and I don't think she liked it.

It wasn't a prizefight. It started when one of the bouncers yelled, "Hey yo, here we go!" There was no bell. There was no ceremony of leaping through the ropes, holding up the gloves while the crowd roared, slipping off the robe.

Instead two guys squeezed between chairs and into the space at their center amid cheers and fist-pumps from the audience—who, while I'm not squeamish, I was starting to hate. Nothing uglier than a slumming suburbanite unless it's a recent MFA with an ironic mustache. All there to celebrate their superior fortune. I squared my own conscience with the fact that I was there just to keep getting laid, and maybe to get laid more often, by a woman half my age. Which excuses pretty much everything.

One of the combatants, whom I took to be Jihad Joe because I didn't think a black guy would call himself the Aryan Menace, looked to be in his early thirties. He'd obviously seen a lot of hard road but his face was still largely unlined. He was wearing old gray sweatpants, army surplus rough-out boots, and what looked to be about four sweatshirts, one over the other, with the top layer sleeveless. He'd wrapped his neck and forehead in Ace bandages and had on a pair of plastic swimming goggles. He carried a bicycle chain with a heavy lock at its end.

Initially I thought he was overmatched by his opponent, who was an inch taller and probably thirty pounds heavier. But then I thought maybe not. The Aryan Menace should have called himself the Celtic Self-Inflicted Wound. That extra thirty pounds was in a big cirrhotic belly. His head was the size of a car battery. Under stringy thinning hair his face was mean and bloated. He'd opted against padding and instead wore too tight jeans, sneaks, and a sleeveless t-shirt. On his right shoulder I could see a Screaming Eagle tattoo with a Ranger patch inked above it. Well, when you cut the capital gains and estate taxes to zero something's got to give. Starting with the VA.

Aryan Menace carried a two-foot length of half-inch pipe with a coupling at its end. Something like a mace. I looked at Jihad Joe's lock and chain and recognized a morningstar. Everything old is new again, I guess.

As I said, there's no bell. Jihad Joe was first in the ring. He got as far back from the entrance as he could and started circling, holding the end of the chain in his right hand and stretching it across his abdomen, swinging the lock with his left in a tight fast circle. The moment Menace entered the circle, Jihad stopped and dropped into a combat crouch, almost like a linebacker, lock still spinning.

Menace didn't waste time. He probably figured that as soon as he got inside the radius of the chain it was useless as a weapon. So he just launched himself straight at Jihad with his pipe raised and other forearm out to protect his head from a swing.

He almost made it. Jihad was a little slow letting go of the chain with his left and deploying it at full length but he was able to catch Aryan across the cheek with the lock. But because he hadn't had time to wind up there was no momentum behind it; the lock hurt and that was about it.

The blow had swung Aryan around. The crowd—which apparently still thought it was at a WWF event—roared and laughed. Including the Iranian. But his new position was not so good for Jihad, because it meant that Aryan was behind him, and he couldn't turn to face him before the pipe came down, missing his head but bouncing pretty hard off his left collarbone. Because the chain was in his right, he didn't drop it, but you could hear the gasped fuck and he staggered. I wondered how long this bout would last.

I never found out. I glanced over at the Iranian. She no longer appeared to be having a good time. In fact her olive complexion had become—literally—green.

Aryan had backed up a little and was about to take another bang at Jihad. But Jihad had recovered a little faster than his opponent had expected and got off a hammer thrower's shot to Aryan's forehead. Aryan turned a millisecond before impact or he'd've been dropped in the Hudson later that night. But because he turned, he just caught the flying sharp edge of the lock across his forehead. And the combatants were just a few feet from us in our prized front row seats.

Scalp wounds are bloody. Really bloody. Aryan staggered, trying to hold the edges together with his hand, blood leaking from between his fingers. He stumbled forward. Straight towards us. He was a foot away when he dropped his hand and spun to face his opponent with the pipe held high. As he turned, the blood flew in an arc like a spiral arm of the Milky Way, spattering the Iranian with dozens of crimson dots. Mostly on her face. Some on her lips.

She was on her feet in an instant, stumbling for the narrow aisle that the fighters had walked down, palm pressed against her mouth. Naturally I was right behind her. Dukie's brother saw us coming and managed to get the padlock the fire marshal really didn't need to know about off the door just in time.

She had her left arm wrapped around a parking meter as she puked into the gutter. Instinctively I reached forward to hold her hair. With her free hand she batted me away. After she finished her current retch she said, "Don't touch me."

Oh boy. Mission accomplished.

Apparently the Iranian's voicemail wasn't working.

I hadn't heard from her for a week. Substantially longer than the usual rage. Maybe this one was going to stick. I was starting to worry I'd lost some dignity for nothing. Though I hadn't exactly carpet-bombed her with voicemails, I'd left more than one, or actually more than three, and my tone in the last one had a little bit of a whiney edge that made me sound like a sixteen year-old begging for a pity handjob. So I'd stopped calling and spent the balance of the week checking out women my own age and trying to reconcile myself to a life of internet porn.

The Persian being out of the picture for the moment, I was free to focus on a problem much bigger than my aging dingus, namely, the fate of my client and the rest of the Flintstones. Torrington had finally got off the pot and charged Bling with murder two and Galileo with conspiracy. This seemed like something of a stretch; how he was going to prove a common criminal purpose was beyond me. I guess he figured it would be a shame to waste so many ugly potential defendants.

Leaving aside a motion to dismiss predicated on non-humanity, I'd toyed briefly with the idea of simply ignoring the impossible truth, keeping Bling off the stand, and making Torrington try what was basically a bad case. His forensics sucked, the co-defendant hated the victim, and the witnesses were all convicted tattooed felons with funny names and gold teeth who happened to be on the payroll of Big Pimp Bonah Records. Under ordinary circumstances I would gladly have taken my chances with the jury with no testimony from the defendant. These were not, however, ordinary circumstances.

The Men in Black's interest was something I was going to have to deal with one way or the other, and even if they waited until the trial got started to drop the other jackboot, they weren't going to like the acquittal of a non-testifying, undocumented funny-looking killer retard—whose DNA didn't seem exactly, well, *human*. And of course there was a reason for that. Which it was my job to make sure they never discovered. Even though they'd already made it pretty clear they weren't going to just forget. And now, of course, I had to worry about Fred, Wilma, Pebbles, and BamBam back on the Bowery as well.

Unencumbered by erotic pleasure I was spending Friday night at the office trying to figure out how to deal with Blingbling's unique ancestry. With trial out of the question and our homegrown Gestapo already sniffing around the truth, I figured that the best approach was a direct frontal assault. Sliding around in the blood and the mud, uphill, while the bullets whipped past my ears. Hell, worked at the Second Somme, right? So I thought that I'd brazenly submit Weiss's affidavit that Bling's DNA was identical to that of a pre-human, add some remarks to the effect that this was certainly odd, and move to dismiss on the ground that someone who should be a fossil could not be expected to follow the law.

What I was trying to do, sitting at my open window over the drunken stockbrokerly merriment on the street below, was find case law supporting the latter proposition. I'd been hunched over the laptop for a couple of hours trying to ignore the street sounds, which somehow suggested my apparently former girlfriend banging men her own age, and a smoldering cigar stub had rolled onto the 1950's Perry Mason desk I'd just had refinished.

Laymen are often surprised by what the law does *not* say. For example, try as you might, no matter how obvious the principle seems, you will not find a case that says a dog cannot sign a lease. Or at least a *valid* lease. This is because nobody has ever stood up on his hind legs, so to speak, and argued to the contrary.

I'd tried two different searches. The first: the present law on the mitigation of liability by diminished mental capacity. Somewhat hopeless in view of the current Court's teaching that anyone with a pulse has a right, if not a duty, to be executed. The second, and potentially more fruitful: whether an animal under any circumstances could be held answerable to the criminal law.

I retrieved the smoldering stub and fired it up again. As I'd anticipated there were a lot of cases from the fourteenth century in which pigs had been burned at the stake for rolling over and smothering their sucklings. Well, what do you expect; before Netflix people had to make their own entertainment. Granted there were a few cases from trial courts in nineteenth-century Indiana patiently explaining why you couldn't marry your horse, but otherwise the bench was silent.

The cigar's coal was getting dangerously close to my fingers. I was thinking about the probate cases prohibiting bequests to animals. I was thinking about pre-civil war criminal codes distinguishing the culpability of blacks from whites and wondering whether I had the balls to even mention them. I was also wondering whether there were still a couple of beers in the office fridge and how many cigars I had left and how my life had worked out this way. My phone bleeped.

A name I was wondering whether I'd have to forget showed on the caller ID. Well, well, well.

The next morning the sticky note was on my laptop screen instead of the pillow. I saw it on the desk in the study as I stumbled towards the kitchen and coffee. Here we go again. I was sure I shouldn't read it before I'd had at least a pint of restorative. Her farewells tended to be particularly operatic after explosive nights, and I was just waking up after Hiroshima. Dawn had been forcing itself through the blinds as she leaned with her forearms on the dresser while I took her from behind. My hands on her narrow hips as she rose on the balls of her feet and rolled her pelvis to meet and equal each of my thrusts. Our eyes met in the mirror. Her tongue traced lips puffy with lust. She slipped a hand between her legs and cupped my balls and slid forward and dipped into her own wetness. She rose slightly and reached behind with the same hand and slipped a finger into my mouth so that I could taste her. She withdrew it from my greedy suckling to slip it into her own. I came as she licked her fingers.

Ah, but that was then. I shuffled out of the kitchen and into the study. The sticky note was still there, backlighted by my shifting screensavers. This month it was renaissance paintings. Hey, I'm a cultured guy. As I reached to peel it off the scene changed to Piero della Francesca's Ideal City, a quattrocento utopia too perfect for human tenantry, platonic birthday cakes surrounding a piazza empty of our fallible selves.

Oh, well. I took another swallow of Brazilian Espresso Blend and braced myself.

See you later.

What the fuck?

However perplexed I might have been by her sudden about face, Friday night left me able to concentrate Saturday and Sunday. So on Monday I filed my motion to dismiss. With supporting affidavit.

The first response was a text from Braunstein. *U fkng azol u cnt b seryus*. Something told me that I had just seen an example of his spelling without secretarial mediation.

I thought about it for a while and texted back. *It's called science. Dickwad*.

It was late in the afternoon. Though it was still just late October and greenhouse gas had melted the ice caps to the point where entire populations of polar bear and penguins were standing on each others' shoulders on a single ice floe, New York was surprisingly pleasant. At least from what I could see from my window. Young ladies from all walks of life were wearing only so much clothing as was strictly necessary but without looking wilted and damp and crabby, as they still had just a few weeks ago. Hmm. I'd worked all through the previous weekend and my assistant had somehow shouldered the cross of her lady problems to endure my employment until five. I could leave whoever called this late to her. I could take a stroll. I could hit the gym and have a nice dinner and get to sleep early for a change.

Or I could call the Iranian.

Braunstein's response, though first, was not alone. No, not at all. My cell rang at six thirty. It was Frobisher.

"Jesus fucking Christ," he said. "Where the fuck have you been?"

It wasn't an hour at which I'm at my best. "Umm. . .*out?*"

"'Um, out? Um, out'," he whined. "Forget your phone, asshole?"

"I had it turned off. And speaking of turned off, what the fuck are you doing calling me at dawn to call me an asshole? Fuck you."

"Yeah? Fuck me? Get your flabby ass downstairs or go online and read the *Post*. Or the News. Or the fucking *Times*. Then call me back and say 'fuck you.' Because you, my friend, are fucked." The line went dead.

Needless to say his tone had been rather strident. I lay there a minute wondering whether there was any point in trying to sleep another hour before facing what didn't sound like good news.

There wasn't. I got up and padded into the kitchen and turned on the coffee. Somehow I'd managed to set it up a couple of hours before when I'd dragged my middle-aged sex-battered frame back from the Iranian's apartment. Addiction. What can I say. Of course I hadn't set the timer to accommodate a crisis I hadn't known was approaching. So I sat and waited for the chirpy burble and stimulating aroma to cut through the fog so I could pour a cup. Clearly I'd need my strength.

I opened Refdesk and clicked on newspapers. First the *Post*.

Oh, Jesus.

HIP-HOP SLAY DEFENSE SHOCKER:
HE'S A CAVEMAN!

Under the screaming headline was a video clip from Bling's brief local access career. Got to hand it to him, he could dance. He was wearing a trucker hat sideways, a Lakers hoodie, and about as much assorted jewelry as Cleopatra. Beneath it were head shots of Braunstein, Torrington, and me.

Braunstein and Torrington were obviously a lot more media savvy than I. Braunstein looked like a coiffed bulldog; Torrington, a tough gang-busting Mick. Nice crisp shots. I, on the other hand, was represented by a blurry little image that it took me a second to recognize as having been lifted from my Homeland Passport. I looked as though I was straining at stool. And they spelled my name wrong.

I clicked over to page three. It got much worse.

SO THAT WHY HE DUM: TWDN SLAY SUSPECT A GENETIC THROWBACK, MOUTHPIECE SEZ

(Manhattan). In a brazen ploy that's shocked courthouse circles and the nation, former rap icon and current murder suspect Blingbling—real name still unknown—claims that charges should be thrown out—because he's a Neanderthal!!!

Loyal Posties will remember that earlier this year Blingbling was accused of killing hip-hopper Einstein Spinoza in the Bedford mansion of TWDN rapmeister Newton Galileo. The evidence—eyewitness statements and the smoking gun in Bling's hand—all pointed to the deformed entertainer.

But yesterday, Post sources reveal, Bling's attorney asked the court to toss the kill counts because the supposed shooter was a throwback to another age.

His attorney—who did not return calls to the cell number his assistant gave us--

Oh, God, Imelda, how many times have I told you. I shambled as fast as I could back to the bedroom and picked up the phone and hit the Recents. Yep. There they were. All at around the time the Iranian was nuzzling my scrotum.

--claims that Blingbling shouldn't step up and face the music because,

according to court papers the Post has obtained, "he suffers from a previously unknown hereditary disorder that renders him incapable of conforming his behavior to the law."

The Post sez:

Wha?

But listen to more from Mr. Raley:

"As shown in the attached affidavit"—from Yale prof Gil Weiss, who the Post learned has just flown the coop to cheese-eating surrender monkey American "ally" France on a "sabbatical" that was supposedly "long planned"— "the defendant is genetically identical to Homo Neanderthalis, a long-extinct cousin to the human race and an entirely separate species whose intellectual capacities have long been the subject of scholarly debate. The manner in which Neanderthal DNA appeared in a defendant before this Court will no doubt fuel scientific controversy long after these litigants and their counsel are dust. But there can be no doubt that this defendant, through some mystery another generation will resolve, was born without the capacity to live in the twenty-first century; rather, his gifts fit him to another world, long gone, of glacier and mastodon."

Well, the thing about litigants and their counsel being dust was pretty good. And so was the bit about another generation. But the other world long gone may have been a little bit over the top.

But wait. There was more.

Bling's shyster isn't alone in his science fiction defense. He has the support of formerly well-reputed Yale anthropologist Weiss. Who says Bling is identical to long-gone Neanderthals. (And let's not forget that evolution is just Charles Darwin's guess.)

Sounds good. Until you find out that Weiss was Raley's Yale roommate. Helloooo? Yale? Roommates?

Not that there'd be anything wrong with that.

I had forgotten my coffee. Probably because my heart was pounding fast enough without it. I took a couple of hot swallows—which the *Post* seemed to think I liked—and clicked over to the *Times*. Not quite so prominent. Page three of the metro section, above the fold.

IF NOT LAWYER'S FANTASY, RAP DEFENSE'S IMPLICATIONS BROAD

(Manhattan) Special to the Times.

Blingbling may be unique in American pop culture: He's had his fifteen minutes of fame—three times.

First, as the oddly misshapen court jester to rap royalty TWDN, Blingbling teetered on the edge of C-List celebrity when his patrons nudged him from hanger-on to performer, financing a local access show in which Bling not only danced in his uniquely energetic style but, unfortunately, interviewed fellow rappers too. Unfortunately because his speech was even less intelligible than his interviewees' street talk. The show was cancelled after its second airing.

Bling's next quarter hour in the bright lights was his arrest for the murder of Einstein Spinoza this spring. The evidence against him appeared damning—consistent eyewitness testimony and his fingerprints on the murder weapon, if only the barrel.

But it is his effort to extricate himself from legal jeopardy that may give Bling a permanent place in the collective memory.

Today, in essence, he pled not guilty on account of prehistory.

Gotta love the *Times*. Consistent. Two hundred well chosen words to get to the topic sentence.

In a motion to dismiss filed this morning, Bling argued that because his genetic makeup "for reasons perhaps never to be known," as his lawyer says, is identical to protohuman Neanderthals, long extinct, he cannot be held culpable under criminal laws enacted by modern humans for modern humans.

The motion raises three questions: anthropological, legal, and political.

Science far-fetched but not impossible

At first Bling's claim seems absurd. How can any twenty-first century defendant claim genetic identity to a species that died out twenty thousand years ago?

Yet internationally-renowned Yale anthropologist Gil J. Weiss provided an affidavit detailing his exhaustive review of Bling's DNA and concluded that "despite my initial disbelief—and indeed my continuing astonishment—I have no alternative but to tell this court that the defendant is for all intents and purposes a Neanderthal." He goes on to speculate—his word—that Bling might represent a mutation or fragments of Neanderthal DNA carried in his various ancestors—long thought impossible—that suddenly found expression in him.

NYU paleoanthropologist James Raymond told the Times that "Weiss's a great man and his science is good, but mutation is a trillion-to-one bet." He went on to say that assuming the accuracy of Weiss's findings—which he could not challenge—it was more likely that Bling is part of a tiny surviving community of Neanderthals, not so different from the so-called Hobbits of Flores Island in Mahdist-dominated Indonesia.

Legal questions thorny

Neither Manhattan Assistant District Attorney Jack Torrington nor officials with the Justice or Homeland Security Departments would respond to the Times inquiries concerning the legal basis for these surprising claims. Former Harvard Law School professor and pre-Patriot Amendment Constitutional law expert Lawrence Clan, reached in his self-imposed exile in London, had more to say. "Well, first of all, I think this exposes the absurdity of questioning science in our fundamental law, to the benefit of religion"--

My God. That was ballsy. The *Times* would be moving the presses offshore soon. If they were smart.

--"but turning to this case, I wonder whether any court in the present system can fairly hear a claim predicated on the scientific validity of evolution, given the so-called Fair to Faith clauses in the Amended First Amendment."

You and me both, Larry.

Political repercussions just beginning

Though appointed officials maintained their silence, the elected have not been so reticent. Connecticut's former junior Senator--

Oh, God, I thought, here we go. I scrolled down a few lines.

--"Forgive me the immodesty of quoting myself, but when I stood in the well of the Senate urging the passage of the Fair to Faith clauses I said, We have to look at the intent of our Founders. And what did they have in front of them? The Origin of Species? No. That wouldn't be written for a hundred years. But what they did have was the Bible. The Old Testament—what my people, who are American people, despite the fact that we are few and what many would call foreign, because in our suffering we have passed through many lands, call the Talmud—and the Book of Genesis told the Founders, and us, how we all came to be. So because our Constitution was written long before what I'm sure were well-meaning scholars came to ask questions about our Creator we have to look at what our Founders thought. And all the Founders had to work with was Genesis. And what was good enough for them is good enough for me."

Reaction has not been so restrained in the so-called Red States. Rev. Jimmy James Prettyman, Pastor of the Full Gospel Tree of Life Cathedral of Hope in Null, Texas—an air-conditioned edifice that seats as many as the Yale Bowl and in far greater comfort, whose parking lots would cover all of Manhattan south of Grand—had some harsh things to say. "I'm not surprised that a couple of East Coast Ivy League fairies double teamed, if you get me, to bail out this murdering street trash so-called musician with a bunch of God-slandering nonsense." Prettyman's opinion carries even greater weight than his enormous congregation would suggest; he enjoys a relationship with the President so close that he's sometimes called "the Pope of the Potomac." Sources close to the Texas White House hinted that the President had briefly considered posting a comment on the case on his personal website, www.christiscoming.com, but ultimately rejected the notion as unseemly.

No matter how questionable the science or outlandish the claims, it is clear that Blingbling's defense has reignited the national controversy over evolution that the Fair to Faith clauses were intended to end. How it will play out—for science, religion, and the defendant—have yet to be seen.

The Times reminds its readers that evolution is just a theory and that many scientists and scholars believe that there are other, equally reasonable, explanations for our presence in this beautiful and complex universe. For competing views visit www.creationscience.deptsocialintegrity.us.gov.

This article is Fair to Faith.

My twelve-ounce mug was empty. After a refill. The combination of caffeine and adrenaline made my pulse rattle in my ears like a snare drum. I was starting to think about having a cigar, but that early, what with everything else, I'd have a stroke around lunchtime.

I was going to have to talk to Frobisher and have his mysterious backers talk to their press flacks. And I was going to have to talk to Bling. Soon.

I glanced at the time. Not even eight. Okay, I should probably check the blogosphere. TruthSoldier first. Just to take the pulse of the trailer parks along the information superhighway. I clicked the bookmark.

Four spinning cherrytops rotated over a twenty four point header. A siren screamed through my laptop's speakers.

American Neanderthal?

I was having that cigar after all.

Undisclosed location, two years later.

Captain Graner is nervous. A mood hitherto absent from a repertoire that seemed limited to variations on rage and sadistic glee. But the evidence leaves no doubt. Hands whose tremor he can barely conceal pluck at his uniform; he licks lips that instantly dry. His head is slightly bowed and occasionally twitches. He blinks constantly. As he paces the narrow ambit of my cell his arrogant strut unpredictably abandons him then returns with redoubled force, leaving him a cowering wreck one minute and preening bantam the next.

"Now listen--" he begins in a schoolboy's crackling falsetto. An explosive forced cough. "Fucking Marlboros," he says in a baritone half an octave below his usual timbre. "Anyway, listen up, monkey boy. You got a visitor coming. Important visitor. I'd tell you who, but it wouldn't mean nothing to you."

I wondered who could have aroused such alarm. As always a new development produced conflicting emotions: hope that it presaged release rapidly replaced by the sinking certainty of death's imminence. And in any captivity—or mine, at least—even the slightest deviation from the norm assumed disproportionate significance. Any visitor was an event; one powerful enough to make Graner nervous, epochal.

"Even if you pretend you can read," Graner continued, now finally settled back in his normal tone. "Say, anybody ever catch you with the paper upside down? Tell you what, one of these days I'm gonna bend the rules just a little and set up a little exam. See you try to read something. Out loud. Maybe we'll make it a little show. Friday night, maybe. The whole base. Prisoners too. No, maybe not Friday, that's sand-nigger Sunday, they'll close their eyes and stick their fingers in their ears and whimper about Allah and then we'll be cutting another couple down off the shower heads next morning. Boys may not know much but they do know how to tie a good solid knot in a towel. Thought they weren't supposed to kill themselves, but hell I guess there's a loophole somewhere, maybe some kind of get out of jail free card if you've already blown up enough Jews. Whatever. You up for a little show, monkey? Let us see how smart you really are?"

His anxiety momentarily mitigated, he leers at me as I cringe on my bunk. Naturally the prospect of seeing again the printed word fills me with

127

elation; I feel like leaping to my feet, shaking his hand, and proudly taking the challenge. But I know he thinks me a pathetic fraud so I must hunch shoulders and hang head as though terrified of so humiliating a public exposure.

But of course that is all he wanted. "Don't worry, Bonzo," he says, tapping my lowered head with his riding crop. "No show for you." I whimpered with what I hoped would be taken for gratitude. "No, we're going to--"

He stops as my cell door is flung open. Something tells me to keep my eyes lowered. Graner's boots meet as he snaps to attention. "Ma'am!"

About a yard from Graner's roughouts I see black stiletto heels. Behind them, at a respectful distance, oxblood wingtips the size of barges. "Right," says a female voice, tired but edged with authority. "Listen, Graner, think you can scare me up a chair? Or are they all down in that gay S and M nightclub you call an interrogation room?" She didn't wait for Graner to answer beyond an audible gulp. "Hey, whatever, you're a hero and these guys are all dead enders. Who cares? Just make sure if there's an autopsy you've rinsed out any DNA, know what I mean? But seriously—a chair? Just one. You can leave, junior."

Boots and wingtips shuffle nervously. The boots more so than the wingtips. "Ma'am," says another male voice. Deeper. "I really don't think it's a good idea for you to be alone--"

"Oh, can it, kid," she says impatiently. "This guy isn't hurting anybody. Right, monkey boy?" I whimper softly and hunch deeper. "See? Now how about that chair. And give us a little time. Half an hour."

The men hesitate but slowly shuffle out. I keep my eyes fixed on her feet. Above which I can see the sharp creases in her black trousers.

The door slams and locks. A full minute of silence. "Okay, monkey," she says. "Just you and me now. You can drop the prehistoric retard act. Look up." Naturally I not only remain frozen but screw my eyes shut. "Look up. *Look at me.*" A manicured nail raps the top of my head.

Slowly I abandon my half-fetal hunch. The figure before me is tall, even allowing for the stiletto heels. The harsh angles of her painfully thin figure are emphasized by the severity of her Homeland Police officer's uniform, black broken only by the eye-and-lightning-bolts armband and her gold badges of rank, which I presume to be among the highest. Still I cannot look at her face.

The nail touches the point of my chin and tilts my head upward. *"Look at me."*

Her face is inches from mine, framed by her long blonde hair, dusty from countless tintings. Her face is every bit as angular as her body, boney as the Elephant Man's. Despite expert makeup and barely detectable surgery, at this range it is evident that she is no longer young, nor has she been for some time. *"Look at me."* Even whispered her voice remains harsh; perhaps, after a lifetime of media rage crowned by absolute power, nothing else is possible.

My worst fear realized. It is the General herself. I try not to flinch and cower as she settles next to me on my narrow bunk. Though I have little contact with my jailers and less with my fellow captives, almost upon my arrival I had heard that the General made monthly visits to our prison to take her pleasure from its inmates. I had heard as well that her bedfellows did not long outlive her love, and that sometimes their deaths actually coincided with its climax.

I struggle not to shudder as her hand touches my shoulder. Her breath tickles my ear. "Tell me," she says, "Has anybody told you about Jesus?"

It is now beyond even my seemingly unlimited capacity for self-deception to persist in hope. If I had any chance of survival, why would the General have made my salvation a personal priority?

Despite the clarity—and likely brevity—of my future, a more congenial explanation bubbles up through muddy despair. Perhaps the General wants to make a positive example of me. An inspiration to others. See the primitive terrorist dupe transformed by the love of Christ. I imagine myself appearing on her weekly television show, crooning gospel in the background as she harangues the nation towards new heights of probity and security. She will hold the microphone to my willing lips as I tearfully admit that I was created in sin by Iranian bioengineers and further corrupted by the ghetto in which I was planted. But that my Savior's blood had washed clean my wicked heart. Together we will kneel and give thanks.

Its manifest absurdity notwithstanding, I manage to cling to this delusion for a few minutes. My grip on reality reestablishes itself and with it, despondence. Whatever the General's purpose, it is not to give me a second chance at a television career.

You are, of course, familiar with my brief humiliating turn on the stage.

My adoption as court freak by hip-hop royalty. Dancing to general hilarity at their shows. A music video that met disappointing sales as a Christmas novelty item at inner-city WalMarts. The tabloid photographs taken on pre-dawn streets outside clubs as my patrons brawl with rivals or reel into their white Escalades, still clutching their Cristal. And my truncated career as a local television personality. At first I had thought the idea further proof of my masters' business ineptitude, evident even to me; their snickers and guffaws in the audience during my first taping demonstrated that it was, rather, confirmation of their cruelty. Had Fate not intervened that night in Bedford, I am certain that I would have ended my days as a chew toy for their starved pit bulls as the entourage shrieked with drunken glee.

You are not, however, likely to know what preceded my short-lived approximation of fame. And the General's appearance makes clear that I have little time.

When it was decided that I would enter the world of commerce, the elders had not thought far beyond the desirability of a little extra cash. They had failed to take into account the fact that none of us had ever acquired the habits of the workplace, nor of work itself. Your people had broken themselves over centuries from agrarian laxity to industrial discipline. From earliest childhood your schools train you to punctual arrival and departure, to time sliced into uniform increments demarcated by ringing bells and dedicated to discrete topics, brief meals in echoing cafeterias. You are raised for the factory. We, on the other hand, were never adapted even to the slow rhythms of agriculture. A hundred millennia of hunting and gathering, urban or rural, required cooperation, but not the clock.

Particularly because we are neurologically incapable of telling time. Digital or analogue, our innumeracy defeats both. Which I discovered on my first day on the job.

The shop was already busy when I arrived. I had bathed and groomed as well as I could before the banging on the mensroom door became impossible to disregard. The self-confidence I had thus acquired immediately vanished when I found Mario standing at the front desk, the fat man seated beside him. The fat man was beaming. Mario was not.

"Hey, what the fuck?" He made a show of looking at his watch. "You know what time it is? No? Have a look, eh?" He thrust his watch in my face. It might as well have been Sanskrit. "You see that? What time is it, eh?" From my sinking head and shaking shoulders he inferred the obvious. "What, you can't tell time?" He took my silence for assent. He turned to the fat man. "See? Not his fault. He can't tell time."

"He's a retard," the fat man said.

"Not his fault he's a retard. You, it's you're fault you're a fat bastard. Hey," he said to me, pinching my earlobe. "You gonna be late again?"

I shook my head. It wasn't easy. He had a tight grip on my ear.

The fat man grunted. Without relaxing his hold Mario led me back to his chair, to the audible amusement of the other barbers and the morning's customers. Finally he released me and took my head in his meaty paws. "Look me in the eye," he said. Despite every impulse to crawl into myself I did what he asked. "Are you gonna make me look like an asshole?" I didn't respond. He shook my head, firmly but somehow gently. "Answer."

"No," I said at last.

He held my eye for a long time. "Okay, then," he said. "I trust you. Don't let me down." He handed me a push broom. "This now your best friend."

I took it and he gusted laughter. "Bullshit! *I'm* your best friend! That broom your *wife*!"

That evening at the Nest, the elders convened to consider how best to get me to work on time. An alarm clock was out of the question; none of us would ever be able to set it. And while street noise often woke us throughout the night it was insufficiently reliable to depend on it for my continued employment. Finally it was decided to post a watch. Two of the younger men would perch in an eastward facing window and take turns catnapping while awaiting dawn. At the first graying of the horizon—which we knew, whatever the season, would long precede the opening of the shop—I would be hurriedly awakened and dressed for work. My workplace, fortunately, was less than a twenty-minute walk away. Thus my second day on the job began with the assistant manager finding me seated on the steps into the shop, eager to begin my day's work.

He found me there the next day, too, and every day thereafter. Rapidly gaining me a reputation for hard work and Mario for good judgment. Always the first to arrive and the last to leave, uncomplaining through fourteen-hour days and six-and-a-half-day weeks. I suspected that my working conditions were entirely illegal, but like any other undocumented worker, I was happy to have the job.

131

And it shortly became clear that my virtues went beyond simple diligence. Within a week I began to see which barbers were busiest and when. I carefully coordinated my rounds through the shop so that hair did not pile in haystacks around their stations. When they were slow I made sure that their garbage cans were emptied and their magazines neatly stacked. Ever mindful of your people's proclivity for jealous rage I made sure not to neglect the younger, idler craftsmen. If their floors were bare I polished their chairs—an enterprise which, if otherwise entirely pointless, earned me their momentary gratitude.

Nor did I ever forget my patron. I was usually at least three hours into my workday when he arrived to find his station freshly cleaned and supplied, the morning's papers neatly folded on the cracked vinyl of the waiting chair, his tools lined up like surgical instruments. I paid particular attention to the mirror and its halo of brassiered starlets and Juventus stalwarts lovingly clipped from magazines. Most mornings his approaching squabble gave me enough notice so that I could greet him with a Styrofoam cup of coffee from the machine in the back room. No matter how bad the coffee, he always made a point of sipping it appreciatively and pinching my ear.

My hard work soon began to pay off. "Pay" being the operative word. Obviously there were many reasons I had been in no position to negotiate salary at the time I was hired, first among them being an inability to count and second, membership in another species. Despite a hundred millennia of evidence to the contrary, the elders and I had simply trusted that your people would treat me fairly and give me whatever my work deserved. At the end of my first week the fat man called me aside. "You're doing good, kid," he said. "This is for you." He pressed what seemed to be a lot of folding money into my hand. Ducking my head and grinning my thanks I backed away.

Fortunately, Mario had seen the transaction. "What'd he give you? Lemme see."

I extended the wad, still dizzy at my newfound wealth. "Motherfucker!" Mario exploded. "You know how much this is?"

Rattled and beginning to tremble I shook my head.

"*Seventeen fucking bucks.* You know what that means?"

Now quaking I shook my head again.

"I didn' think so. Hey, you don' worry, *you* didn' do nothing wrong."

Fuming aloud in what I took to be Sicilian, he lumbered off in the fat man's direction. It was clear that there was some problem with the amount I had received for my labor. I assumed that it was too little: the money had come from the fat man; Mario was my friend and the fat man's enemy. Therefore he had no reason to be angry. Unless of course what the fat man had given me somehow reduced the amount owed to Mario. But "owed" was a concept even less suited to my brain structure than "amount," so I abandoned that source of anxiety and turned instead to whether I had suddenly invited a great deal of unwanted attention. Just as I decided that I could probably make it to the stairs undetected, Mario rounded the corner with a thick, rumpled envelope outstretched before him.

"*Now* it's payday," he said, thrusting the packet into my hand. "Go ahead. Count. Oh. Right. Okay, I count for you. Now watch. Maybe you learn something." He pulled out a stack of crinkled bills and began to rattle off twenty, forty, sixty, and numbers I presumed to be higher still. "There you go. Two hundred." He crammed the bills back into the envelope. "Here. Put this in your pocket. Front not back. You put it in the back some asshole on the street got it. Maybe get yourself a wallet, okay?" He put a hand on my shoulder. "Look, you don't give that away, you don't spend it all. You keep working hard and you get more. This is America, right? This is New York!" He slapped my cheek gently. "Okay, back to the broom."

When I returned to the Nest that evening, the elders were stunned at our good fortune. Even if they were somewhat unsure as to its extent. We were confident that two hundred was more—possibly much more—than seventeen, but the precise relationship might as well have been quantum mechanics. Fortunately, our facility with images afforded some guidance. The portraits on the currency were easily remembered and recognized. Some years earlier, two of my uncles had prepared a table of approximate equivalencies between specific former presidents and common items. A Washington—of course only I knew his name—was a Hershey's bar; a Lincoln a six pack of batteries or a large Frappucino. The distinguished faces on the rarer bills were still mysteries as none of us had ever received one.

Over successive evenings we studied Jackson's austere features as though he might suddenly speak and give up his secret. Finally, however, I hit upon an expedient. Alone among my fellows I was reasonably familiar with the concept of "change," having seen it made dozens of times a day without really understanding its purpose. The next day I cautiously approached a cashier who had always been kind and extended a Jackson. As I began my carefully rehearsed request, she looked up from her drawer. "Break that for you, hon?" I grinned and nodded. "Fives okay? Or you want singles?"

"Fives," I said, covering my uncertainty.

She snapped off four bills and thrust them into my hand. "Have a good one."

For the rest of the day I made my head ache with the implications of my experiment. Four Lincolns comprised a Jackson. That being so, what made up a Lincoln?

Though I hadn't previously consulted the Nest, I decided to test a hypothesis empirically. As I left the shop that night, I stopped at the Nuts-4-Nuts stand at the corner. The vendor had always been friendly. I extended a Lincoln with quaking hand and with painstaking deliberations said, "Change, please?"

Without looking up he said "Sorry, not without—" He then saw me. "Oh. Okay, for you, what the fuck, it's the end of the day." He took the bill and handed me five more in return. "Have a good one, boss." I mumbled thanks and headed on my way.

That night our best minds bent to the task. If four Lincolns made a Jackson, how could it be that it took *five* Washingtons to make a Lincoln? Had there been some mistake? Or was there some sort of progressive effect, so that it would require only three Jacksons to constitute the next largest unit, whatever it was, until the process ended in singularity? Naturally we left for another generation the question of why sometimes a single bill would purchase many items, when on other occasions a single item required many bills. In any event, as I finally begged for leave to sleep—after all, I was the only one who had to get up for work the next day—the group was bent over a stretch of floor we had not yet decorated. When dawn came and I was awakened, I saw that they had begun the rough outline of a table in the form of an elegant marine allegory, in which five minor Washingtons were swallowed by a grouper-sized Lincoln, who in turn disappeared down Jackson's baleen maw.

Cautiously confident that we at last had a handle on your financial ecology, the elders began to part with the presidential portraits I brought home. First all of our boomboxes had fresh batteries; shortly thereafter every room had a boombox. The St. Marks Place sidewalk vendors were the greatest beneficiaries of our newfound wealth. Having the double advantages of working at night and being just a few rungs further from the bottom than ourselves, we felt, if not safe, not entirely exposed in our mumbled negotiations over their outspread blankets covered with stolen radios, old pornography, and empty Grolsch bottles. Otherwise we confined our financial transactions to quick, anxious midnight exchanges in hole-in-the-wall bodegas and newsstands.

Except, of course, for Starbucks. It was only there that we were willing to risk open daylight connection with the wheels of commerce. At first we thought to scatter our purchases among many outlets so that our sudden startling appearance would not lead to rumor, suspicion, and an eventual extinguishing pogrom. Because the chain then had yet to deeply penetrate the still-ungentrified reaches of the Lower East Side in which we lived, this strategy required our going so far afield that our emissaries returned after hours with beverage turned tepid. Fortunately, we discovered that in the southern reaches of Manhattan, at least, our looks raised no alarm. Barristas long inured to the eccentricities and affectations of the East Village barely lifted an eyebrow in response to a mumbled order from an oddly deformed caffeine and chocolate junkie. Thus, while we instinctively knew never to risk going out as a body--indeed never in groups larger than two and then only late at night—a single Neanderthal could become a regular on the Bowery without drawing attention to himself.

As my career progressed my rewards expanded beyond the monetary. Despite the fat man's hostility—which itself was beginning to fade towards grudging acceptance—the other barbers were becoming to look on me as something of a pet, or perhaps a mascot. In my first month Mario returned from his own lunch with a hot dog for me and laughed when I ignored the bun and inhaled the meat. Shortly other barbers began to bring me unadorned franks and naked burgers when they came back from their breaks. As the weather turned colder some of my co-workers took to bringing me cast-off clothes which they presented with a quiet, "Here, thought this might fit you."

I acquired my name in an episode that then seemed to complete my acceptance in your world. I mentioned earlier that before my introduction to the working world our sole source of cash had been the coins and singles our young men earned dancing on the streets for the entertainment of queued-up clubgoers. Given the solidity of our frames it is perhaps a cause for surprise that we can dance at all and genuine astonishment that we can dance so well. Whether it is a talent wired in our genes and nervous systems or a skill honed over millennia of bored isolation, we really are quite good. One day in early winter, as the festive season was nearing its peak, I was cleaning the breakroom in the back reaches of the shop. A few barbers and a middle-aged cashier, a heavy-set lady who to mark the approaching holiday wore an incongruous elf hat, sat drinking brackish coffee and watching an elderly television. After a few cycles through the basic cable offerings, they finally settled on a music video station that happened to be playing Michael Jackson's "Beat It."

What can I say? It had been my favorite from the moment I heard it. Unconsciously I began to tap my feet, twitch my hips, sway my shoulders. As the music began to take control I heard one of the barbers say, "Hey, check out the retarded guy."

Naturally I froze. I barely dared look at my audience. But to my amazement when I did they were grinning. Not with contempt but with what appeared to be genuine pleasure. "Hey, honey," said the cashier. "Keep it up. You're good."

Hesitantly at first, but with increasing confidence, I finished the number. By some twist of fate three more tunes followed, all danceable, without a commercial break. When I finished the fourth—a proto-rap piece that must have gone back to the early nineties—I came out of my trance to find that I had gathered a crowd. Perhaps a dozen of my co-workers. Mortified and panicked—had I not spent my entirely life scrupulously avoiding the attention I had just demanded?—I grabbed my broom and made to hurry off, head bowed.

But I was stopped by a wave of applause. Of course I initially thought they were mocking me. But their faces said otherwise; they beamed with real enjoyment. And something else as well: pride. I had become one of their own, their special-needs stepchild, and my surprising little achievement was as great a source of pleasure as a first grader's drawing magnetically affixed to a refrigerator.

In an agony of embarrassment—tinged, I must admit, with just a little of my own pride—I stood in the center of the room, my head still hanging. Conveniently enough. For a Dominican stylist who came to work each day festooned with more jewelry than an Aztec princess approached me with one of his necklaces—a gilt lasso of three feet's circumference—in his hands. Leaving only four for himself. As he draped it over my shoulders he said, "Yo, Chilly, moves like that you need some bling." The room erupted in delighted laughter. Among which was my own. When I returned to the Nest that evening, my chain was passed from hand to hand in wonder. Though my natural inclination—as I'm sure you know by now we are not in the least possessive—was to leave it with my fellows to be shared during the day, I knew better. To appear at work unadorned would risk offending my benefactor. Thus the next morning I entered the shop with what for a chronically terrified evolutionary fugitive amounted to a swagger, my golden collar swinging like a knight's.

Thus, I acquired my name. When I had left work the previous night I was "the retarded guy." The next morning, "Bling". By lunch I was Blingbling.

And the rest, as they say, is history.

Motion hearing. Manhattan, late November.

"Lot of traffic," I said to my driver.

He grunted. For him, that was effusive. We were taking one of our ever-changing circuitous routes to Centre Street. This time through Chinatown. Which, on this late-autumn midweek midmorning, should not have been solid with cabs.

I decided to try another conversational gambit. "Think it's construction?"

"You wish," he said.

Startled by his loquaciousness I had no choice but to agree. "You're right," I said. "I wish."

I knew it would be bad, of course. For the first day or so I tried to take the press heat myself. The foreign media at least seemed interested in the issues; half their calls came from science correspondents trying to track down the elusive Professor Weiss. The other half, of course, wanted my take on the effect my defense would have on our embattled empire's religious delusions. Which I usually conceded was an excellent question before the phone went down.

The domestic press was much worse. The national outlets were still trying to pretend they were something other than the publicity arm of a trailer park theocracy, so the call usually came from someone with a JD or at least a working knowledge of criminal procedure as Patriotically Amended. But because their panties were in a sweaty bunch over the Fair to Faith clause of the Amended First Amendment I was inevitably asked, "Doesn't your defense require a judge to find that God didn't create Man in His own image?"

Again, excellent question. Again, the phone went down.

I decided to let somebody else answer the phone after the death threats began. The first few, surprisingly, came by email. I say surprisingly because I always figured that anyone smart enough to use email was smart enough to know that "dead" had an "a" in it. Or at least knew that the little red spellcheck line meant something was amiss. But no. HEY JESUS HATER NU YORK QWEER U R DED. Of course it was entirely possible that the message had come from a member of the Harvard Law School faculty whose prose style had been corrupted by excessive texting. But somehow I doubted it, though the Q rather than a K bespoke a certain degree of

138

literacy, perhaps deliberately concealed. Not unlike Jack the Ripper's notes to the London press. An historical comparison that I am sure would occur to the cops if they found my bowels removed with surgical precision and looped over a gaslight.

Once I got a request for an interview with what was left of NPR. I almost did it until I found out that it was from an Alabama affiliate that had a five AM Sunday show called Talking to Heathens.

The emails were followed by voicemails. At that point I called Flemming. Not his jurisdiction, obviously, but he had friends. There was a cop at my front door the next morning to walk me to my office. And I guess Flemming made sure word got around. First I got phone calls from the kind of heavy-hitters who represented Five Families capos, asking what they could do. Then I got lunch invitations from white shoe Wall Street firms who sent around hire cars with private security who shepherded me up freight elevators to private dining rooms overlooking Ground Zero. Junior partners in Turnbull and Asser shirts and Charvet ties logged pro bono hours telling me how much they respected what I was doing. Which kind of alarmed me. I thought I was just doing my job, which really shouldn't have merited comment. Their admiration flowed not from that, however, but from the fact that in this case it entailed sticking my thumb in the eye of the Religious Right that was now running the country. Which was not the safest thing to do. And once lunch was over they urged me back through the service entrance and down to the street from whence I came.

Of course I had to give up my weekly visits to the Flintstones. Which I found surprisingly difficult. I'd historically fled any relationship with a woman with kids. So it was no small wonder, especially to me, that I'd found myself looking forward to time-traveling back to the Clan of the Cave Bear as eagerly as any divorced dad anticipated a soccer game.

And the Iranian had made herself scarce. Which I didn't find surprising, but hurtful nonetheless. But then again her life was tough enough without having to stand by her man as he blasphemed against every Abrahamic religion, hers included, while her cousins simultaneously gassed our boys in the Iranian mountains. No, her life was plenty tough enough.

So when I went downtown to Centre Street it was in a Crown Vic with a whip antenna, which the police in their innocence believed was unmarked, driven by a heavyset middle-aged man with a mustache in a cheap blazer and Rockports, which the police also believed was plainclothes.

We were on our way to the preliminary hearing on our motion to dismiss. Preliminary because I didn't expect the court to decide an issue this complex on the briefs; instead it would hear us huff and puff and set the case down for a full evidentiary hearing in about three months. Which meant four or five days of testimony broken up by frequent recesses for guilty pleas in Spanish and sentencings in Russian, followed by four months of judicial silence punctuated by a brief incomprehensible decision in which my client and I were leaned over the rail and repeatedly sodomized. The usual, in other words.

Any rational person, of course, would have known by now that the usual was the last thing I could expect.

My last shreds of self-delusion were stripped away as my car finally edged onto Centre Street, and I saw why traffic had been blocked all around Lower Manhattan. Maybe I should've listened to the radio in the shower that morning.

There were two or three thousand people on either side of a traffic lane barely kept open by cops in riot gear. Most of the crowd had the fried-Twinky hypertensive bulk of out of towners. Though maybe their faces were that good Mid-American scarlet because were screaming and waving signs that said things like MAN IN GOD'S IMAGE and BIBLE IS OUR LAW and JESUS DIED FOR AMERICA and MR. PRESIDENT, EXECUTE BLING and HIP-HOP KILLS REAL (WHITE)AMERICANS and even RALEIGH WON'T MAKE A MONKEY OUT OF ME. The last of which really impressed me, partly because it sounded like something from "Inherit the Wind," partly because they'd spelled my name right. Which was not repeated in the signs that started to batter our windshield once the mob had penetrated the clever ruse of a cop car with untinted windows. My suddenly well-known profile was now clearly visible. The crowd on either side surged forward and fists started to pound the roof and doors. Fat red faces pressed against the windows, mouths gaping words I couldn't make out over the siren my driver had just started. Someone just ahead of us with a plastic shopping bag in his hand wound up for the pitch and an instant later the bag splattered runny brown over the windshield.

"Shit," I said.

"That it is," said my driver.

As the crowd pressed in ahead of us, nearly closing the street completely, I heard a couple of pops. Plumes of dense white mist exploded around us.

"Tear gas," said my driver. He flicked something on the dashboard and the air conditioner roared. We crawled forward another couple of feet. Through the shit-smeared windshield I could see the Jerry Springer types gagging and retching yet still somehow able to hold their position blocking our progress. Then City cops in body armor and brainbucket helmets carrying assault rifles broke through.

"I was you," said my driver, his tone just the same as when he'd ordered a large light-two sugars earlier that morning, "I'd get down."

"I'm way ahead of you," I said from the floorboards. But I wasn't sure he could hear me through the Barbour over my head.

Half an hour later I was waiting to be admitted to chambers. Braunstein, of course, was already there. Not a hair out of place. "Nice ride in?"

Once the SWAT guys had broken through, it hadn't taken us more than ten minutes to make it to the judges' underground parking garage. Half a dozen hard-faced middle-aged men with gold shields clipped to their belts closed in as I got out of the car. They hustled me to the elevator. Because we weren't on "Law and Order" they didn't respond with streetwise ripostes to the witty lawyerly banter with which I was covering my shakes.

On the other hand, I wasn't killed in transit. Which made me really glad to be a New Yorker. Anyplace else in patriotically amended America, the cops would've let the mob through and my personal denouement would've looked like the last five minutes of "Braveheart."

"Nice ride in?" Braunstein said again. He actually looked a little concerned.

I took a deep breath. "Yeah," I said. "Fine. I managed to avoid soiling myself."

"Right," he said, just barely cracking a smile. "West Side Highway. Smart. FDR, you'd be sitting in shit."

"Day's still young," I said. "Look who we got."

"Right," he said. "Blackandblue. I'd known, I'd be here in Depends."

Justice Black had done no harm to the bar or the people of New York in twenty years as an appellate public defender, entertaining our higher courts with witty and well-reasoned briefs on behalf of felons who were pretty much fucked anyway. Then a hiccup in our otherwise perfectly functioning system of patronage—a *Times* investigation into the Brooklyn machine—

had kicked him onto the trial bench as a Good Government nominee. Ever since he had tortured the trial bar with his conviction that no matter who was in front of him, he was the smartest guy in the room. He liked to pretend that his nickname came from bitter lawyers who'd come to court unprepared and been on the receiving end of a justified judicial pummeling. In fact, it came from his taste for Latino rough trade. Monday mornings he'd stumble around with his glasses scotch taped together and bruises on his forehead, mumbling about muggings, when every cop in the courthouse knew he'd been in a Yonkers underpass motel getting it high and hard from Pedro.

I was less than one of his particular favorites because a few years before I'd seen him waddling into the Angelika with his wife. I'd just got myself a skinny decaf latte to ease my way into slumberland during one of the few foreign movies—actual celluloid; anything digital could spread behind the firewalls—the Patriotic Media Council had allowed into the Home of the Free. I tried to remain a respectful five paces behind as they squeezed their way down the aisle, looking anywhere but at them.

But he'd caught my horrified stare as one of the fattest women in Manhattan took a full minute to wedge herself into a seat. For a terrible instant our eyes met, and I knew his little nod was no collegial greeting, but a promise of payback; he had seen the look on my face. Which was promptly forthcoming, in ways small and big: vacations destroyed by continuances denied, adverse evidentiary rulings just this side of reversible error.

So I was less than happy when the court officers led us to Black's chambers through a set of service corridors and fire stairs so circuitous even Jack Ruby couldn't find us. The great jurist waved us to seats. His flabby triceps flopped around inside short sleeves. "Sit, gentlemen, sit, we're all friends here," he said, face split in that jack-o-lantern grin that usually meant you were about to be sanctioned. There were four customers' chairs in front of his battered veneer desk. Braunstein and I took two on the right. Torrington took one at the far left, thus dodging our contagion. I tried to catch his eye. We'd had a couple of little chats after I filed the motion and I wanted to know whether the deal was on. But he was looking at anything but me.

"Well, well, well. Quite a case here, quite a case, quite a day we're going to have." He swiveled in his government-issue big shot chair so that

I could see the screensaver crawling on the monitor behind his desk.

"Oh, that's new, Your Honor," I said. "'Stately plump Buck Mulligan yadda yadda.' *Ulysses*, right? Used to be whatever it was from *Finnegan's Wake*."

I don't know why I kept trying. Somehow I'd latched onto the delusion that if Black recognized that I wasn't one of the semi-literate outer borough baboons whose whinings usually burdened his days, all would be forgiven. I'd never been right before.

And I sure wasn't now. "'Yadda, yadda,' Mr Raleigh? '*Yadda yadda*'? Ah yes." He steepled his fingers, his icy eyes glinting behind LensCrafter frames. "I'd forgotten that you had the advantage of an Ivy League education. How foolish we must seem to you. How pretentious--"

"You got that right, Your Honor," said Braunstein. Black stopped as though tasered. Torrington was startled enough to actually look at us. "I don't know how many times I broke this guy's balls about this Yale crap since we got started on this piece of shit but hey, he won't learn. So anyway, where we going with this?"

Black unsteepled his fingers and folded his hands on his desk. He fixed Braunstein with his piggy blue eyes. There was a long moment in which no one spoke. The only sound in the room was Black hyperventilating. I studied the tips of my shoes and thought to myself Oh God, at last there's someone he's going to hate more than me.

No such luck. Eventually Black got control of himself and choked out, "Perhaps we should hear from Mr. Raleigh."

I tore my attention from my footwear and was about to deliver my pitch when, true to form, Black continued. "Perhaps Mr. Raleigh will explain why rather than simply changing his plea to not guilty by reason of diminished capacity he instead decided to burden this court, this city, and this *country*, may I say, with a motion whose determination would require this court to incorporate into our jurisprudence the very best of juvenile science fiction."

"Well—" I began, eloquently enough.

"You know, Mr. Raleigh," said Black, "before you respond perhaps I should have a court reporter here. For your own protection. Because, sir, as I'm sure you're aware, were I to find that your motion were advanced without a good faith belief in its soundness I'd have no alternative but to refer you for disciplinary proceedings. Which, given the expense you've caused the state, would no doubt imperil your license to practice."

I'd already had shit thrown at me once that day. Twice was too much.

"Whatever you think is right, Judge," I said. "In fact, please. And when we've got a reporter here I want to repeat what you just said. And if you don't, I think my good friends here, being senior members of the trial bar, will be happy to provide affidavits."

Braunstein smiled and spread his hands. "Gotta speak the truth," he said. Torrington just stared at a spot four feet above the judge's head. Which itself was pointed a little to the right of my line of sight, his eyes burning a hole in the wall behind me.

"Because, Your Honor," I continued, "if you suggest that a motion advanced with supporting affidavits from a Yale anthropologist does not comply with both the statute and my ethical obligations, I think you should say so, and state your grounds, on the record. For *your* protection."

I've never known minutes to really pass like hours unless I was having a cystoscopy, but I will tell you that before Black spoke I had plenty of time to plan a second career in Uniontown, PA working for the Post Office. My father, I figured, still had a few chits to call in. Not so bad; lots of exercise, done by four, Yuengling drafts still under a buck and plenty of single moms to rub up against.

Just before I'd decided to call a realtor, Black broke the silence. "Mr. Raleigh," he said, "you are quite correct. Your papers, on their face—and let me emphasize, *on their face*—appear to meet the requirements of the statute and of course your ethical obligations. And let me emphasize, *appear*."

I had to box him in. And this was too much fun to stop anyway. "Your Honor's emphasis doesn't suggest that in the absence of countervailing evidence he's formed any opinion as to the validity of my moving papers?"

Black's voice was strangled. "Certainly not."

"Then I suppose we can proceed without a reporter." And then, malevolent idiot that I am, I opened my briefcase and said, "Oh—sorry, Judge. I should've asked earlier. What happened?"

Black pulled his attention from the court file he'd buried his head in. "What?"

"Your eye."

"My *eye*?"

"Yes, sir. Looks like you got a hell of a shiner a while ago. Bump into a doorknob?"

A snort sounded. Surprisingly to my left. "Sorry," said Torrington, his hand over his mouth. "Allergies." Braunstein kicked my ankle as he reached down to open his own briefcase.

Black stammered and pulled a pocket mirror from a desk drawer. "It does still show, doesn't it?" he said anxiously, sliding his glasses onto his forehead and peering at his reflection. "That—oh, I uh, had the flu last week and um, as I was running to heed nature's call I stumbled and struck my face on the doorjamb. Ha! I'd almost forgotten. Thank you, Mr. Raleigh, for your concern."

"Not at all, Your Honor," I said placidly.

"Yes!" said Black. He dropped the mirror into its drawer and slammed it shut. "Flu. In any event, gentlemen, I'm sure you'll all agree that Mr. Raleigh's motion will require an evidentiary hearing. Am I correct?"

Torrington stirred. "Your Honor, while I agree that this defendant's motion is, as you say, facially compliant—and I think Your Honor's emphasis is apt, facially compliant—with the statute, I think Your Honor is correct in saying that it is also facially absurd."

Never miss an opportunity to kiss ass. That's how prosecutors grow up to be judges. Black hummed and smirked.

"But that said, Your Honor, I think we have to afford Mr. Raleigh his right to embarrass himself in front of the world if that's what he thinks is in his client's interest. After which, of course, I'm sure he'll change his plea as your Honor suggests."

"Well, Mr. Torrington, perhaps Mr. Raleigh thinks, as did Bernard Shaw, that there's no such thing as bad publicity."

"Behan," I said.

"Sir?"

"Brendan Behan. 'There is no such thing as bad publicity except your obituary.'"

I'd never actually had the word 'apoplectic' pop into my mind during a conversation before. Clearly Black was thinking about being responsible for my obituary. "Sorry, Your Honor," I said. "I do a lot of crosswords. Can't help myself sometimes."

"He sure can't," said Braunstein, breaking his unaccountable silence. "So excuse me, gentlemen, but I got to be in two other courts today, so maybe we should just schedule the evidentiary and get this show on the road?"

"Your Honor," said Torrington, "I'd love to accommodate Mr. Braunstein but as you know there's been extensive Federal interest in this case. So I have to insist—I've been *instructed* to insist, if you all follow me--"

The room suddenly got five degrees colder. We followed.

"--that any rulings in this case, including the entry of scheduling orders, take place in open court on the record."

Black punched a button on his phone. "Bring them in," he said.

The speaker squawked, "Okay."

"Mr. Torrington," said Black, "I've received the same instructions, from different masters, perhaps, but the same instructions nevertheless. Gentlemen, I am sorry." He did seem genuinely apologetic, which notched my general anxiety to Xanax levels. "I have a full courtroom out there. This is a very contentious case for many reasons. Our security here is good but not perfect. Precautions must be taken."

The door behind his desk opened. A cop walked in carrying what looked like a bunch of black life vests. They seemed heavy. "Okay, gents," the cop said, "stand up and we'll get you fitted. Judge, DA, you know the drill, you put 'em on yourselves."

I was the last to stand, and the last to realize what they were. "Easy, boss," said Braunstein as the cop cinched the Kevlar tight. "I just got this from the tailor."

My heart was pounding in my throat as the cop dropped my vest over my head and started strapping me in. "What," I whispered to Braunstein. "No helmets?"

"Hard shot with a pistol unless he's right behind you, Abe," he whispered back. "But keep moving anyway. And do me a favor—don't sit too close to me."

My boxers were sodden as we lined up to go through the judge's door into the courtroom. Braunstein was behind me. His hand fell on my shoulder. "Hey, lucky you. You got the one with the bullseye!"

Black had one of those big old Manhattan courtrooms with thirty foot ceilings and oak paneling and murals of boats towed by mules named Sal on the old Erie Canal that used to make me think, when I was much younger, that I was Clarence Darrow. Or at least Sam Waterson.

Not so today. Black's bailiff and law assistant went out first. There was a short hallway between chambers and the judge's door behind the bench. As it opened we were hit by the meanest courtroom buzz I'd ever heard, worse than the sentencing of a serial child rapist or the acquittal of an Orthodox rabbi who'd fallen asleep at the wheel and plowed through a Dominican Day parade. To name just two of my efforts to make the world a better place.

It got worse as Torrington went through, but I heard someone yell, "He's the DA!" and it sunk back to its previous ugly grumble. I was next. I tried to keep my head down without looking cowed, hoping to maintain my self-respect while pretending to be someone else. No dice.

At the back of the well of the court, lined up in front of the bar, were a dozen SWAT cops in the same riot gear as their buddies on the street. Assault rifles across their bellies. Comforting until I realized that when the crossfire began it would likely be over my dead or soon to be so body. Another squad was deployed on either side of the aisle, and more at the back. Otherwise the courtroom was occupied by the ugliest bunch of white people I ever saw.

They apparently had the same opinion of me. As soon as I came through the door and hurried down the steps around the witness box and towards counsel table, trying not to hold my briefcase across my chest to stop a bullet, I was recognized. A fat man with a mullet stood up. "THAT'S THE BASTARD! THAT'S RALEIGH!" He pointed straight at me.

I tried not to duck but I think I did a full-body twitch. Fortunately he didn't have a gun. He was just making sure that everybody was looking at the right guy when they started screaming abuse. As I made my way to the table, in what I like to think was a dignified sprint, two cops on the aisle were dragging him from his seat and frog-marching him out.

The roar in the courtroom was too much for a middle-aged man with an earbud habit to pick out individual words. I wedged my supposedly bulletproof torso into a chair and started unpacking my briefcase, reasonably confident that the layers of Kevlar-clad cop behind me would stop anything headed my way.

Braunstein took the chair next to me. "Like I told you," he said, "you're gonna get a lot of business out of this case. See, already you're the people's hero. Smart move."

Black was on the bench. He was less than twenty feet away so I could see that his face was shiny with sweat. As he swung the gavel the left side of his face exploded in a tic. Like most bullies he was completely gutless, which ordinarily would have given me a lot of satisfaction to see proven. Especially in public. But at this moment I really wanted him to be a hero. For my sake.

As the gavel fell again I glanced over at the state's table. Torrington was not alone. To his right were a couple of stony-faced men in gray suits, white shirts, and red-and-blue ties. The uniform of Homeland plainclothes. As one of them inclined his head towards Torrington to speak, I saw the glint of rimless glasses and recognized Major Strasser.

Shit. Shit shit *shit*. Okay, maybe he was just there to observe. A happy delusion that Braunstein immediately shattered. "Hey," he said, nudging me through my body armor, "I think we got a problem. Torrington has that fuckwad with him. Something tells me we're not gonna be in this courtroom too long." His face was tight, and that worried me more than seeing Strasser in the first place. "Something tells me we're gonna miss it."

I hadn't had enough time to think about it, but I couldn't figure out why Homeland had insisted on open court when it would have been far easier to disappear us all. Maybe it was going to rig the hearing to conclusively disprove evolution by showing that Bling was just a human freak and Adam and Eve rode dinosaurs. Or maybe it just needed law enforcement to be seen to be on Jesus' side. Or maybe I was just an increasingly frantic mouse in a maze.

Black was swinging the gavel like John Henry the Steel Driving Man. To no avail. The courtroom mob scented his fear and hooted for blood. Black dropped the gavel and ran his fingers through his haystack of gray hair, his shoulders shuddering as he hunched forward on the bench. Major Strasser, at the next table, tapped Torrington on the shoulder and inclined his head towards the bench. Torrington shook his head no. Strasser nodded yes. Twice. Hard. Then he pointed at the judge.

Counterintuitively I felt kind of bad for Torrington. Lawyers aren't supposed to do what Washington just then clearly wanted. Torrington put his hands flat on the table in front of him and stared at the ceiling for a full minute. Negotiations for his soul complete, he pulled his Kevlar-burdened self out of his chair and started towards the bench. Without looking at defense table.

Braunstein and I stood up simultaneously. "Your honor, is this a sidebar?" I said.

The roar behind us passed the decibel level usually associated with lynch mobs. Between the shrieks and cries for my client's dismemberment and my own, I could make out the bull-throated roars of cops telling people to shut the fuck up and sit the fuck down.

"Judge, this is wrong!" Braunstein shouted. "What the hell, prosecution ex parte, fuck the Patriot Act, this is a *court*! *Nobody* gets to talk to the court by himself! *Let the record show that the prosecution is now giving the Court a back rub!* "

Torrington was at the bench, behind Black, his hand on his quaking shoulder. Braunstein was around the table and on his way to the judge. Myself just behind. My eyes tearing and lungs filling with the pepper spray that was beginning to waft forward from the cheap seats.

Major Strasser was a little quicker around his table. He planted himself between Braunstein and me and the bench.

The drab man was not very big, smaller even than my elegant friend. But he stopped Braunstein in his tracks. And, of course, me behind him. Strasser shook his head slowly from side to side and pointed back at our table.

If it was just me I would have gone back to the table and sat down and made a big show of shaking my head in disbelief as I packed my briefcase. Then I would have run out of the courtroom and out of New York back to Uniontown, PA where my elderly parents kept my bedroom as a shrine to my junior high school science fair triumphs. The room in which I would spend every night curled in the fetal position sobbing softly around a bourbon bottle awaiting the inevitable knock on the door. After which the Men in Black would lead me downstairs into a smoked-windowed SUV and an IV drip that would break whatever was left of my will before I got to whatever Freedom Friendly state I'd been renditioned to. Where after a few waterboardings I'd've given up all I had and more. At the last cycle they'd just keep pouring the water so that my last words would be an explosive gurgle. While my parents went to their graves wondering how this all had happened.

But it wasn't just me.

I had a client downstairs in the pen, who while he didn't deserve what seemed likely to happen to him, did deserve a defense. Or at least a lawyer. So as Braunstein and Strasser stood nose to nose trying to eyeball each other to death, I nipped around them up the two short steps to the bench.

I was right behind Torrington, who was right behind Black. From this perspective I could understand why Black had lost it. The courtroom was one degree north of pandemonium. The rednecks were throwing themselves against a cordon the SWAT guys had formed to protect the well of the court. Some of the cops were swinging batons or rifle butts into thick trailer-park skulls. So far the thin blue line was holding.

So far.

Torrington was bent close to Black. I grabbed the DA's shoulder and stuck my mouth next to his ear. "What the *fuck* are you doing?"

He barely turned his head. Just loud enough for me to hear, he said, "Ending this fucking case. Look at your buddy,"

Distracted as I was by the antics of the Bible thumpers with the cops, I hadn't noticed Braunstein and the Homeland golems. Braunstein was staring with bent head at a stiff looking bluebacked document Strasser held in front of him.

"Wow," I said. "Just like TV. And?"

"That's a D notice. Now maybe you want to go back through that door and wait till we tell you what to do next."

Braunstein's face was ashen. I guessed mine was too.

"Shit," I said. Then I did what I was told.

Undisclosed location, two years later

Captain Graner just left.

He wasn't here long. He came with his assistant, as usual. As usual, he stood with his hands behind his back at parade rest while she sat on the concrete shelf that serves this cell as a seat, transcribing in her laptop the barked interrogation that I long ago realized was an assignment he had created for himself, for even the most stupid of his superiors would not have trusted him with a mission of any importance. Again he pressed me about my fluency in Arabic, my knowledge of aircraft, the hatred I and my kind bore for America. As usual, with downcast eyes I muttered my denials.

You will be surprised that all my denials were equally true. Antipathy is as foreign to us as jealousy or rage because, perhaps, of the slow, thick blood that enabled us to thrive through millennia of world-girdling rivers of ice. Or because of the later millennia in which we did not prosper, when dwindling numbers made internecine conflict racial suicide, the limit of anger shrank to a momentary irritation which might rouse the nest first to a chittering anxiety and then daylong make-up cuddles.

That said, I can tell you that neither in ancient bardic chants nor present-day gossip around the boombox was a harsh word ever spoken about you. It never occurred to us that whatever you visited on us, disaster or petty slight, was the product of malice. Rather, you were simply part of the natural world to which we so precariously clung, no more to be blamed than calving ice floe or murderous bear.

Given your easy hatreds you may doubt me. Nevertheless, it is true. I continue to wonder whether your habit of mutual extermination because of an offending eye shape or skin color or form of worship springs from that time in which you coexisted with us. Whether you satisfy your thirst for our blood, the blood of the true Other, with that you have drunk so many times from your own veins.

And I wonder, too, whether when I am at last dead that thirst will finally be slaked. Am I that rough beast, his hour come at last, that slouches towards Bethlehem to die? Am I your Second Coming? Will it redeem you, make you whole, when you at long last bury or burn the final evidence of the genocide that made you yourselves, masters of all the world?

But I digress. A luxury I can ill afford. Time now is short.

151

At the conclusion of his perfunctory interrogation—his last questions had to do with whether I had bought hundred pound sacks of nitrate fertilizer—Captain Graner took his hands from behind his back. In the left was a thick packet of grease-darkened yellow paper. I twitched; the odor of fatty meat had hung in the room since his arrival, but I assumed it had been a trick of our unreliable air conditioning, venting the mess hall into my cell. Now its source was revealed as otherwise.

"Okay, monkey man," he said. "Enough questions. You've been good. Here's a little something." Awkwardly he extended the packet.

His assistant stopped typing. My eyes were fixed on the concrete floor.

"Come on," he said. "Take it. Me to you."

My eyes still down, I unsteadily extended my hand. Into it was thrust a heavy wad of oily lukewarm paper. I dared to raise my eyes. It was covered with red script obliterated by leakage.

"From the mess hall," said Graner. "Go ahead, unwrap it."

I did as I was told. In my hands was a sesame seed bun from which peeked the edges of two slabs of gray meat festooned with shredded lettuce, leaking a viscous white sauce.

"Burger King," said Graner. "We outsource. All yours."

I burst into tears.

"No, hey, calm down, don't thank me, no big deal, honest, umm okay honey we're done here now, see you later monkey man." I fell back onto my bunk, the burger still in my hands, and wailed and rocked. Blind with weeping I knew that they had left only when I heard the door slam shut and triple bolt.

Graner was wrong. Not entirely; there was just a shred of sudden unexpected gratitude in my response. But largely. I knew that his gesture was motivated by the certainty that I would soon be dead.

At last I regained my composure. Freed from fear by the complete absence of its evil twin: hope. The burger was now cold.

I do not have much time.

I will ignore the public events that led me here. My remaining moments limit me to the private.

I met with Mr. Raleigh the day before I was to appear in court. Providentially he had managed to maintain my separation from the other prisoners when I was transferred to Manhattan; from what little I had seen, the suburban criminal was as nothing to his metropolitan colleague. The transit from my solitary cell to the conference room was an occasion of terror. Despite the brevity of my public career, apparently I was well remembered on the street. *"Yo, BLING!"* howled my fellow convicts-to-be, hurling themselves against their bars or strutting bow-legged back and forth, hands curled into armpits in an ook-ook-ooking simian parody. Humiliated and verging on panic, I shambled shackled down the corridor, head down, a jailer on either side.

That afternoon Mr. Raleigh was as cocky as a terrier. "Listen," he said, "you're going to want to worry. But don't. You'll be in the courtroom for two minutes max. Then you're out. That's the good news. The bad news is there'll be about two hundred screaming idiots in the courtroom. Don't let 'em scare you. There'll also be at least a dozen big armed cops between you and them, plus another couple around you at all times."

I uncapped his elegant pen. I still preferred to write. Possibly showing off, possibly because I took such pleasure in his antique writing instruments. *What will become of me?*

I thought that for just an instant his canine jauntiness slipped. But just for an instant. "Short term or long?"

An easy answer so I spoke it aloud. "Both."

He smiled crookedly. "First the easy part. As I've told you before, once we've entered the plea the court will schedule a hearing on the motion to dismiss. The court will want more briefs before the hearing. This is, shall we say, a novel issue, and no judge is going to shoot from the hip. It's going to take a while, probably months. During that time you enjoy the hospitality of the Empire State. What I think is likely to happen is that if the motion ever gets decided the case gets dismissed. Which *should* mean you walk out of here a free man.

"If we don't, we have to try your case like any other defendant and win or lose. If we lose, you go to jail for at least twenty years. I don't think we will, though I can't guarantee it, because the forensics on your side are so strong and the witnesses against you are so bad.

"These are not ordinary circumstances. No, not at all. But this is the tricky part. We have laws that were intended for sex offenders that let the state put you away in a mental institution even after you've served a criminal sentence. They may argue you're a public menace and try to go that route. Or they may try another way. But whatever reasoning they use they don't want you out giving interviews about life in the Stone Age, that's for sure. You're just too much of a problem for the Administration. Hell, you read the papers." I swelled with pride; indeed I do. "The mouth-breathers amended the Constitution just one step short of criminalizing modern science and here you go proving evolution."

I don't, actually. *You didn't evolve--*

"I know, I know, but you get my point. In any event on the one hand the Administration—which has plenty of support even here, where the Patriot Amendments failed by a landslide—so wants you to disappear that if you weren't such a matter of public record they'd have chained you to an old cigarette machine and dropped you into Sheepshead Bay by now." I cringed, and for once he didn't reassure me. "It's true. Face facts. Getting ahead of this with the motion to dismiss was your best life insurance. If we'd sat still after they finally got the DNA right you'd've been disappeared by now. And maybe me too." Again his cockiness slipped for a moment.

Quickly restored. "But we got ahead of it, and we're both still here. So what happens to you?

"Very simple. Nobody wants to try this case; they don't want you walking around loose; you don't want to spend your life in a nut hatch. So we cop a plea. In exchange for which you get twenty years probation and house arrest. Special condition of probation is absolute media silence. But here's the beauty part. You're under the supervision of Professor Gil J. Weiss. In France."

I sat stunned. Twenty years? I would expire before my sentence; as I told you, we eat a lot of meat. And I would never see the Nest again. My head spun, and for a moment I thought I would vomit. Our kind has never done well with isolation; I had endured my separation better than could any of my cousins, possibly because of my long immersion in your world, but every night spent without the warmth of snoring kindred had felt like an amputation. Had it not been for Mr. Raleigh's recording messages from the Nest I might have lost my mind.

Raleigh was still talking. "It's not a done deal by any stretch. But the prosecutor and I have been talking. So it looks like exile." He grinned crookedly. "Ooh la la."

But there was a reason, after all, that I had spent so much time away from the others. A reason I had not simply died from loneliness. I am, after all, different. My head righted itself. My stomach settled.

France.

I waited for hours for the call to court that never came. Deprived of any stimulation I rehearsed in my mind everything I had ever read about my place of exile. With growing excitement I imagined myself seated at an outdoor table sipping *chocolat*, reading the International Herald Tribune, like a jazz age expatriate. Would I learn French? Would its rapid cadences fit my mouth better than English? Would galleries welcome me? Should I get a beret? Thus I whiled away the time, as happily as anyone shackled and manacled ever had.

But my attorney's entrance exploded all my hopes.

Gone were the Airedale strut and crooked grin; he shambled into the conference room with bowed head, beaten. As he passed me to take his chair I smelled neither cigar nor cologne, but the acrid whiff of fear.

He sat with elbows on the table, hands folded, fingers occasionally twining with anxiety. He did not meet my eye. "Look," he said, futilely attempting a smile, "I wouldn't be signing up for any French lessons right now, Pierre."

I sat mute, the pen and virgin paper before me.

"I have nothing but bad news," he said. "Really bad. Let me just get it all out and then ask questions. Okay?"

I nodded. It was all I could do.

"Okay. Okay. First, the District Attorney isn't interested in a plea. Of any kind. You're not going to France. And that, I'm afraid, is the *good* news.

"Next is the really bad news. The case is over in New York. In fact, the case is over, period. I can't fucking *believe* this." His clasped hands were shaking. "Look. Blame me. But filing the motion to dismiss completely fucked us up. The DA referred it to Homeland and they passed it up to the Czar and she took it to the Patriot Tribunal. And the Tribunal issued what's called a D Notice. From Subsection D of Section 114 of the Patriot Amendments Enabling Statute, giving it exclusive jurisdiction over any and all actions, civil or criminal, in which it finds a threat to national security. That means that once the notice is issued it, and only it, has the case. Subject to its own special procedures, some of which are contained in the Classified Annexes of the United States Code and the Federal Rules of Criminal and Civil Procedure. And that, my friend, means it gets to decide cases according to rules only it knows."

He finally met my eye. His were red-rimmed. "You're a pretty well read guy," he said. My despair notwithstanding, a little bubble of pride welled up. Only to burst. "Do you know what the Star Chamber was?" I shook my head. "Never mind. By the way, I should tell you we probably can't count on these conversations being confidential any more. Maybe I should remember that myself. Ah, fuck 'em anyway." His shoulders quivered a moment; I still wonder what he was suppressing.

In a moment he had recovered himself. "It gets worse from here. The Tribunal not only took jurisdiction but decided the motion to dismiss. Under its rules—that is, those parts of the rules I'm allowed to know—I can't let you see the decision. I was allowed to read it—once—before it was burned in front of me. Pursuant to statute. Jesus *Christ*. I can't believe this. Sorry. Sorry." He was crying now. He took his bright silk handkerchief from his suit pocket and dabbed streaming eyes. "Anyway, I am permitted to tell you that it was signed by at least one Justice of the Supreme Court, the Attorney General, the Homeland Czar, and two federal judges appointed after passage of the Patriot Amendments. Other than that I can't tell you, because their names were blacked out.

"But I can tell you the gist of the decision. In fact I'm required to. The Court specifically found that you are not human and thus not bound by law and therefore not criminally liable for any act you may or may not have done. Accordingly it did not reach the factual basis for your prosecution.

"But it further found that because you aren't human you are an animal. Property. Thus, not subject to any legal protection except those that the states afford beasts from cruelty. And because of your exceptional status as a human-seeming animal, the federal government's interest in preventing terrorism or unrest disruptive to national security as a result of theological issues arising therefrom, and in the absence of any property interest in you that might be protected by the Due Process Clause—that means you don't have an owner—the federal interest, under the Supremacy Clause, requires that you be immediately remitted to the custody of the Homeland Police for its disposition.

"I am so sorry."

Oddly parallel we both sat with bowed head and clasped hands. At last I reached for the pen. His hand snaked around my wrist. "Don't write," he whispered, his face close to mine. "The pad is government property now. Speak. Quietly. I can understand you and maybe they can't."

I struggled to articulate clearly. "Can we appeal?"

He shook his head. "Sorry," he whispered. "Not even the Supreme Court has jurisdiction any more."

"Then I'm lost," I said.

He kept his slender fingers curled around my thick wrist. Our eyes met over the table. This time he did not look away. "Yes," he said, "you are."

After a moment he withdrew his hand and dropped his gaze. "There's something worse."

I'm afraid I snorted a laugh. Mr. Raleigh replied in kind. "Right," he said. "What could be worse. But I'm afraid something is." He looked me in the eye again. Later I gave him credit for doing so. "I'm afraid I've been very sloppy. I don't know why but Homeland wasn't surveilling me. Maybe they just fucked up. But they didn't know about the Nest. Not until somebody who was close to me got into my laptop. Where I had a couple of notes. The order requires me to turn over everything I know about other, similar animals. Or face prosecution myself. I'm sorry."

We were both very still for a very long time. I reached for the pen. This time Mr. Raleigh didn't stop me.

What will you do?

"I don't know," he said.

Judgment. Manhattan, later that day.

When I got home the street was a lot quieter than when I'd left.

Not surprisingly. At either end of the block was a very serious looking man with a wire in his ear and a blue windbreaker with HOMELAND POLICE in big yellow letters. Another stood next to the entrance to my building. No reporters, no trucks with satellite uplinks. The D Notice, of course. Once filed media coverage of the case was barred. Though, given the kind of balls the American press had these days, it was probably superfluous. They'd smash their own presses if the Homeland Czar asked. Pussies.

But speaking of pussies, here I was. I thanked my driver and got a grunted "no problem."

I nodded to the Homeland cop. The Homeland cop nodded back. "In for the night?" he asked.

"Where would I go?"

He smiled sourly, raised the mic pinned to his windbreaker and muttered some cop talk. Another nod and he walked off. Guess they figured I could take care of myself. Or, more to the point, be trusted to spend the night cowering under the bed.

There was a holiday wreath on the front door that hadn't been there this morning. Beginning to look a lot like Christmas. Feeling all warm and snuggly inside I let myself in and walked up the flight to my apartment.

"Honey, I'm home," I said. Just to hear myself say it. On my way to the kitchen, where I was pretty sure I had enough beer, I passed the open study door. Just out of the corner of my eye I could see my laptop open on the desk. I ignored it. That'll show her.

I happily counted ten bottles of several varieties. More than enough— well, enough—to see me through. I popped a Stella without taking off my coat or turning on the kitchen light. It went down pretty fast. I put the empty on the counter and opened a Sixpoints Bengali Tiger. Something with a little more heft to fortify me for what was coming next.

No time like the present. Strasser had given me two passwords to open a document I didn't know I had. In those terrible minutes after he'd read the Patriot Tribunal order in Black's chambers he'd seemed—briefly— apologetic. "I know our methods seem harsh, Mr. Raleigh," he said. "Not so harsh as our enemy's. Here." He extended a slip of paper—torn from a memo pad with the Homeland seal—and pressed it into my damp hand.

"These codes protect a document on your laptop. She wanted to explain herself." Stunned, I took the note. Not until my car was nosing out into traffic an hour later did I connect the dots to the morning months ago when I had awoken to find a cheery yellow sticky note from the Iranian stuck to a running laptop that should not have been running. I gagged.

I walked down the hall Tiger in hand and settled into the Aeron in front of the desk. Tap tap tap. There it was.

I am so sorry.

Well, there's a start, I thought. Funny, though, no hey-stud-muffin salutation.

You are reading this when you know what I have done. I know that it has done terrible things to your client and may do terrible things to you. I did not want any of those things to happen. But I had no choice.

Of course not. Nobody who fucks over anyone else ever thinks he does.

That's how he lives with himself after.

As you know I was born here. But my parents and brothers were not. The men who made me do what I did said that there were many irregularities in their petitions for asylum. I don't know whether this is true but it would not surprise me. And that one of my cousins is a Shari'a judge in Shiraz. Which is true. They told me that this was not enough to detain me but more than enough for the rest of my family. I did not believe them at first. I refused to tell them anything and said I would not talk to them any more. But a few days later my father called to tell me that Homeland had raided my brothers' store in Newark and arrested them and their workers and impounded all the rugs as contraband. I found the card the Homeland man had given me and called him. He asked whether I thought my brothers would prefer to be interrogated in Poland or Panama. He added that after my parents were picked up one would go to Liberia and the other Jordan; did I think that my mother would like Africa?
So you see I had no choice.

Neither did I. I flipped open the humidor on the desk and decapitated a Punch robusto. The co-op board was the least of my worries now. It and its non-smoking building could go fuck themselves. I got it fired up and returned to the text.

As soon as I agreed to do as he asked, the Homeland man had my brothers freed and their stock released. I asked only that I be allowed to explain myself to you. Since you are reading this I see he kept his word.

I would love to tell you that I love you and so make this thing even more tragic than it is. We would both love that, I think, like something out of Casablanca, how dramatic and noble. Or ignoble. But you and I both know that I did not. I was and am, however, so very fond of you. And I want you to know that my rages of the past few months were directed not at you but at myself and what I was doing. And I want you to know, too, that I never got into bed with you for any reason other than wanting to.

Oh, good. I feel so much better. And hey, I bet you don't feel like a complete treacherous slut now, either.

I won't ask you to forgive me.

Good.

But I do ask you to believe that I'm sorry for what I have done to you.

Roxana D.

Up until that moment I hadn't really been angry. Why not I can't imagine. But the "Roxana D." would have made me throw the Tiger against the wall if there weren't a few good swallows left. See, Iranians don't have middle names. A Farsi oversight. Always a problem when they're filling out forms requesting middle initials. I always called her darling. So she started listing her middle initial as D. As in Roxana Darling. One of those cute fun things that make relationships between middle-aged men and their young Persian betrayers just so darn adorable.

Speaking of betrayal, I had some thinking to do.

The Tiger was gone. Just in the nick of time. I picked up another in the

160

kitchen and finally got rid of my coat. I flipped on the lights in the living room and slumped on the couch, beer in one hand and remote in the other. Though I briefly toyed with spending the balance of the night—and, who knows, my freedom—sucking down beers in front of a blank screen, I at last sacked up enough to hit the on button.

Gee, only eighty stations? Seems like just yesterday—okay, five years ago—we had four hundred. But unlimited worldwide access is just one of the many ways the bad guys beam their evil thoughts into the heads of unsuspecting Americans. One missing dirty bomb swept away not only most of our civil liberties, but many of our more sophisticated entertainment options as well.

Many, but not all. Before I got home I'd thought it was about time for my annual replay of *Casablanca*. A nice black and white movie about black and white choices. Pretty much what I had in front of me. But something told me that if I were Rick and Bling were Lazlo, he wasn't getting onto that plane to Lisbon.

The eerily prescient Iranian, however, had handily poisoned my favorite movie for my next several incarnations. As I surfed through our Patriotically-truncated media, I thought about a long walk along the river or, hell call me crazy, reading instead. But having already decided to drink ten beers on a school night and piss off my neighbors with Dominican shadegrown, a rational healthy decision somehow seemed wrong. So I settled in for a night in front of the tube.

After two more beers I'd begun to think that a midnight swim in the Hudson would've been a better choice. National networks' late night offerings would lead a reasonable person to think the South had won the Civil War. Just as I was about to tackle the dilemma of early bed or a bar, I happened to stumble across AMC. Which was in the last half hour of a movie that you probably haven't seen called *13 Rue Madeleine*.

I have. I saw it once before. In my grandfather's living room on the black and white TV. Above it his pictures of FDR, John L. Louis, and the Holy Family. (Grampap was an immigrant, a coal miner, and a Catholic.) I was maybe seven, so my dad had to explain a lot to me. But he wasn't around just now, so I hit the Info button instead.

Yeah, there it was. World War II. Jimmy Cagney is an OSS agent parachuted into Vichy France to get to a scientist before a Nazi double agent does the same. Jimmy gets the scientist onto a plane to London, but before he can get on himself the SS arrives, and as Jimmy makes his break the bad guys get him. He desperately reaches for his cyanide pill—he knows a lot, and every man has his breaking point—but drops it as a Nazi slugs him from behind.

I watched slack-jawed as back in London Jimmy's OSS handlers explained a mission to a roomful of American bomber pilots in leather jackets. All of them smoking. Those were the days. Their job was to demolish a building in Lyons at 13 Rue Madeleine. Gestapo headquarters. Altitude zero. A murmur of protest; caps get set at angles even more rakish. "Zero altitude? What the--?"

Jimmy's boss takes center stage and tells the boys that it's only fair that they know why they're taking their lives in their hands. Jimmy is even now being tortured by the Nazi thugs. We cut to Jimmy dangling from shackles in a Lyonnaise dungeon, his back crosshatched with bleeding stripes as a grinning Nazi winds up to give him another. Nothing compared to what we do every day in Freedom Friendly holding facilities, but then again, nothing compared to what the Nazis actually did, either.

Every man has his breaking point, says Jimmy's boss. He knows all of our plans for the invasion. Nodding solemnly the pilots grind out their smokes and adjust their hats to more somber tilts. We cut again to Gestapo HQ. Air raid sirens wail; bombs crash. Terrified, the head SS man throws open the dungeon door.

Cagney's eyes are blackened and his mouth bloody. Nevertheless he throws back his head in triumphant laughter as a last bomb detonates and the frame dissolves in fire and smoke.

Speaking of fire and smoke, my cigar had gone out. As I relit I remembered asking my father why the Americans had blown up our own guy. And more importantly, why our guy was laughing. He patiently explained that we were doing the right thing because under enough pressure any man would talk and if he talked many men would die. And that Cagney was laughing because now he knew that he would never talk. So he won.

Maybe a little heavy for a seven year old. But not too heavy for me now.

I threw open a window. If I craned my head at just the right angle I could see the Hudson. Suddenly that was very important. Just as important as smoking the rest of my cigars and drinking the rest of my beer, because very soon neither might be available.

I stuck my head out the window again and looked at the street. Empty. At least of cops. The Men in Black apparently still figured that both the press and I were scared enough to be trusted.

I thought about the other things that could shortly cease to be options. I picked up the phone and speed-dialed the Iranian, but recognized its futility and my ratlike desperation before the first ring and hung up—though not without wondering what the combination of guilt sex and pity sex might be like. There were some outcall services I'd represented I knew I could trust, so I started to scroll through my contacts. But then my rational mind reasserted itself. Whatever happened, I wasn't going to be arrested tomorrow or next week. So it wasn't necessary to shriek and claw the dirt like a gerbil sliding backwards down a python's gullet. I had enough time to organize getting laid. Maybe more than once.

But speaking of getting organized, I had to figure out how to deal with the consequences of what I'd just now decided to do, which kind of ruled out finishing the rest of the beer but fortunately, not the cigars.

I put my coat back on. It was time for that walk. But not to the Hudson. The other way. The Lower East Side. There were people there I had to see.

Undisclosed location, two years later

The door has just closed behind Captain Graner. He has explained what's about to happen. His last words were, "I'm real sorry."

The Homeland Czar has decided that my evolutionary singularity raises the possibility that I am a bioterror weapon. Created by Mahdists or other evil elements bent on America's extermination. Made, not begotten. How could it be otherwise? For if I am who I claim to be, why, humanity must have evolved from lower animals. An impossibility equally contrary to the Word and the law.

Again, I digress. Are you surprised? Monkeys are so easily distracted.

The Czar has determined that as a bioterror weapon my inner workings must be explored. Thus I am to be dissected. But in order to ensure that the handiwork of Islamofascist bioengineers is properly understood, the dissection is to take place before my death.

I am to be vivisected. As a kindness, Graner explained, I will be almost completely unconscious while this takes place.

Almost completely.

There is no room in my heart for terror. This may surprise you. Instead there is only hope.

Yesterday I was granted one of my rare sojourns into daylight. Perhaps a favor from my jailers, knowing what decision had been made. As I shuffled across the asphalt through steaming tropical air, I caught sight of another orange-clad figure, shackled and handcuffed like myself, pushed along his way by a pair of black-clad hometroopers. Male, slightly built and slightly stooped with iron-gray hair. Oddly familiar, especially for this place.

The other captive was half a dozen yards away, head down, stumbling as his guards thrust him onward. As he passed he turned his face from his feet. Our eyes met. His were almost invisible among bruises. "They got away," said Mr. Raleigh. "I got to them in time. *They got away.*"

A rifle butt between the shoulder blades sent him sprawling face down, arms outstretched, cruciform. The soldiers began to kick him in the ribs. He tried to get up, but one of his guards ground a boot into his neck. For his sake I hoped that it broke. Sadly it did not; the last I saw of Mr. Raleigh he was curled into a fetal ball, on his side, arms raised to protect face, and knees raised to protect genitals from the hometroopers' angry kicks.

They got away. So Graner had lied all along. What a shock.

I have too little time left to speculate how Mr. Raleigh reached the Nest without detection. Nor can I address the deeper question of why he would have put himself at risk—now, obviously, realized—for a people not only not his own, but whom his own had instinctively hunted to the verge of extermination since it came into being.

As I wait for the last turn of the keys I wonder how the Nest will conceal itself now. My face—*our* face—was on the front page of every tabloid in every corner newsbox for weeks. Though now displaced by military disasters and domestic atrocities, the image will no doubt linger for a while. Perhaps my people will abandon the daylight altogether to seek refuge in train tunnels rather than disused warehouses, returning to the womb of the First Mother, who had so long ago sheltered us from world-walking blizzard. To subsist for a year or two on rats and fast food scraps. Then, once I am forgotten, to make their way west from one strip mall dumpster to the next until they are at last safe in the woods of the Alleghenies.

But no matter how they survive, they will survive. My own failure to do so is of no consequence.

There is more. My people have teetered on the precipice so long that each day of continued existence is a welcome surprise. What leaves me almost too stunned for gratitude is that our salvation—for today, at least—has been purchased by a human's sacrifice of himself. I can only guess at his motive. But his actions show that your instinctual antipathy for the Other may at last be overcome by something else. Perhaps there is hope.

The world is so big and we are so small, all of us. We are in it for so brief a time. I wonder, when death comes, will it be a wall or a door? Or will it be a wind that scatters my soul like leaves?

The key is in the lock. I love you all. Goodbye.

Acknowledgements

First, I have to thank Tom Perrotta and the late Richard Selzer, whose limitless generosity and friendship not only made this book possible, but made it possible for me to call myself a writer at all. As important has been the unflagging encouragement of Pat Kaplan, without which I would not have started down this road.

While adversity is not to be sought, it is not without its uses, chief among which is revealing your true friends. I have more and better than I deserve: Randi and Jeremy Vishno; Felicia and Rick Gordon; Rosemary and Steve Jacobs; Deb and Charlie Price; Tom McNamara; Phil Weber; Trey Ellis; John Crowley; Lou Bayard; Sylvia Madrigal; Colleen Kinder; Penn Rhodeen; Brett Flamm; Kevin Dehghani; Claudia Baio; Tara Knight; and Carlos Candal.

Nor can I omit Chad Prevost, without whose boundless energy, enthusiasm, and creativity the initial version of this work would never have seen the light of day.

And without the loyalty, wisdom, and enterprise of Shawn "Crawdaddy" Crawford, it would have vanished as though it never was—my gratitude cannot ever be sufficiently expressed.

And finally I must thank Sharon Witt, my best friend, to whom I have the undeserved good luck to be married.

The Calliope Group would like to thank K.M. West for her fresh take on the book during revisions.

Acknowledgements